走進李伯大夢

美國短篇小說精選

英|漢|對|照

Washington Irving 等 _ 著

羅慕謙 _ 譯

CONTENTS

CONTENTS

1

■ 華盛頓·歐文

Rip Van Winkle

李伯大夢

■ Washington Irving (1783-1859)

Whoever has made a voyage up the Hudson[1] must remember the Kaatskill mountains. They are a dismembered[2] branch of the great Appalachian family, and are seen away to the west of the river, swelling up to a noble height, and lording it over[3] the surrounding country. Every change of season, every change of weather, indeed, every hour of the day, produces some change in the magical hues and shapes of these mountains; and they are regarded by all the good wives, far and near, as perfect barometers[4].

When the weather is fair and settled, they are clothed in blue and purple, and print their bold outlines on the clear evening sky; but sometimes, when the rest of the landscape is cloudless, they will gather a hood of gray vapors about their summits, which, in the last rays of the setting sun, will glow and light up like a crown of glory.

At the foot of these fairy mountains, the voyager may have descried[5] the light smoke curling up from a village, whose shingle-roofs gleam among the trees, just where the blue tints of the upland melt away into the fresh green of the nearer landscape.

---

1 Hundson (River) 哈德遜河（位於美國東北部的河流）
2 dismember [dɪsˈmembər] (v.) 使不連接
3 lord it over . . . 在……面前擺架子、逞威風
4 barometer [bəˈrɑːmɪtər] (n.) 氣壓計（用以預測天氣）
5 descry [dɪˈskraɪ] (v.) 遠遠看到

　　航行過哈德遜河的人，一定都會記得卡士奇山。卡士奇山是阿帕拉契山脈一條斷落的支脈，從河上遙望，就坐落在遠遠的西邊，高聳壯麗，傲視著四周的平地。每當季節要更替，天氣要轉換，甚至隨著每個時辰的推進，卡士奇山的色調與形狀都會跟著變化，所以遠遠近近的主婦，都把卡士奇山視為最佳的天氣預報員。

　　天氣晴朗穩定時，山脈是藍色和紫色的，在晚霞中顯現出清晰的輪廓。但有時候周圍的天空都清朗無雲，山頂上卻聚積著一團灰濛濛的霧氣，在落日的映照下閃閃發亮，彷彿一頂榮耀的皇冠。

　　在這座美麗山脈的山腳下，航行者可能還會看到村莊升起的裊裊炊煙。村舍的屋瓦在樹林間閃爍，遠遠望去，蔚藍的山脈在這裡逐漸轉為翠綠，與樹林合而為一，蔓延成眼前的綠色大地。

It is a little village of great antiquity, having been founded by some of the Dutch colonists, in the early times of the province, just about the beginning of the government of the good Peter Stuyvesant[6], (may he rest in peace!), and there were some of the houses of the original settlers standing within a few years, built of small yellow bricks brought from Holland, having latticed windows and gable fronts, surmounted with weathercocks.

In that same village, and in one of these very houses, (which, to tell the precise truth, was sadly time-worn and weather-beaten), there lived, many years since, while the country was yet a province of Great Britain, a simple, good-natured fellow, of the name of Rip Van Winkle. He was a descendant of the Van Winkles who figured so gallantly in the chivalrous days of Peter Stuyvesant, and accompanied him to the siege of Fort Christina.

He inherited, however, but little of the martial character of his ancestors. I have observed that he was a simple, good-natured man; he was, moreover, a kind neighbor, and an obedient henpecked[7] husband. Indeed, to the latter circumstance might be owing that meekness of spirit which gained him such universal popularity; for those men are most apt to be obsequious[8] and conciliating abroad, who are under the discipline of shrews at home.

---

6 Peter Stuyvesant（1592-1672）荷蘭於北美洲的殖民地總督（1644 被迫
　將殖民地讓給英國）
7 henpecked [ˈhɛnpɛkt] (a.) 怕老婆的
8 obsequious [əbˈsiːkwɪəs] (a.) 順從的；卑躬的

8 ■ Rip Van Winkle

Peter Stuyvesant

　　這座小村莊歷史很悠久了，是早期荷蘭移民所建立的，始於彼得‧史蒂文森（願他安息！）開始擔任荷蘭總督之際。當初荷蘭移民所建的房屋，有些還在村裡屹立了好幾年，牆是荷蘭帶過來的小黃磚砌成的，窗戶是格子窗，正面有山形牆，屋頂上豎著風信雞。

　　好多年以前，當這個國家還受英國統治時，在這座小村莊裡，就在一棟這樣的屋子裡（老實說，屋子飽受歲月與風霜的侵蝕，變得又破又舊了），住著一個叫李伯‧凡‧溫可的純樸老實人。在彼得‧史蒂文森總督那個充滿騎士精神的時代，他的祖先展現了英勇的氣概，跟隨總督攻打克利斯丁那堡。

　　然而，李伯並沒有遺傳到多少祖先的戰鬥性格。我剛說過了，他是一個純樸的老實人，此外他還是個和藹可親的鄰居，而且是個溫順懼內的丈夫。也許就是因為家有悍妻，他才養成了這麼溫和的脾氣，讓他在外面的人緣這麼好。

❶ 李伯大夢

Their tempers, doubtless, are rendered pliant and malleable in the fiery furnace of domestic tribulation[9], and a curtain-lecture is worth all the sermons in the world for teaching the virtues of patience and long-suffering. A termagant[10] wife may, therefore, in some respects, be considered a tolerable blessing; and if so, Rip Van Winkle was thrice blessed.

Certain it is, that he was a great favorite among all the good wives of the village, who, as usual with the amiable sex, took his part in all family squabbles[11]; and never failed, whenever they talked those matters over in their evening gossipings, to lay all the blame on Dame Van Winkle.

在家受到悍妻管教的男人，在外往往也是個好好先生。在悍妻的烈火下，他們無疑都練就了溫和柔順的個性。老婆的訓示，比世上所有宣揚忍耐吃苦的講道都有用。所以從某些角度看來，家有悍妻反而是一種福氣，如果真是如此，那麼李伯真是三生有幸了。

可以確定的是，村子裡的婆婆媽媽都很喜歡他。每次只要李伯跟老婆發生口角，婦女們都會站在李伯這一邊，而且傍晚時分聚在一起說三道四時，一定會數落李伯夫人的不是。

---

9   tribulation [ˌtrɪbjʊˈleɪʃən] (n.) 苦難
10 termagant [ˈtɜːrməgənt] (a.) 愛鬥嘴的（女人）
11 squabble [ˈskwɑːbəl] (n.) 爭吵

A termagant wife may, therefore, in some respects, be considered a tolerable blessing; and if so, Rip Van Winkle was thrice blessed.

The children of the village, too, would shout with joy whenever he approached. He assisted at their sports, made their playthings, taught them to fly kites and shoot marbles, and told them long stories of ghosts, witches, and Indians. Whenever he went dodging about the village, he was surrounded by a troop of them, hanging on his skirts, clambering on his back, and playing a thousand tricks on him with impunity[12]; and not a dog would bark at him throughout the neighborhood.

The great error in Rip's composition was an insuperable aversion to all kinds of profitable labor. It could not be from the want of assiduity or perseverance; for he would sit on a wet rock, with a rod as long and heavy as a Tartar's[13] lance, and fish all day without a murmur, even though he should not be encouraged by a single nibble. He would carry a fowling-piece on his shoulder, for hours together, trudging through woods and swamps, and up hill and down dale, to shoot a few squirrels or wild pigeons.

He would never refuse to assist a neighbor even in the roughest toil, and was a foremost man at all country frolics for husking Indian corn, or building stone-fences; the women of the village, too, used to employ him to run their errands, and to do such little odd jobs as their less obliging husbands would not do for them.

---

12 impunity [ɪmˈpjunətɪ] (n.) 免於受罰
13 Tartar [ˈtɑːrtər] (n.) 韃靼人（過去為一尚武的遊牧民族，現為俄羅斯的少數民族之一）

村裡的小孩子也都很喜歡他，一看到他就高興地歡呼。李伯陪他們玩耍，幫他們做玩具，教他們放風箏和打彈珠，還跟他們講鬼怪、巫婆和印地安人的故事。每次他在村裡閒晃，總會有一群小孩圍著他，抓著他的衣服，爬在他的背上，用各種方式捉弄他，但是他永遠也不會生氣。村裡的狗，也從來不會對他吠一聲。

李伯性格上最大的缺點，就是厭惡所有能夠賺錢的工作。但是他不是不勤奮，也不是沒毅力。他可以坐在潮濕的大石頭上，握著一根跟韃靼人的長矛一樣長、一樣重的釣竿，釣一整天的魚，即使魚竿動也沒動一下，他還是一句怨言也沒有。他也可以連著好幾個小時背著獵槍，跋山涉水，翻山越嶺，就為了獵幾隻松鼠或野鴿。

當鄰居需要幫忙時，不管是多麼粗重的工作，他都來者不拒。地方上有剝玉米皮或砌石牆的活動時，他一定跑第一。村裡的婦女都會找他跑腿，或是請他做些自家丈夫不願意做的雜務。

In a word, Rip was ready to attend to anybody's business but his own; but as to doing family duty, and keeping his farm in order, he found it impossible.

In fact, he declared it was of no use to work on his farm; it was the most pestilent[14] little piece of ground in the whole country; everything about it went wrong, and would go wrong, in spite of him. His fences were continually falling to pieces; his cow would either go astray, or get among the cabbages; weeds were sure to grow quicker in his fields than anywhere else; the rain always made a point of setting in just as he had some out-door work to do; so that though his patrimonial[15] estate had dwindled away under his management, acre by acre, until there was little more left than a mere patch of Indian corn and potatoes, yet it was the worst-conditioned farm in the neighborhood.

His children, too, were as ragged and wild as if they belonged to nobody. His son Rip, an urchin begotten in his own likeness, promised to inherit the habits, with the old clothes of his father. He was generally seen trooping like a colt at his mother's heels[16], equipped in a pair of his father's cast-off galligaskins[17], which he had much ado to hold up with one hand, as a fine lady does her train[18] in bad weather.

Rip Van Winkle, however, was one of those happy mortals, of foolish, well-oiled dispositions, who take the world easy, eat white bread or brown, whichever can be got with least thought or trouble, and would rather starve on a penny than work for a pound.

總之，別人的事情他都樂意幫忙，自己的事情他就不想做。養家活口和照料田地這種事，他覺得自己完全做不來。

他還說，去照料他那塊田一點用處也沒有，因為那塊田是那一帶最倒楣的一塊地，除了他自己以外，田裡所有的東西都連帶遭殃。籬笆老是壞掉；養的母牛不是走丟，就是踩到甘藍菜園裡；雜草永遠長得比農作物還快；只要他得在戶外工作，天空就開始下起雨。於是，祖傳的田地在他的照料下一畝一畝地減少，最後只剩一小塊地還種著玉米和馬鈴薯，但是這塊田地真是村裡最貧瘠的一塊田了。

他的孩子也是衣衫襤褸，又皮又野，像是沒爹沒娘的孩子。他的兒子小李伯長得就跟他一模一樣，將來除了會繼承老爸的舊衣裳，勢必也會遺傳到老爸的個性。他經常像隻小馬似地緊緊跟在媽媽身後，穿著一條爸爸不要的寬大馬褲，一隻手拉著褲管，就像高貴的淑女在雨天時拉起裙擺那樣。

但是李伯天性樂觀，他人憨憨的，脾氣很好，什麼事都看得開，吃好吃壞都無所謂，只要不用動腦、不用費工夫就好。他寧願少一分錢餓肚子，也不願為了一鎊錢去工作。

---

14 pestilent ['pɛstɪlənt] (a.) 擾人的；令人不愉快的
15 patrimonial [ˌpætrɪ'moʊnjəl] (a.) 祖傳的
16 at someone's heels 緊跟著某人
17 galligaskins [ˌgælɪ'gæskɪnz] (n.) 馬褲或寬鬆的褲子
18 train [treɪn] (n.) 長裙拖在地上的下襬

If left to himself, he would have whistled life away in perfect contentment; but his wife kept continually dinning in his ears[19] about his idleness, his carelessness, and the ruin he was bringing on his family. Morning, noon, and night, her tongue was incessantly going, and every thing he said or did was sure to produce a torrent of household eloquence.

Rip had but one way of replying to all lectures of the kind, and that, by frequent use, had grown into a habit. He shrugged his shoulders, shook his head, cast up his eyes, but said nothing. This, however, always provoked a fresh volley from his wife; so that he was fain to draw off his forces, and take to[20] the outside of the house—the only side which, in truth, belongs to a henpecked husband.

Rip's sole domestic adherent was his dog Wolf, who was as much henpecked as his master; for Dame Van Winkle regarded them as companions in idleness, and even looked upon Wolf with an evil eye, as the cause of his master's going so often astray. True it is, in all points of spirit befitting an honorable dog, he was as courageous an animal as ever scoured the woods—but what courage can withstand the ever-during and all-besetting terrors of a woman's tongue?

19 din in someone's ears 喋喋不休地說
20 take to . . . 逃往……

如果可以，他會整天吹著口哨，這樣心滿意足地過一輩子。但是他的老婆總是在他耳邊嘮叨，說他又懶惰又粗心，家都快被他毀了。她從早到晚唸個不停，不管李伯說什麼或做什麼，一定都會被她數落。

　　老婆開罵時，李伯只有一個應對的辦法，而且因為用多了，都已經變成了一種習慣。他會聳聳肩，搖搖頭，望著天空，一語不發。但是這種反應往往只會把老婆惹得更火大，所以這時他也樂得棄甲投降，逃到屋外。而說實話，家門之外也才是懼內丈夫唯一的歸屬。

　　家裡唯一跟李伯感情要好的，就是他的狗狗「小狼」。小狼就跟主人一樣怕李伯夫人，因為在李伯夫人的眼裡，他們倆就是一起遊手好閒的難兄難弟，她甚至認為小狼就是李伯誤入歧途的罪魁禍首。沒錯，就一條狗而言，小狼算是林子一帶驍勇的動物了，但是再怎麼英勇，哪敵得過女人的嘮叨不休？

The moment Wolf entered the house, his crest fell, his tail drooped to the ground, or curled between his legs, he sneaked about with a gallows air, casting many a sidelong glance at Dame Van Winkle, and at the least flourish of a broomstick or ladle, he would fly to the door with yelping precipitation.

Times grew worse and worse with Rip Van Winkle as years of matrimony[21] rolled on; a tart temper never mellows with age, and a sharp tongue is the only edged tool that grows keener with constant use.

　　小狼只要一走進家門，頭就低下來，尾巴不是垂到地上，就是夾在兩腿中間。牠緊張兮兮、躡手躡腳地在家裡亂竄，時不時偷瞄李伯夫人，只要李伯夫人一拿起掃帚或湯杓，牠就汪汪大叫，往門口跑。

　　結婚以來，李伯的日子一天比一天難過。因為尖酸刻薄的個性不會隨著歲月而消失，尖牙利嘴的本事也只會越磨越高強。

---

21 matrimony [ˈmætrɪmoʊni] (n.) 婚姻

For a long while he used to console himself, when driven from home, by frequenting a kind of perpetual club of the sages, philosophers, and other idle personages of the village; which held its sessions on a bench before a small inn, designated by a rubicund portrait of His Majesty George the Third. Here they used to sit in the shade through a long, lazy summer's day, talking listlessly over village gossip, or telling endless sleepy stories about nothing.

But it would have been worth any statesman's money to have heard the profound discussions that sometimes took place when by chance an old newspaper fell into their hands from some passing traveler.

　　有好一陣子，每當他被趕出家門，他就會去找村子裡那些總聚在一起聊天的社會賢達、哲人和閒混之士。這些人都會坐在小酒館前的長椅上開講。小酒館的門口掛了一張英王喬治三世的畫像，畫像上的國王臉色紅潤。漫長慵懶的夏日，他們會坐在樹蔭下，有一句沒一句地聊著村子裡的八卦，或是說著沒完沒了、令人打盹的言之無物之事。

　　但是如果偶然路過的路人所帶來的舊報紙落入他們的手中，這時他們頗有深度的討論，倒是值得政客們掏錢來聽聽了。

Here they used to sit in the shade through a long, lazy summer's day, talking listlessly over village gossip, or telling endless sleepy stories about nothing.

How solemnly they would listen to the contents, as drawled out by Derrick Van Bummel, the schoolmaster, a dapper learned little man, who was not to be daunted by the most gigantic word in the dictionary; and how sagely they would deliberate[22] upon public events some months after they had taken place.

The opinions of this junto were completely controlled by Nicholas Vedder, a patriarch of the village, and landlord of the inn, at the door of which he took his seat from morning till night, just moving sufficiently to avoid the sun, and keep in the shade of a large tree; so that the neighbors could tell the hour by his movements as accurately as by a sun-dial. It is true, he was rarely heard to speak, but smoked his pipe incessantly.

His adherents, however (for every great man has his adherents), perfectly understood him, and knew how to gather his opinions.

When any thing that was read or related displeased him, he was observed to smoke his pipe vehemently[23], and to send forth short, frequent, and angry puffs; but when pleased, he would inhale the smoke slowly and tranquilly, and emit it in light and placid clouds; and sometimes, taking the pipe from his mouth, and letting the fragrant vapor curl about his nose, would gravely nod his head in token of perfect approbation[24].

22 deliberate [dɪˈlɪbərɪt] (v.) 討論；商議
23 vehemently [ˈviːəməntli] (adv.) 猛烈地；激烈地
24 approbation [ˌæprəˈbeɪʃən] (n.) 認可

　　村裡的小學老師德瑞克‧凡‧布墨，他短小精幹，學識豐富，字典上最長的字也難不倒他。大家會嚴肅地聽著他拉長音調朗讀報上的內容，然後鄭重其事地討論幾個月前發生的事情。

　　大家都以尼可拉斯‧維德為意見領袖。他是村子裡德高望重的長老，也是這間酒館的老板。他從早到晚都坐在酒館門口，偶爾為了避開太陽、躲進樹蔭時才會挪動一下身子，所以鄰居都可以從他的位置來判斷當時的時辰，就跟日晷一樣準確。他很少開口說話，總是在一旁不停地抽著菸斗。

　　不過他的擁護者（每個偉人都有擁護者）非常了解他，知道怎麼猜出他的想法。

　　要是別人朗讀或述說的內容不合他的意，他就會猛吸菸斗，氣憤地頻頻吐煙。但如果合他的意了，他就會慢慢、靜靜地吸菸，吐出輕盈溫和的煙霧，有時候還會拿下嘴上的菸斗，任芳香的煙霧縈繞在鼻子邊，然後鄭重地點頭表示贊同。

From even this stronghold the unlucky Rip was at length routed[25] by his termagant wife, who would suddenly break in upon the tranquility of the assemblage, and call the members all to nought; nor was that august personage, Nicholas Vedder himself, sacred from the daring tongue of this terrible virago[26], who charged him outright with encouraging her husband in habits of idleness.

Poor Rip was at last reduced almost to despair; and his only alternative, to escape from the labor of the farm and the clamor of his wife, was to take gun in hand, and stroll away into the woods. Here he would sometimes seat himself at the foot of a tree, and share the contents of his wallet with Wolf, with whom he sympathized as a fellow-sufferer in persecution.

"Poor Wolf," he would say, "thy mistress leads thee a dog's life of it; but never mind, my lad, whilst I live thou shalt never want a friend to stand by thee!"

Wolf would wag his tail, look wistfully in his master's face, and if dogs can feel pity, I verily believe he reciprocated[27] the sentiment with all his heart.

In a long ramble of the kind, on a fine autumnal day, Rip had unconsciously scrambled to one of the highest parts of the Kaatskill mountains. He was after his favorite sport of squirrel shooting, and the still solitudes had echoed and re-echoed with the reports of his gun.

25 rout [raʊt] (v.) 擊敗並趕走
26 virago [vɪˈrɑːɡoʊ] (n.) 潑婦；悍婦
27 reciprocate [rɪˈsɪprəkeɪt] (v.) 回報；酬答

但不幸的，就連這個大本營，最後也還是被悍妻攻破。她會突然闖進他們平靜的聚會，把每個成員都罵得一無是處。就連年高德劭的尼可拉斯‧維德也逃不過這個潑婦的利嘴，她指責他帶壞她老公遊手好閒。

　　可憐的李伯最後都快走投無路了。要避開田裡的工作和老婆的嘮叨，唯一的辦法就是拿起獵槍、逃到山林裡。有時候他會坐在樹下，跟小狼一起分享口袋裡僅剩的糧食。小狼和他同病相憐，他很同情小狼。

　　「可憐的小狼，女主人讓你的日子很不好過，但是別擔心，只要我活著，我就永遠是你最忠誠的朋友！」他會這樣對著小狼說。

　　小狼聽了會搖搖尾巴，悲憫地看著主人。如果狗也有憐憫之心，我相信牠此時正全心全意地回應主人的同情。

　　一個晴朗的秋日，也是在這樣的山林漫步中，李伯不知不覺爬上了卡士奇山的山頂。他在獵松鼠，這是他最喜愛的消遣，靜謐的山林中迴盪著槍響聲。

Panting and fatigued, he threw himself, late in the afternoon, on a green knoll, covered with mountain herbage, that crowned the brow of a precipice[28].

From an opening between the trees, he could overlook all the lower country for many a mile of rich woodland. He saw at a distance the lordly Hudson, far, far below him, moving on its silent but majestic course, with the reflection of a purple cloud, or the sail of a lagging bark, here and there sleeping on its glassy bosom and at last losing itself in the blue highlands.

On the other side he looked down into a deep mountain glen[29], wild, lonely, and shagged, the bottom filled with fragments from the impending cliffs, and scarcely lighted by the reflected rays of the setting sun. For some time Rip lay musing[30] on this scene; evening was gradually advancing; the mountains began to throw their long blue shadows over the valleys; he saw that it would be dark long before he could reach the village; and he heaved a heavy sigh when he thought of encountering the terrors of Dame Van Winkle.

As he was about to descend, he heard a voice from a distance hallooing: "Rip Van Winkle! Rip Van Winkle!" He looked around, but could see nothing but a crow winging its solitary flight across the mountain.

---

28 precipice ['prɛsɪpɪs] (n.) 懸崖；峭壁
29 glen [glɛn] (n.) 峽谷
30 muse [mjuz] (v.) 沉思；冥想

　　將近傍晚的時候，他已經走得氣喘吁吁，筋疲力竭，便在懸崖頂端一個長滿青草的小土丘上躺了下來。

　　從樹隙間，他可以俯瞰山下整片茂密的林地。他遠眺著山下壯闊的哈德遜河，河水寧靜而莊嚴地流動著，明鏡般的河面上，這裡映著一片紫色的雲影，那裡點綴著一張緩緩而行的帆影，最後只見河流消失在藍色的高地上。

　　另一邊是一片蠻荒淒涼的深邃山谷，底端佈滿了峭壁落下的碎石，落日餘暉無法照到。李伯就這樣在那躺了好一會兒，忘神地欣賞眼前的風景。夜色逐漸降臨，群山開始在山谷上罩上深藍的長影。他知道自己天黑之前是趕不回村子了，一想到回去後又要面對李伯夫人的毒罵，他就深深地嘆了一口氣。

　　在他正準備下山時，聽到遠方傳來一個聲音喊道：「李伯！李伯！」他四下張望，只見到一隻烏鴉在山間孤單地飛過，沒有看到其他什麼動靜。

He thought his fancy must have deceived him, and turned again to descend, when he heard the same cry ring through the still evening air, "Rip Van Winkle! Rip Van Winkle!"—at the same time Wolf bristled up his back, and giving a low growl, skulked to his master's side, looking fearfully down into the glen.

Rip now felt a vague apprehension[31] stealing over him; he looked anxiously in the same direction, and perceived a strange figure slowly toiling up the rocks, and bending under the weight of something he carried on his back. He was surprised to see any human being in this lonely and unfrequented place, but supposing it to be some one of the neighborhood in need of his assistance, he hastened down to yield it.

On nearer approach, he was still more surprised at the singularity[32] of the stranger's appearance. He was a short, square-built old fellow, with thick bushy hair, and a grizzled beard. His dress was of the antique Dutch fashion—a cloth jerkin strapped round the waist— several pairs of breeches, the outer one of ample volume, decorated with rows of buttons down the sides and bunches at the knees. He bore on his shoulders a stout keg, that seemed full of liquor, and made signs for Rip to approach and assist him with the load.

---

31 apprehension [ˌæprɪˈhenʃən] (n.) 憂慮；擔心
32 singularity [ˌsɪŋgjʊˈlærɪti] (n.) 奇特；異常

他覺得一定是自己聽錯了，轉身準備下山，卻聽到靜謐的暮色中又響起同樣的呼聲：「李伯！李伯！」小狼頓時背毛直立，低吟了一聲，縮到主人腳邊，害怕地望向旁邊的山谷。李伯感到一股莫名的恐懼襲上心頭。

他不安地望向山谷，結果看到一個奇怪的身影，正慢慢地從山谷爬上來，駝著背地馱著重物。他很吃驚會在這麼荒涼偏僻的地方看到人，他想這個人應該是附近村子裡的人，看起來很需要幫忙，於是他便快步走過去。

當他走近看到那陌生人的奇特外貌時，更是吃驚了。這是一個身材矮小、長得粗粗壯壯的老頭，他的頭髮又粗又密，還留著灰色的鬍子。他穿著荷蘭的傳統服裝——上半身穿著呢馬甲，腰間束著皮帶——層層的馬褲，最外面那條又寬又大，褲管兩側鑲著成排的釦子，膝蓋部分也有成簇的釦子。背上揹了一個結實的木桶，裡面似乎裝滿了酒。他跟李伯做手勢，要他過去幫忙。

Though rather shy and distrustful of this new acquaintance, Rip complied with his usual alacrity; and mutually relieving each other, they clambered up a narrow gully, apparently the dry bed of a mountain torrent. As they ascended, Rip every now and then heard long rolling peals, like distant thunder, that seemed to issue out of a deep ravine[33], or rather cleft between lofty rocks, toward which their rugged path conducted.

He paused for an instant, but supposing it to be the muttering of one of those transient thunder-showers which often take place in mountain heights, he proceeded. Passing through the ravine, they came to a hollow, like a small amphitheater[34], surrounded by perpendicular[35] precipices, over the brinks of which impending trees shot their branches, so that you only caught glimpses of the azure sky, and the bright evening cloud.

During the whole time Rip and his companion had labored on in silence; for though the former marveled greatly what could be the object of carrying a keg of liquor up this wild mountain, yet there was something strange and incomprehensible[36] about the unknown, that inspired awe and checked familiarity.

---

33 ravine [rə'viːn] (n.) 深谷；峽谷
34 amphitheatre ['æmfɪˌθɪətər] (n.) 圓形露天劇場
35 perpendicular [ˌpɜːrpən'dɪkjʊər] (a.) 垂直的
36 incomprehensible [ɪnˌkɑːmprɪ'hensɪbəl] (a.) 不可思議的

李伯雖然有些羞澀，也有些戒心，但是他還是一如往常，欣然地答應了。他們同心協力，一起爬上一個狹窄的溝壑，這溝壑顯然是一條山澗乾涸的河床。李伯不時聽到一陣陣綿長的隆隆聲，彷彿遙遠的雷聲，似乎是從哪個山谷深淵傳上來的，不然就是從這條崎嶇小路盡頭的岩石裂縫中傳過來的。

　　他停下來想聽清楚，想想應該是高山裡常見的雷陣雨的低吼，便又繼續往前走。穿過山谷後，他們來到一片猶如圓形露天劇場的空地，周圍是陡直的峭壁，峭壁頂端的樹木伸出樹枝，遮住了天空，只能從枝葉的縫隙之間瞥見蔚藍的天空和炫耀的晚霞。

　　這一路上，他們兩個人都沒有講話。儘管李伯很好奇為什麼要揹這樣一桶酒來到這深山野外，但是這個陌生人有一種不尋常且深不可測的調調，令他感到敬畏，所以他不敢隨意探問。

On entering the amphitheater, new objects of wonder presented themselves. On a level spot in the center was a company of odd-looking personages playing at ninepins[37].

They were dressed in a quaint outlandish fashion; some wore short doublets, others jerkins, with long knives in their belts, and most of them had enormous breeches, of similar style with that of the guide's. Their visages, too, were peculiar; one had a large head, broad face, and small piggish eyes; the face of another seemed to consist entirely of nose, and was surmounted[38] by a white sugar-loaf hat, set off with a little red cock's tail.

They all had beards, of various shapes and colors. There was one who seemed to be the commander. He was a stout old gentleman, with a weather-beaten countenance; he wore a laced doublet, broad belt and hanger, high-crowned hat and feather, red stockings, and high-heeled shoes, with roses in them.

The whole group reminded Rip of the figures in an old Flemish[39] painting, in the parlor of Dominie Van Schaick, the village parson, and which had been brought over from Holland at the time of the settlement.

---

37 ninepins [ˈnaɪnˌpɪnz] (n.) 九柱滾球戲（即早期的保齡球遊戲）
38 surmount [sərˈmaʊnt] (v.) 居於……之上；在……頂上
39 Flemish 法蘭德斯地區的（法蘭德斯 Flanders 位於今法國北部、比利時和荷蘭西南部一帶）

On a level spot in the centre was a company of odd-looking personages playing at ninepins.

　　走進空地後，出現了更多奇怪的景象。中間的平地上，一群形貌奇特的人正在玩滾球。

　　他們穿著古怪的奇裝異服，有些人穿著緊身短上衣；有些人穿著背心外套，皮帶上佩著長刀；他們大家幾乎都穿著寬大的馬褲，就跟把李伯帶來這裡的那個人一樣。這些人的長相也很奇怪，有一個傢伙的頭很大、臉很寬，眼睛卻像豬眼睛一樣小；有一個傢伙整張臉就只看到一個大鼻子，頭上戴著一頂圓錐狀的白色帽子，帽子上插著一小根紅色雞毛。

　　他們每個人都蓄著鬍子，但是鬍子的形狀和顏色各有不同。其中有個傢伙看起來像是這群人的領袖。他是個身材粗壯的老頭，有一張飽經風霜的臉，穿著束帶緊身上衣，腰間繫著一條寬皮帶，佩戴著一把短刀，頭上戴著插有羽毛的高頂帽，腳上穿著紅色的長襪子，和一雙繫著玫瑰花結子的高跟皮鞋。

　　在村子牧師多米尼·凡·夏克家的客廳裡，有一幅描繪法蘭德斯風景的老畫作，是殖民時期從荷蘭帶過來的，這群人讓李伯聯想到這幅畫裡的人物。

❶
李伯大夢

What seemed particularly odd to Rip was, that though these folks were evidently amusing themselves, yet they maintained the gravest faces, the most mysterious silence, and were, withal, the most melancholy party of pleasure he had ever witnessed. Nothing interrupted the stillness of the scene but the noise of the balls, which, whenever they were rolled, echoed along the mountains like rumbling peals of thunder.

As Rip and his companion approached them, they suddenly desisted[40] from their play, and stared at him with such a fixed statue-like gaze, and such strange uncouth, lackluster[41] countenances, that his heart turned within him, and his knees smote together. His companion now emptied the contents of the keg into large flagons[42], and made signs to him to wait upon the company. He obeyed with fear and trembling; they quaffed the liquor in profound silence, and then returned to their game.

讓李伯感到特別奇怪的是，這群人儘管表面上在玩著遊戲，卻個個神情肅穆，一語不發，他從沒見過這麼死氣沉沉的聚會。空地裡一片安靜，只聽得到球滾動時在山間所造成的如雷轟般的聲音。

李伯和老頭走向他們時，他們突然停下動作，目不轉睛、面如死灰地盯著李伯，盯得李伯渾身發毛、雙腿發軟。這時老頭把木桶裡的酒倒進幾個大酒壺，要李伯端給他們。李伯照做，他邊端酒、邊發抖。那群人安安靜靜地痛快暢飲後，又繼續玩他們的遊戲。

40　desist [dɪˈzɪst] (v.) 停止
41　lackluster [ˈlæklʌstər] (a.) 毫無生氣的
42　flagon [ˈflægən] (n.) （有壺蓋、壺嘴、把手的）大肚壺

. . . though these folks were evidently amusing themselves,
yet they maintained the gravest faces, the most mysterious silence . . .

By degrees, Rip's awe and apprehension subsided. He even ventured, when no eye was fixed upon him, to taste the beverage which he found had much of the flavor of excellent Hollands. He was naturally a thirsty soul, and was soon tempted to repeat the draught. One taste provoked another; and he reiterated[43] his visits to the flagon so often, that at length his senses were overpowered, his eyes swam in his head, his head gradually declined, and he fell into a deep sleep.

On waking, he found himself on the green knoll whence he had first seen the old man of the glen. He rubbed his eyes—it was a bright sunny morning. The birds were hopping and twittering among the bushes, and the eagle was wheeling aloft, and breasting the pure mountain breeze.

"Surely," thought Rip, "I have not slept here all night." He recalled the occurrences before he fell asleep. The strange man with the keg of liquor—the mountain ravine—the wild retreat among the rocks—the woebegone[44] party at ninepins—the flagon—"Oh! that flagon! that wicked flagon!" thought Rip—"what excuse shall I make to Dame Van Winkle?"

---

43 reiterate [riːˈɪtəreɪt] (v.) 反覆
44 woebegone [ˈwoʊbɪɡɑːn] (a.) 滿面愁容的；愁眉苦臉的

　　李伯內心的恐懼與不安逐漸消失。他甚至還趁沒人看到的時候，大膽地偷喝酒。那酒嚐起來像上等的荷蘭杜松子酒。他本來就愛喝酒，所以喝完第一口，馬上忍不住喝了第二口。喝完一口又想喝一口，他一口接一口地喝了壺裡的酒，最後漸漸失去意識，變得迷茫恍惚。他的頭越垂越低，接著就進入了沉沉的夢鄉。

　　他醒來時，發現自己正躺在那個長滿青草的小土丘上，他就是在這裡遇到山谷裡的老頭的。他揉揉眼睛，發現已是陽光燦爛的早晨了。鳥兒在樹叢間蹦跳歌唱，老鷹在空中盤旋，翱翔在山間清新的微風中。

　　「我該不會在這裡睡了一夜吧！」他心想。他想起睡覺之前所發生的事情，想起揹著酒桶的怪老頭，還有那片山谷，他們在山岩間辛苦地攀爬，還有鐵著臉玩滾球的那些人，他也想起了酒壺。「噢！酒壺！要命的酒壺！我要怎麼跟李伯夫人解釋？」李伯想。

On waking, he found himself on the green knoll whence
he had first seen the old man of the glen.

He looked round for his gun, but in place of the clean, well-oiled fowling-piece, he found an old firelock lying by him, the barrel encrusted [45] with rust, the lock falling off, and the stock worm-eaten. He now suspected that the grave roysterers of the mountains had put a trick upon him, and having dosed him with liquor, had robbed him of his gun.

Wolf, too, had disappeared, but he might have strayed away after a squirrel or partridge. He whistled after him and shouted his name, but all in vain; the echoes repeated his whistle and shout, but no dog was to be seen.

He determined to revisit the scene of the last evening's gambol, and if he met with any of the party, to demand his dog and gun. As he rose to walk, he found himself stiff in the joints, and wanting in his usual activity.

　　他四下尋找他的槍，但是躺在他身邊的，不是他那把擦得光亮、上好油的獵槍，而是一把老舊的火槍，槍管都生鏽了，扳機都脫落了，槍柄也蛀壞了。他開始懷疑是山裡那幫嚴肅的酒鬼在捉弄他，先用酒把他灌醉，再把他的槍偷走。

　　小狼也不見了，不過牠可能是跑去哪裡追松鼠或山鶉了。他吹口哨，叫喊小狼的名字，但是沒有回應。他的口哨聲和呼喊聲在山間迴盪，但是就是不見小狼的蹤影。

　　他決定回去昨晚那群人玩滾球的地方，找到他們以後一定要跟他們討回他的狗和槍。他想站起身子，卻發現自己關節僵硬，不如平時那樣的靈活。

---

45 encrust [ɪnˈkrʌst] (v.) 覆以外皮

"These mountain beds do not agree with me[46]," thought Rip, "and if this frolic should lay me up[47] with a fit of the rheumatism[48], I shall have a blessed time with Dame Van Winkle."

With some difficulty he got down into the glen: he found the gully up which he and his companion had ascended the preceding evening; but to his astonishment a mountain stream was now foaming down it, leaping from rock to rock, and filling the glen with babbling murmurs.

He, however, made shift to scramble up its sides, working his toilsome way through thickets of birch, sassafras, and witch-hazel; and sometimes tripped up or entangled by the wild grape vines that twisted their coils or tendrils from tree to tree, and spread a kind of network in his path.

At length he reached to where the ravine had opened through the cliffs to the amphitheater; but no traces of such opening remained. The rocks presented a high impenetrable wall, over which the torrent came tumbling in a sheet of feathery foam, and fell into a broad deep basin, black from the shadows of the surrounding forest.

「睡在山裡頭對我實在不太好，要是這一晚害我染上風濕病，每天得躺在家裡，那我跟李伯夫人就真有好日子過了。」他想。

他勉強走下山谷，找到前天傍晚他跟老頭爬上的山溝。但是令他吃驚的是，山溝裡現在竟然變得流水淙淙，溪水在岩石間飛濺，整片山谷都是潺潺的水聲。

於是他改沿著小溪邊往上爬，吃力地在樺樹、黃樟樹和金縷梅的樹叢間前進。野葡萄藤伸出的卷鬚纏繞在樹枝之間，在他的前進的路上佈下一張張錯綜複雜的網，不時把他絆倒或纏住。

最後他終於爬到山谷那塊可以穿過峭壁、通向空地的地方，然而原來峭壁上的缺口卻不復存在。山岩在他眼前形成一堵無法穿越的高牆，山岩的前面，山澗嘩嘩流下，激起一片白色的水花，最後流入一塊又深又廣的窪地，窪地在四周森林的陰影下一片漆黑。

46 not agree with somebody 有害某人之健康
47 lay somebody up 使臥病在床
48 rheumatism [ˈruːmətɪzəm] (n.) 風濕病

❶
李伯大夢

Here, then, poor Rip was brought to a stand. He again called and whistled after his dog; he was only answered by the cawing of a flock of idle crows, sporting high in air about a dry tree that overhung a sunny precipice; and who, secure in their elevation, seemed to look down and scoff at the poor man's perplexities[49].

What was to be done? The morning was passing away, and Rip felt famished[50] for want of his breakfast. He grieved to give up his dog and gun; he dreaded to meet his wife; but it would not do to starve among the mountains. He shook his head, shouldered the rusty firelock, and, with a heart full of trouble and anxiety, turned his steps homeward.

As he approached the village, he met a number of people, but none whom he knew, which somewhat surprised him, for he had thought himself acquainted with every one in the country round. Their dress, too, was of a different fashion from that to which he was accustomed.

They all stared at him with equal marks of surprise, and whenever they cast eyes upon him, invariably stroked their chins. The constant recurrence of this gesture induced Rip, involuntarily, to do the same, when, to his astonishment, he found his beard had grown a foot long!

49 perplexity [pər'pleksɪti] (n.) 困惑
50 famished ['fæmɪʃt] (a.) 非常飢餓的

可憐的李伯走到這裡只能就此打住了。他又開始吹口哨，呼喊小狼的名字，但是回應他的只是一群烏鴉嘎嘎的叫聲。烏鴉在高空圍著一棵懸在峭壁邊的枯樹打轉，峭壁被太陽照得發亮。烏鴉高高在上，牠們正往下看，似乎是在嘲笑李伯這個可憐的傻子。

怎麼辦？就快中午了，沒吃早飯的李伯飢腸轆轆。他不願放棄他的狗和槍，也怕見到老婆，但是餓死在這山中也不是辦法。他搖搖頭，扛起生鏽的火槍，憂心忡忡地走上回家的路。

走在通往村子的路上，他遇到了幾個人，但是這幾個人他都不認識，這就有點奇怪了，因為村子這一帶的人他應該都認識的啊。這些人的穿著也很奇特，不是李伯熟悉的裝扮。

他們每個人都一臉驚訝地瞪著他看，而且只要眼光一落到他身上，就開始摸自己的下巴。這個動作看多了，李伯不自主地也摸起自己的下巴，結果這一摸，他發現自己的鬍子竟有三十公分長！

He had now entered the skirts of the village. A troop of strange children ran at his heels, hooting[51] after him, and pointing at his gray beard. The dogs, too, not one of which he recognized for an old acquaintance, barked at him as he passed. The very village was altered: it was larger and more populous. There were rows of houses which he had never seen before, and those which had been his familiar haunts had disappeared. Strange names were over the doors—strange faces at the windows—everything was strange.

His mind now misgave him; he began to doubt whether both he and the world around him were not bewitched. Surely this was his native village, which he had left but the day before. There stood the Kaatskill mountains—there ran the silver Hudson at a distance—there was every hill and dale precisely as it had always been—Rip was sorely perplexed—"That flagon last night," thought he, "has addled my poor head sadly!"

It was with some difficulty that he found the way to his own house, which he approached with silent awe, expecting every moment to hear the shrill voice of Dame Van Winkle. He found the house gone to decay—the roof fallen in, the windows shattered, and the doors off the hinges.

51 hoot [hu:t] (v.) （不尊敬地）狂笑

　　他這時走進村子。一群他不認識的孩子追著他跑，手指著他灰色的鬍子哈哈大笑。街上的狗，他一隻也認不出來，也都對著他吠。村子變了，變得更大、更熱鬧了。成排的房子，都是他以前沒見過的，而他熟悉的地點卻已不復見。門上寫著陌生的名字，窗口探出陌生的臉龐——他所看到的一切都變得陌生了。

　　他開始擔心起來，懷疑自己和這個世界是不是都被施了魔法。沒錯，這是他出生的村子，他前一天才離開的村子。卡士奇山矗立在這裡，銀色的哈德遜河在那邊遠遠流過，每座山丘與山谷都在原來的位置，李伯實在想不通。「昨晚那壺酒把我可憐的腦袋都搞糊塗了！」他想。

　　他花了好些功夫才找到回家的路。他膽顫心驚地悄悄走近，心想隨時都會聽到李伯夫人尖銳的聲音。他發現屋子破舊不堪，屋頂已經塌陷，窗戶都破了，門也脫落了。

A half-starved dog that looked like Wolf was skulking[52] about it. Rip called him by name, but the cur[53] snarled, showed his teeth, and passed on. This was an unkind cut indeed.—"My very dog," sighed poor Rip, "has forgotten me!"

He entered the house, which, to tell the truth, Dame Van Winkle had always kept in neat order. It was empty, forlorn, and apparently abandoned. This desolateness overcame all his connubial[54] fears—he called loudly for his wife and children—the lonely chambers rang for a moment with his voice, and then all again was silence.

　　一隻餓得半死不活、看起來像小狼的狗，畏畏縮縮地在屋外亂竄。李伯叫牠，但狗只是張牙露齒地對他低吠了幾聲，然後走開。這真是一個無情的打擊。「我自己的狗，都不認識我了！」李伯嘆了口氣。

　　他走進屋裡。李伯夫人一向都把屋裡打理得井井有條，但是現在屋子裡空無一物、冷冷清清的，顯然已經沒有人住在這裡了。屋子裡的淒涼景象，讓李伯一時之間忘了對老婆的懼怕，他開始大聲呼喊老婆和孩子的名字。呼喊聲迴盪在空蕩蕩的屋子裡，最後又恢復一片寂靜。

52　skulk [skʌlk] (v.) 鬼鬼祟祟地走
53　cur [kɜːr] (n.) 惡狗；雜種狗
54　connubial [kəˈnubiəl] (a.) 夫妻間的；婚姻的

It was with some difficulty that he found the way to his own house, which he approached with silent awe, expecting every moment to hear the shrill voice of Dame Van Winkle.

He now hurried forth, and hastened to his old resort, the village inn—but it too was gone. A large rickety wooden building stood in its place, with great gaping windows, some of them broken, and mended with old hats and petticoats, and over the door was painted, "The Union Hotel, by Jonathan Doolittle." Instead of the great tree that used to shelter the quiet little Dutch inn of yore, there now was reared a tall naked pole, with something on the top that looked like a red nightcap, and from it was fluttering a flag, on which was a singular assemblage of stars and stripes—all this was strange and incomprehensible.

He recognized on the sign, however, the ruby face of King George, under which he had smoked so many a peaceful pipe, but even this was singularly metamorphosed[55]. The red coat was changed for one of blue and buff, a sword was held in the hand instead of a scepter, the head was decorated with a cocked hat[56], and underneath was painted in large characters, "GENERAL WASHINGTON."

There was, as usual, a crowd of folk about the door, but none that Rip recollected. The very character of the people seemed changed. There was a busy, bustling, disputatious tone about it, instead of the accustomed phlegm[57] and drowsy tranquility. He looked in vain for the sage Nicholas Vedder, with his broad face, double chin, and fair long pipe, uttering clouds of tobacco smoke, instead of idle speeches; or Van Bummel, the schoolmaster, doling forth the contents of an ancient newspaper.

他加快腳步走向他偷閒的老地方——村裡的小酒館，但是小酒館也不見了。矗立在那裡的是一棟東倒西歪的大木屋，開著幾扇大窗戶，有些窗戶都已經破了，用舊帽子和舊襯裙勉強補起來，門的上方漆著「聯合旅館，強納森‧杜立德經營」幾個字。原來總是為這間安靜的荷蘭小酒館投下一片庇蔭的大樹不見了，現在直立在那裡的是一根光光禿禿的長木竿，木竿頂端有一個像頂紅色睡帽的東西，上面飄揚著一面旗子，旗面上是一堆星星和條紋之類的奇特圖案。這一切對李伯來說，都顯得如此陌生而不可思議。

　　不過他還是在門口的畫像上認出了喬治三世國王紅潤的臉龐，他就在這個畫像下不知愜意地抽了多少菸斗，只是畫像也變了樣。原來的紅袍變成了藍黃相間的外套，手裡的權杖也換成一把劍，頭上戴著一頂捲邊三角帽，畫像下方寫著「華盛頓將軍」這幾個大字。

　　酒館門口就跟往常一樣聚集了一群人，但沒有一個人是李伯所認識的。這些村民的個性好像也變了，他們鬧哄哄的，說起話來誰也不讓誰，一點都沒有以往那種慵懶平靜的樣子。他在人群中尋找村子的長老尼可拉斯‧維德的身影，想找到他那一張寬臉孔、雙下巴，嘴裡還含著長菸斗，吐出層層的白煙，不和大家說著言不及義的閒話。他也尋找著小學老師德瑞克‧凡‧布墨正在為大家朗讀舊報紙的身影。

55　metamorphose [ˌmetəˈmɔːrfoʊz] (v.) 使變形
56　a cocked hat 古時的捲邊三角帽
57　phlegm [flem] (n.) 冷靜；鎮靜

In place of these, a lean, bilious-looking fellow, with his pockets full of handbills, was haranguing[58], vehemently about rights of citizens—elections—members of Congress—liberty—Bunker's hill[59]—heroes of seventy-six[60]—and other words, which were a perfect Babylonish jargon to the bewildered Van Winkle.

The appearance of Rip, with his long grizzled beard, his rusty fowling-piece, his uncouth dress, and the army of women and children that had gathered at his heels, soon attracted the attention of the tavern politicians. They crowded round him, eying him from head to foot with great curiosity. The orator bustled up to him, and, drawing him partly aside, inquired, "on which side he voted?"

Rip stared in vacant stupidity. Another short but busy little fellow pulled him by the arm, and rising on tiptoe, inquired in his ear, "whether he was Federal or Democrat."

Rip was equally at a loss to comprehend the question; when a knowing, self-important old gentleman in a sharp cocked hat, made his way through the crowd, putting them to the right and left with his elbows as he passed, and planting himself before Van Winkle, with one arm akimbo[61], the other resting on his cane, his keen eyes and sharp hat penetrating, as it were, into his very soul, demanded in an austere tone, "What brought him to the election with a gun on his shoulder, and a mob at his heels, and whether he meant to breed a riot in the village?"

李伯找不到他們的身影，他只看到一個激動的瘦子在口袋塞滿了傳單，正激昂地講著什麼公民、選舉權、國會議員、自由、邦克山戰役、一九七六年的英雄等等的，一頭霧水的李伯一句也聽不懂。

李伯在這裡一出現，他那長長的灰鬍子、肩上生鏽的獵槍、一身破舊的衣裳，還有身後跟來的一群婦女與小孩，馬上就引起了酒館裡這些政治家們的注意。他們紛紛圍住他，好奇地從頭到腳打量他。剛才那名演說者衝向他，把他拉到一邊，問道：「您投票給哪一邊？」

李伯呆呆地望著他。一個小個子抓著他的手臂，踮起腳尖，附在他的耳邊說：「他問你是聯邦派還是民主派的？」

李伯依舊一臉茫然，他聽不懂他在講什麼。這時候，一個樣子很神氣的老紳士，他戴著一頂捲邊三角帽，用手肘推開左右的人群一路擠過來，在李伯面前站定，然後一雙手叉在腰上，一隻手歇在枴杖上，他銳利的雙眼和尖銳的帽簷，彷彿直穿進李伯的靈魂似的。他嚴厲地問道：「你為什麼肩上扛著一把槍、身後帶著一群暴民來投票？你是不是想在村子裡鬧事？」

58 harangue [həˈræŋ] (v.) 高聲訓斥
59 Bunker's Hill 邦克山（在波士頓附近，在此指邦克山戰役，美國獨立戰爭初期首場大型戰役）
60 seventy-six 指美國獨立的年份 1776 年
61 akimbo [əˈkɪmbou] (a.) 手叉腰的

❶
李伯大夢

"Alas! gentlemen," cried Rip, somewhat dismayed, "I am a poor quiet man, a native of the place, and a loyal subject of the King, God bless him!"

Here a general shout burst from the bystanders—"a tory[62]! a tory! a spy! a refugee! hustle him! away with him!" It was with great difficulty that the self-important man in the cocked hat restored order; and having assumed a tenfold austerity of brow, demanded again of the unknown culprit, what he came there for, and whom he was seeking. The poor man humbly assured him that he meant no harm, but merely came there in search of some of his neighbors, who used to keep about the tavern.

"Well—who are they?—name them."

Rip bethought himself[63] a moment, and inquired, "Where's Nicholas Vedder?"

There was a silence for a little while, when an old man replied, in a thin, piping voice, "Nicholas Vedder? why, he is dead and gone these eighteen years! There was a wooden tombstone in the churchyard that used to tell all about him, but that's rotten and gone too."

"Where's Brom Dutcher?"

"Oh, he went off to the army in the beginning of the war; some say he was killed at the storming of Stony-Point—others say he was drowned in a squall[64] at the foot of Antony's Nose. I don't know—he never came back again."

「不是的！這位先生，我只是一個可憐的小老百姓，是這個村子裡的人，我忠心效忠國王，國王萬歲！」李伯有些驚慌地喊道。

周圍的人一聽，立刻大喊起來：「保皇黨的！保皇黨的！間諜！難民！趕走他！趕走他！」頭上戴著三角帽的神氣老紳士費了好大的勁，才恢復現場的秩序。他皺起眉頭，擺出一副比剛才還要更嚴肅的神情，再次質問這名陌生的罪犯，問他來這裡有什麼目的，到底是要來找誰的。可憐的李伯謙卑地向他保證，他無意傷害任何人，他之所以來這裡，只是想找幾個常在酒館裡蹓躂的鄰居。

「好，那你的鄰居是誰？叫什麼名字？」

李伯想了一下，開口問道：「尼可拉斯·維德在哪裡？」

大家一片沉默，一會兒後才有一個老人用微弱的尖嗓門答道：「尼可拉斯·維德？他早就死啦，都死了十八年了！教堂的墓地本來有塊木碑記載著他的生平，現在都朽掉了。」

「那布藍·杜齊在哪裡？」

「他戰爭爆發後就去從軍了。有人說他在史東尼角一役中喪生了，也有人說他在一場暴風雨中，在安東尼鼻山的山腳下溺斃了。我也不知道，總之他再也沒有回來過。」

62 tory ['tɔːri] (n.) 保皇黨員；保守黨員
63 bethink oneself 考慮
64 squall [skwɑːl] (n.) 夾帶雨雪的一陣狂風

"Where's Van Bummel, the schoolmaster?"

"He went off to the wars, too, was a great militia general, and is now in Congress."

Rip's heart died away at hearing of these sad changes in his home and friends, and finding himself thus alone in the world. Every answer puzzled him too, by treating of such enormous lapses of time, and of matters which he could not understand: war—Congress—Stony-Point;—he had no courage to ask after any more friends, but cried out in despair, "Does nobody here know Rip Van Winkle?"

"Oh, Rip Van Winkle!" exclaimed two or three. "Oh, to be sure! that's Rip Van Winkle yonder, leaning against the tree."

Rip looked, and beheld a precise counterpart of himself as he went up the mountain: apparently as lazy, and certainly as ragged. The poor fellow was now completely confounded[65]. He doubted his own identity, and whether he was himself or another man. In the midst of his bewilderment, the man in the cocked hat demanded who he was, and what was his name?

"God knows!" exclaimed he, at his wit's end[66]; "I'm not myself—I'm somebody else—that's me yonder—no—that's somebody else got into my shoes—I was myself last night, but I fell asleep on the mountain, and they've changed my gun, and everything's changed, and I'm changed, and I can't tell what's my name, or who I am!"

「那小學老師德瑞克・凡・布墨呢？」

「他也去從軍，還是一個優秀的民兵將軍，他現在在國會裡。」

聽到家鄉和朋友這些悲哀的改變，李伯意識到自己現在是孤孤單單地留在這個世界上，他心都涼了。他們的每一句話他都越聽越糊塗，這麼多年的時間，這麼多他無法理解的東西：戰爭、國會、史東尼角。他沒有勇氣再去詢問其他友人的下落，絕望之中，他大喊道：「那有人知道李伯・凡・溫可這個人嗎？」

「噢，李伯・凡・溫可！」兩、三個人喊道：「知道啊！李伯・凡・溫可就在那裡，就靠在樹那邊。」

李伯一看，看到一個和他上山的樣子很相像的男人：這個男人顯然跟他一樣懶惰、一樣衣衫襤褸。可憐的李伯完全糊塗了，他開始懷疑自己的身分，懷疑自己不再是自己，而是變成了另一個人。這時一個頭戴三角帽的老人問他是誰，叫什麼名字。

「只有老天才知道！」已經不知所措的李伯大喊道：「我不是我自己了，我是另外一個人。那邊那個人就是我，不對，那是別人鑽進我的身體。我昨天晚上還是我自己，後來我在山上睡著了，然後他們就把我的槍換掉，把什麼都換掉，甚至把我也換掉了，我根本不知道我的名字，也不知道我是誰！」

65 confound [kənˈfaʊnd] (v.) 使困惑
66 at one's wit's end 不知所措；智窮計盡

The bystanders began now to look at each other, nod, wink significantly, and tap their fingers against their foreheads. There was a whisper, also, about securing the gun, and keeping the old fellow from doing mischief; at the very suggestion of which, the self-important man in the cocked hat retired with some precipitation[67].

At this critical moment a fresh, comely woman pressed through the throng to get a peep at the gray-bearded man. She had a chubby[68] child in her arms, which, frightened at his looks, began to cry. "Hush, Rip," cried she, "hush, you little fool; the old man won't hurt you." The name of the child, the air of the mother, the tone of her voice, all awakened a train of recollections in his mind.

"What is your name, my good woman?" asked he.

"Judith Gardenier."

"And your father's name?"

"Ah, poor man, Rip Van Winkle was his name, but it's twenty years since he went away from home with his gun, and never has been heard of since—his dog came home without him; but whether he shot himself, or was carried away by the Indians, nobody can tell. I was then but a little girl."

Rip had but one more question to ask; but he put it with a faltering[69] voice: "Where's your mother?"

---

67 precipitation [prɪˌsɪpɪˈteɪʃən] (n.) 倉促輕率的行動
68 chubby [ˈtʃʌbi] (a.) 圓圓胖胖的
69 faltering [ˈfɑːltərɪŋ] (a.) 畏縮的；結結巴巴的

圍觀的人群開始你看我、我看你，又是點頭、又是使眼色的，還用手指拍拍額頭。人群中有人低聲説，應該要把槍枝保管好，以免這個老頭亂來。一聽到這個建議，戴著三角帽的神氣老人就倉皇走掉了。

　　在這個關鍵的時刻，一個年輕漂亮的婦女擠到人群前面，想看看這個留著灰色鬍子的老人。她懷裡抱著一個圓圓胖胖的小娃娃，小娃娃一見到李伯，就嚇得哇哇大哭。婦女説道：「別哭，小李伯，別哭了，傻孩子，老爺爺不會對你怎麼樣的。」娃娃的名字和母親的神態與聲調，立刻勾起李伯一串串的回憶。

　　「小姐，你叫什麼名字？」他問。

　　「茱蒂・賈登尼。」

　　「你父親叫什麼名字？」

　　「唉，我可憐的父親叫做李伯・凡・溫可。他二十年前扛著獵槍出門後，我們就再也沒有他的消息了。當時他的狗自己跑回來，至於我父親，他到底是自己開槍打死自己了，還是被印地安人抓走了，沒有人知道。當時我的年紀還很小。」

　　李伯還想問另外一個問題。他結巴地問道：「那你母親呢？」

"Oh, she too had died but a short time since; she broke a blood-vessel in a fit of passion at a New England[70] pedler."

There was a drop of comfort, at least, in this intelligence. The honest man could contain himself no longer. He caught his daughter and her child in his arms. "I am your father!" cried he—"Young Rip Van Winkle once—old Rip Van Winkle now! Does nobody know poor Rip Van Winkle?"

All stood amazed, until an old woman, tottering[71] out from among the crowd, put her hand to her brow, and peering under it in his face for a moment, exclaimed, "Sure enough! it is Rip Van Winkle—it is himself! Welcome home again, old neighbor. Why, where have you been these twenty long years?"

Rip's story was soon told, for the whole twenty years had been to him but as one night. The neighbors stared when they heard it; some were seen to wink at each other, and put their tongues in their cheeks: and the self-important man in the cocked hat, who, when the alarm was over, had returned to the field, screwed down the corners of his mouth, and shook his head—upon which there was a general shaking of the head throughout the assemblage.

70 New England，美國東北部一區，包括今日緬因、新罕布什爾、佛蒙特、麻薩諸塞、羅德島和康乃迪克等州。據說因此區地形風景與英國海岸相似，因而被命名為「新英格蘭」。
71 totter [ˈtɑːtər] (v.) 踉踉蹌蹌；步履蹣跚

「噢，她前一陣子才去剛世。她跟一個新英格蘭的小販吵架，氣得腦血管破裂。」

這個消息裡至少含有一點安慰。李伯再也忍不住了，他把女兒和孫子一把擁進懷裡。「我就是你的父親！我以前是李伯，現在是老李伯了。沒有人認識可憐的李伯嗎？」他喊道。

大家聽得都楞住了。這時一個老太太跟跟蹌蹌地走到前面，把手舉到眉毛前，盯著李伯的臉看了好一會兒，然後驚呼：「是啊！他就是李伯，他就是李伯本人。老鄰居，歡迎你回來啊，你這二十年都到哪裡去了呀？」

李伯立刻把事情的經過一五一十地告訴大家，這整整二十年對他來說只是一夕之間的事。村民們聽得目瞪口呆，有些人互相眨眨眼，做著鬼臉。戴著三角帽的神氣老人在一場虛驚後，又走了回來。他噘著嘴，搖搖頭。眾人一看到他搖頭，也都跟著搖起頭來。

It was determined, however, to take the opinion of old Peter Vanderdonk, who was seen slowly advancing up the road. He was a descendant of the historian of that name, who wrote one of the earliest accounts of the province. Peter was the most ancient inhabitant of the village, and well versed in[72] all the wonderful events and traditions of the neighborhood. He recollected Rip at once, and corroborated[73] his story in the most satisfactory manner.

He assured the company that it was a fact, handed down from his ancestor the historian, that the Kaatskill mountains had always been haunted by strange beings. That it was affirmed that the great Hendrick Hudson, the first discoverer of the river and country, kept a kind of vigil[74] there every twenty years, with his crew of the Half-moon; being permitted in this way to revisit the scenes of his enterprise, and keep a guardian eye upon the river, and the great city called by his name.

That his father had once seen them in their old Dutch dresses playing at ninepins in the hollow of the mountain; and that he himself had heard, one summer afternoon, the sound of their balls, like distant peals of thunder.

To make a long story short, the company broke up, and returned to the more important concerns of the election. Rip's daughter took him home to live with her; she had a snug, well-furnished house, and a stout cheery farmer for a husband, whom Rip recollected for one of the urchins that used to climb upon his back.

不過大家決定聽聽老彼得・凡德東怎麼說，這時他正慢慢向酒館這邊走過來。他的祖先是歷史學家，當地最早的一份歷史紀錄就是他的祖先所寫的。彼得是村子裡最年長的居民，熟知當地所有的軼事與傳統。他立刻就想起李伯這個人，並且非常肯定地證實了李伯的事情。

Peter was the most ancient inhabitant of the village

　　他告訴大家，根據他歷史學家的祖先所說，卡士奇山上的確一向就有奇怪的東西出沒。他說，偉大的亨卓克・哈德遜，也就是發現哈德遜河和這個地方的人，每二十年都會帶他「半月號」船上的船員在山上守夜，重訪他發現的這片大地，並守護依他命名的這條河流與城市。

　　他的父親就曾在山上的空地親眼看到他們穿著荷蘭傳統服飾在玩滾球，而他自己也曾在一個夏日午後親耳聽到他們隆隆的滾球聲，聽起來就像遠方傳來的雷聲。

　　長話短說，人群最後散開了，留下的人又回到更重要的選舉問題上。李伯的女兒把李伯帶回家一起住。她有一間溫暖舒適的屋子，和一個健壯、開朗的務農老公，李伯認出他就是以前常爬到他背上的一個小頑童。

72　be versed in . . . 精通；通曉
73　corroborate [kəˈrɑːbəreɪt] (v.) 證實
74　vigil [ˈvɪdʒɪl] (n.) 守夜；警戒

As to Rip's son and heir, who was the ditto of himself, seen leaning against the tree, he was employed to work on the farm; but evinced a hereditary disposition to attend to any thing else but his business.

Rip now resumed his old walks and habits; he soon found many of his former cronies[75], though all rather the worse for the wear and tear of time[76]; and preferred making friends among the rising generation, with whom he soon grew into great favor.

Having nothing to do at home, and being arrived at that happy age when a man can be idle with impunity, he took his place once more on the bench at the inn door, and was reverenced as one of the patriarchs of the village, and a chronicle of the old times "before the war."

　　至於李伯的兒子兼繼承人，就是之前靠在樹邊、跟李伯一個樣子的小李伯，他受雇於別人的農場。他完全遺傳了父親的性格，他樂於幫忙別人，自己的事情卻不願意做。

　　李伯又恢復以前到處蹓躂的老習慣。他很快就找到不少以前的朋友，但是經過歲月的摧殘，他們每個人都老了，所以李伯寧願多跟年輕人打交道，而他也很快就建立起極佳的人緣。

　　現在李伯在家沒事做了，而且也到了享清福的年紀，於是他又開始天天坐在酒館門口的長凳上。他被村民尊為村裡的一位長老，是一位「戰前歷史」的專家。

---

75 crony ['kroʊni] (n.) 老友；摯友
76 the worse for the wear and tear of time 經歲月的摧殘而年老不堪

. . . and preferred making friends among the rising generation,
with whom he soon grew into great favor

It was some time before he could get into the regular track of gossip, or could be made to comprehend the strange events that had taken place during his torpor. How that there had been a revolutionary war—that the country had thrown off the yoke of old England—and that, instead of being a subject of his Majesty George the Third, he was now a free citizen of the United States.

Rip, in fact, was no politician; the changes of states and empires made but little impression on him; but there was one species of despotism[77] under which he had long groaned, and that was—petticoat government.

Happily that was at an end; he had got his neck out of the yoke of matrimony, and could go in and out whenever he pleased, without dreading the tyranny of Dame Van Winkle. Whenever her name was mentioned, however, he shook his head, shrugged his shoulders, and cast up his eyes; which might pass either for[78] an expression of resignation[79] to his fate, or joy at his deliverance.

He used to tell his story to every stranger that arrived at Mr. Doolittle's hotel. He was observed, at first, to vary on some points every time he told it, which was, doubtless, owing to his having so recently awaked. It at last settled down precisely to the tale I have related, and not a man, woman, or child in the neighborhood, but knew it by heart.

77 despotism ['despətɪzəm] (n.) 暴政統治；專制獨裁
78 pass for . . . 被看作……
79 resignation [ˌrezɪg'neɪʃən] (n.) 聽天由命；認命

他過了一段時間之後才有辦法跟上村民的閒聊，了解他在山上沉睡的那段時間裡所發生的各種怪事。像是怎麼會發生了獨立戰爭——這個國家脫離了英國的統治——所以他不再是喬治三世國王的子民，而是一個美國的自由公民了。

李伯對政治不感興趣，對於聯邦或帝國的變化，他沒有特別的感觸。他受到的是另外一種暴政，他曾經長期受到壓迫，那就是——老婆的暴政。

幸好這都結束了。他已經擺脫婚姻的枷鎖，可以自由地進出家門，不必繼續在李伯夫人的恐怖統治底下惶恐度日。每當有人提起李伯夫人的名字，他就會搖搖頭、聳聳肩，然後抬頭望著天，那個樣子既像是在向老天認命，又像是在表達解脫的喜悅。

每個來到杜立德旅館的外地人，李伯都會跟他們說起自己的故事。一開始，他講的事情會有點前後不一致，這是因為他才剛大夢初醒的緣故。後來，他經歷的經過才確定下來，這也就是我在此敘述的版本。村子裡的男女老少，無一不對他的故事瞭若指掌。

Some always pretended to doubt the reality of it, and insisted that Rip had been out of his head, and that this was one point on which he always remained flighty. The old Dutch inhabitants, however, almost universally gave it full credit.

Even to this day, they never hear a thunder-storm of a summer afternoon about the Kaatskill, but they say Hendrick Hudson and his crew are at their game of ninepins; and it is a common wish of all henpecked husbands in the neighborhood, when life hangs heavy on their hands, that they might have a quieting draught[80] out of Rip Van Winkle's flagon.

NOTE

The foregoing Tale, one would suspect, had been suggested to Mr. Knickerbocker by a little German superstition about the Emperor Frederick *der Rothbart* and the Kypphäuser mountain: the subjoined note, however, which he had appended to the tale, shows that it is an absolute fact, narrated with his usual fidelity[81]:

"The story of Rip Van Winkle may seem incredible to many, but nevertheless I give it my full belief, for I know the vicinity of our old Dutch settlements to have been very subject to marvelous events and appearances.

不過，總有些人就是不相
信，他們覺得李伯一定是精神
錯亂了，才會編出這樣的故
事。不過那些荷蘭來的老村民
都很相信李伯。

到了今天，他們還是不曾
在夏日的午後聽到卡士奇山傳
來雷聲，但是他們會說，亨卓
克‧哈德遜和他的船員正在玩
滾球。而村子裡每一個懼內的
男人，他們在日子難過的時
候，都希望能喝一口李伯酒壺
裡的酒，然後沉沉睡上一覺。

追述

可能有人會以為，是德國那則關於佛瑞克大帝和克柏浩斯山的
迷信，帶給尼可布可先生靈感，寫出了上面這個故事。故事後附加
的後記，則說明李伯大夢是一個詳實敘述的真實故事：

「很多人可能無法相信李伯的故事，但我個人是百分之百地相
信，因為我知道我們的荷蘭老村子附近經常出現奇奇怪怪的事件。

80　draught [dræft] (n.) 一口
81　fidelity [fɪˈdeləti] (n.) 詳實；精確無誤

Indeed, I have heard many stranger stories than this, in the villages along the Hudson; all of which were too well authenticated[82] to admit of a doubt. I have even talked with Rip Van Winkle myself, who, when last I saw him, was a very venerable old man, and so perfectly rational and consistent on every other point, that I think no conscientious person could refuse to take this into the bargain; nay, I have seen a certificate on the subject taken before a country justice and signed with a cross, in the justice's own handwriting. The story, therefore, is beyond the possibility of doubt."

D. K.

POSTSCRIPT

The following are traveling notes from a memorandum-book of Mr. Knickerbocker:

The Kaatsberg or Catskill mountains have always been a region full of fable. The Indians considered them the abode[83] of spirits, who influenced the weather, spreading sunshine or clouds over the landscape, and sending good or bad hunting seasons. They were ruled by an old squaw[84] spirit, said to be their mother.

She dwelt on the highest peak of the Catskills, and had charge of the doors of day and night to open and shut them at the proper hour.

我還聽過比這個更奇怪的事情，都是在哈德遜河邊的村子裡發生的，而且個個都經過證實，不容一絲懷疑。我甚至還親自跟李伯談過話，他是個令人尊敬的老人，我最後一次見到他的時候，他頭腦非常清楚，事情的來龍去脈也交代得很清楚，我想沒有一個認真負責的人不會把這一點考慮進去。而且，我還看到一份證明這個事件的文件，這個文件被帶到當地一位法官面前，法官還親手簽了名，所以，李伯的故事是千真萬確的。」

尼可布可補記

. . . .

後記

　　以下是尼可布可先生在本子上記下的旅遊筆記：

　　卡士奇山區一向是個充滿傳說的地方。印地安人相信卡士奇山是仙靈居住的地方，仙靈控制著天氣，為大地帶來陽光，也帶來烏雲，可以為狩獵帶來豐收，也可以帶來慘澹的一季。這些仙靈都被一個老女仙靈所統治，據說她是他們的母親。

　　她住在卡士奇山的最高峰，掌管白天和夜晚，每天都要按時開關白天和夜晚的大門。

82　authenticate [ɔ:'θentɪkeɪt] (v.) 證明是真實的
83　abode [ə'boʊd] (n.) 住所
84　squaw [skwɑ:] (n.) 北美印地安女人

❶
李
伯
大
夢

She hung up the new moons in the skies, and cut up the old ones into stars. In times of drought, if properly propitiated[85], she would spin light summer clouds out of cobwebs and morning dew, and send them off from the crest of the mountain, flake after flake, like flakes of carded cotton, to float in the air; until, dissolved by the heat of the sun, they would fall in gentle showers, causing the grass to spring, the fruits to ripen, and the corn to grow an inch an hour.

If displeased, however, she would brew up clouds black as ink, sitting in the midst of them like a bottle-bellied spider in the midst of its web; and when these clouds broke, woe betide the valleys!

In old times, say the Indian traditions, there was a kind of Manitou or Spirit, who kept about the wildest recesses of the Catskill mountains, and took a mischievous pleasure in wreaking all kind of evils and vexations[86] upon the red men. Sometimes he would assume the form of a bear, a panther, or a deer, lead the bewildered hunter a weary chase through tangled forests and among ragged rocks, and then spring off with a loud ho! ho! leaving him aghast on the brink of a beetling precipice or raging torrent.

The favorite abode of this Manitou[87] is still shown. It is a great rock or cliff on the loneliest part of the mountains, and, from the flowering vines which clamber about it, and the wild flowers which abound in its neighborhood, is known by the name of the Garden Rock.

她把新月掛上夜空，把舊的月亮剪成星星。乾旱的時候，居民如果平息了她的怒氣，她就會把蜘蛛網和早晨的露水紡成夏日的雲朵，讓它們從山峰飄出來，一片接一片，就像一團團梳理過的棉絮。片片雲朵被太陽一照，化成輕柔的陣雨落下來，青草開始冒出，水果開始成熟，玉米也開始長高，一小時就長三公分。

When these clouds broke, woe betide the valleys!

　　但是如果惹她生氣了，她會釀出墨黑的烏雲，自己坐在烏雲中間，就像一隻圓腹蜘蛛坐在蜘蛛網中間一般。而當這些烏雲化成雨落下來時，整片山谷都會被淹沒！

　　根據印地安人的傳說，古時候有一個仙靈，出沒於卡士奇山最深幽隱密的荒地，以捉弄印地安人為樂。有時候，他會化身為一隻熊，或者是一隻豹、一隻鹿，誘使困惑的獵人穿過錯綜複雜的森林和嶙峋的山岩一路追去，最後大喊一聲「哈！哈！」，然後跳開，留下獵人目瞪口呆地站在陡峭的懸崖或湍急的山澗邊。

　　這個仙靈最鍾愛的住所現在還看得到。它位在山中最僻靜的大山岩或大峭壁處，上面爬滿藤蔓，周圍開滿野花，人稱岩石花園。

85　propitiate [prəˈpɪʃɪeɪt] (v.) 使息怒；取悅
86　vexations [vekˈseɪʃəns] (n.) （常用複數）傷腦筋的事；令人惱火的事
87　Manitou (n.) （印地安人的）神

Near the foot of it is a small lake, the haunt of the solitary bittern, with water-snakes basking in the sun on the leaves of the pond-lilies which lie on the surface.

This place was held in great awe by the Indians, insomuch that the boldest hunter would not pursue his game within its precincts.

Once upon a time, however, a hunter who had lost his way, penetrated to the Garden Rock, where he beheld a number of gourds placed in the crotches of trees.

One of these he seized and made off with it, but in the hurry of his retreat he let it fall among the rocks, when a great stream gushed forth, which washed him away and swept him down precipices, where he was dished to pieces, and the stream made its way to the Hudson, and continues to flow to the present day, being the identical stream known by the name of the Kaaterskill.

山岩下有一個小湖,經常有孤單的水鳥飛來,還有水蛇躺在湖面的睡蓮葉上曬太陽。

印地安人把這個地方奉為聖地,就算是最大膽的獵人,也不敢走進這一帶打獵。

有一次,有一個獵人迷了路,闖進了岩石花園,看到樹木的枝椏上放了許多葫蘆。

他抓起其中一個葫蘆就跑,然而匆忙之中,葫蘆掉進了石塊之間,一條山澗頓時湧出,把他一路沖到懸崖下。他被摔得粉身碎骨。那條山澗一路流到哈德遜,直至今日仍汩汩奔流,人稱卡士奇河,也就是哈德遜河。

Nathaniel Hawthorne (1804-1864)

胎記

■ 霍桑

The Birthmark

In the latter part of the last century there lived a man of science, an eminent proficient in every branch of natural philosophy, who not long before our story opens had made experience of a spiritual affinity[1] more attractive than any chemical one. He had left his laboratory to the care of an assistant, cleared his fine countenance from the furnace smoke, washed the stain of acids from his fingers, and persuaded a beautiful woman to become his wife.

In those days when the comparatively recent discovery of electricity and other kindred mysteries of Nature seemed to open paths into the region of miracle, it was not unusual for the love of science to rival[2] the love of woman in its depth and absorbing energy. The higher intellect, the imagination, the spirit, and even the heart might all find their congenial aliment[3] in pursuits which, as some of their ardent votaries[4] believed, would ascend from one step of powerful intelligence to another, until the philosopher should lay his hand on the secret of creative force and perhaps make new worlds for himself.

We know not whether Aylmer possessed this degree of faith in man's ultimate control over Nature. He had devoted himself, however, too unreservedly[5] to scientific studies ever to be weaned from[6] them by any second passion. His love for his young wife might prove the stronger of the two; but it could only be by intertwining itself with his love of science, and uniting the strength of the latter to his own.

上個世紀的下半葉，有一個出名的科學家，精通各門自然科學。在我們的故事展開之前不久，他感受到一種比任何化學變化都要強大的心靈吸引力，於是他把實驗室丟給助手看管，然後洗淨被爐火薰黑的俊秀臉龐，沖掉手指上的酸液痕跡，前去跟一位美麗的女子求婚。

在那個時代，電和其他的自然奧秘剛被發現，通往奇蹟之路彷彿被開啟了。人們熱愛科學，那份深情與專注，甚至勝過對於男女的情愛。人類的智慧、想像、心靈，甚至是感情，都能從各種科學探索中找到適宜的養分。就像一些狂熱的科學信徒所相信的，科學探索會帶領他們一步步走上更高境界的智慧，最後解開創造之源的秘密，甚至為自己創造一個新的世界。

我們不知道艾墨是不是也如此深信人定勝天，我們只知道，他毫無保留地獻身於科學研究，任何其他的熱情都不可能使他放棄對科學的追求。他對年輕妻子的愛情，或許勝過對科學的熱愛，但這也是因為愛情緊緊與科學相繫，而且科學的力量也結合到了他自己的身上。

1 affinity [əˈfɪnɪti] (n.) 吸引力
2 rival [ˈraɪvəl] (v.) 比得上；與……匹敵
3 aliment [ˈælɪment] (n.) 養料；食物
4 votary [ˈvoʊtəri] (n.) 信徒；崇拜者
5 unreservedly [ˌʌnrɪˈzɜːrvɪdli] (adv.) 毫無保留地
6 wean somebody from . . . 使某人放棄（興趣、習慣）

Such a union accordingly took place, and was attended with truly remarkable consequences and a deeply impressive moral. One day, very soon after their marriage, Aylmer sat gazing at his wife with a trouble in his countenance that grew stronger until he spoke.

"Georgiana," said he, "has it never occurred to you that the mark upon your cheek might be removed?"

"No, indeed," said she, smiling; but perceiving the seriousness of his manner, she blushed deeply. "To tell you the truth it has been so often called a charm that I was simple enough to imagine it might be so."

"Ah, upon another face perhaps it might," replied her husband; "but never on yours. No, dearest Georgiana, you came so nearly perfect from the hand of Nature that this slightest possible defect, which we hesitate whether to term a defect or a beauty, shocks me, as being the visible mark of earthly imperfection."

"Shocks you, my husband!" cried Georgiana, deeply hurt; at first reddening with momentary anger, but then bursting into tears. "Then why did you take me from my mother's side? You cannot love what shocks you!"

To explain this conversation it must be mentioned that in the centre of Georgiana's left cheek there was a singular mark, deeply interwoven, as it were, with the texture and substance of her face. In the usual state of her complexion—a healthy though delicate bloom—the mark wore a tint of deeper crimson[7], which imperfectly defined its shape amid the surrounding rosiness.

這樣的結合，隨之招來了驚人的後果和深刻的教訓。婚後不久，有一天，艾墨坐在那兒，面有難色地端詳妻子。他的神情越來越不安，最後他終於開口了。

「喬琪娜，你有沒有想過，你臉上的那塊胎記也許可以弄掉？」他說。

「沒有呢。」她笑著說，但當她一察覺到艾墨嚴肅的表情時，立刻又滿臉羞紅。「有很多人都說它很迷人，所以我也就跟著這麼想了。」

「啊，長在別人的臉上也許會很迷人，但長在你臉上就不是了。我心愛的喬琪娜，大自然把你創造得這麼完美，所以這個小小的瑕疵很令我震驚，我不知道該說它是一種缺憾，還是一種美麗，它就像是不完美的塵世的一個印記。」艾墨說。

「它令你震驚，老公！」喬琪娜心痛地喊道。她氣得滿臉通紅，接著哭了起來。「既然如此，你為什麼要把我從我母親的身邊娶走？你怎麼可能愛一個令你震驚的人！」

要了解這段對話，容我說明一下。喬琪娜左邊的臉頰中間有一個胎記，深深地印在她臉部的皮膚上。平常，在她健康而嬌嫩的氣色下，這個胎記會淡淡地呈現出深紅色，在粉紅色的面頰上稍稍露出輪廓，顯得有所瑕疵。

7 crimson ['krɪmzən] (n.) 深紅色

When she blushed it gradually became more indistinct, and finally vanished amid the triumphant rush of blood that bathed the whole cheek with its brilliant glow. But if any shifting motion caused her to turn pale there was the mark again, a crimson stain upon the snow, in what Aylmer sometimes deemed an almost fearful distinctness.

Its shape bore not a little similarity to the human hand, though of the smallest pygmy[8] size. Georgiana's lovers were wont to say that some fairy at her birth hour had laid her tiny hand upon the infant's cheek, and left this impress there in token of the magic endowments that were to give her such sway over all hearts. Many a desperate swain[9] would have risked life for the privilege of pressing his lips to the mysterious hand.

It must not be concealed, however, that the impression wrought by this fairy sign manual varied exceedingly, according to the difference of temperament in the beholders. Some fastidious[10] persons—but they were exclusively of her own sex—affirmed that the bloody hand, as they chose to call it, quite destroyed the effect of Georgiana's beauty, and rendered her countenance even hideous. But it would be as reasonable to say that one of those small blue stains which sometimes occur in the purest statuary marble would convert the Eve of Powers[11] to a monster.

當她突然臉紅時，胎記會變得更模糊，最後消失在猛然湧上的紅暈之中。但身體如果有什麼大動作讓她臉色轉蒼白，胎記就又會出現，就像白雪上的紅斑一樣，清晰得有時會令艾墨觸目驚心。

這個胎記的形狀像一隻人的手，一隻很小的手。以前，喬琪娜的追求者會說，在她出生的時候，有位仙女把她小小的手貼在她的小臉上，留下了這個印記，這象徵著仙女送給她令人傾心的魅力。許多愛得發狂的年輕人，他們為了得到親吻這個神秘手印的特權，甚至甘願冒生命的危險。

不過，毋須諱言，人們對這個仙女手印的看法也天壤之別，見仁見智。一些吹毛求疵的人——這些人無一例外都是女性——她們把這個印記稱為「血手」，說它毀了喬琪娜的美貌，甚至使她變得醜陋可怕。話說回來，說最純淨的大理石雕像上偶爾出現的小藍斑，只需小小一塊，就足以將出自雕刻家鮑爾斯之手的夏娃變成一隻怪物，也不無道理。

8 pygmy ['pɪɡmi] (n.) 侏儒
9 swain [sweɪn] (n.) 戀愛中的青年（特指仰慕者或情人）
10 fastidious [fæ'stɪdiəs] (a.) 挑剔的
11 指美國著名雕刻家 Hiram Powers（1805-1873）

2
胎
記

Masculine observers, if the birthmark did not heighten their admiration, contented themselves with wishing it away, that the world might possess one living specimen of ideal loveliness without the semblance[12] of a flaw. After his marriage,—for he thought little or nothing of the matter before,—Aylmer discovered that this was the case with himself.

Had she been less beautiful,—if Envy's self could have found aught[13] else to sneer[14] at,—he might have felt his affection heightened by the prettiness of this mimic hand, now vaguely portrayed, now lost, now stealing forth again and glimmering to and fro with every pulse of emotion that throbbed within her heart; but seeing her otherwise so perfect, he found this one defect grow more and more intolerable with every moment of their united lives.

It was the fatal flaw of humanity which Nature, in one shape or another, stamps ineffaceably on all her productions, either to imply that they are temporary and finite, or that their perfection must be wrought by toil and pain. The crimson hand expressed the ineludible[15] grip in which mortality clutches the highest and purest of earthly mould, degrading them into kindred with the lowest, and even with the very brutes, like whom their visible frames return to dust.

In this manner, selecting it as the symbol of his wife's liability to sin, sorrow, decay, and death, Aylmer's somber imagination was not long in rendering the birthmark a frightful object, causing him more trouble and horror than ever Georgiana's beauty, whether of soul or sense, had given him delight.

至於男性，這個胎記如果沒有加深他們的愛慕之情，那就是會認為若沒有這個胎記，這個世界便會擁有一個美麗動人、完美無瑕的活標本。艾墨之前沒有這樣想過，但結婚後，他發現自己就有這樣的想法。

　　如果喬琪娜沒有這麼漂亮，如果嫉妒之神能夠找到別的對象嘲弄，他對喬琪娜的感情可能還會因為這隻可愛的小手而加深。這隻小手時而隱現，時而消失，時而又悄然出現，隨著她心中絲絲的情緒波動而忽隱忽現。但是喬琪娜是如此的完美，除了這個胎記以外。他們現在時時刻刻生活在一起，艾墨覺得這個缺憾愈來愈礙眼。

　　這是人類致命的缺陷，自然之神就是這樣，以各種方式在受造物身上留下不可磨滅的烙印，不是意味著萬物的生命短暫有限，就是意味著完美必須以辛勞和痛苦換取而來。這隻緋紅色的小手說明了最崇高、最純潔的受造物，也無法逃脫死亡的魔爪，死亡將他們攫住，貶到最卑賤的地位，甚至與畜生同級。而與畜生一樣，他們有形的軀體最終也將回歸塵土。

　　艾墨就這樣認定這塊胎記是妻子難逃罪孽、悲傷、腐朽和死亡的象徵。他有了這種陰暗的想像後不久，就將這塊胎記視為不祥之物。胎記在他心中引起的煩惱與恐懼，甚至勝過喬琪娜善良的心靈與美麗的容貌所帶來的愉悅。

12　semblance [ˈsembləns] (n.) 外觀；外貌
13　aught [ɔːt] (n.) 任何事物
14　sneer [snɪr] (v.) 嘲笑
15　ineludible [ˌɪnɪˈluːdəbl] (a.) 無法逃避的

At all the seasons which should have been their happiest, he invariably and without intending it, nay, in spite of a purpose to the contrary, reverted to[16] this one disastrous topic. Trifling as it at first appeared, it so connected itself with innumerable trains of thought and modes of feeling that it became the central point of all.

With the morning twilight Aylmer opened his eyes upon his wife's face and recognized the symbol of imperfection; and when they sat together at the evening hearth his eyes wandered stealthily to her cheek, and beheld, flickering with the blaze of the wood fire, the spectral[17] hand that wrote mortality where he would fain[18] have worshipped.

Georgiana soon learned to shudder at his gaze. It needed but a glance with the peculiar expression that his face often wore to change the roses of her cheek into a deathlike paleness, amid which the crimson hand was brought strongly out, like a bas-relief[19] of ruby on the whitest marble.

Late one night when the lights were growing dim, so as hardly to betray the stain on the poor wife's cheek, she herself, for the first time, voluntarily took up the subject.

"Do you remember, my dear Aylmer," said she, with a feeble attempt at a smile, "have you any recollection of a dream last night about this odious[20] hand?"

"None! none whatever!" replied Aylmer, starting[21]; but then he added, in a dry, cold tone, affected for the sake of concealing the real depth of his emotion, "I might well dream of it; for before I fell asleep it had taken a pretty firm hold of my fancy."

在本該是他們最快樂的日子裡，他卻老愛提這個致命的話題，儘管他並非有意，甚至也想避免提起。一開始，這只是一件芝麻小事，但在和各種思緒與感觸緊密相連後，就演變成一切的中心點。

　　晨曦之際，艾墨一睜開雙眼，就看到妻子臉上那塊象徵著缺陷的印記。傍晚時分，他們一起坐在壁爐前，他的目光悄悄移到她的臉頰上，看到那隻幽靈的手在爐火的烈焰反光下忽隱忽現，在他欣然膜拜的地方寫下了死亡的記號。

　　喬琪娜很快就發現這一點，他的凝視令她不寒而慄。艾墨只要一露出那種常見的怪異表情，對她瞥上一眼，喬琪娜紅潤的臉龐立刻會轉成一片慘白，露出那隻緋紅色的小手，就像潔白的大理石上浮雕著一塊紅寶石。

　　這天夜晚，火光漸微，可憐的喬琪娜臉上那塊胎記幾乎看不到。這時，她第一次自己提起這件事。

　　「心愛的艾墨，你還記不記得，」她勉強擠出一個微笑地說道：「你還記不記得昨晚你夢到了這隻可怕的手？」

　　「我不記得！我什麼也不記得！」艾墨嚇了一跳地說，但接著又冷冷地補上一句，好掩飾內心深藏的憂慮，「我有可能是夢到了，因為我在睡覺之前，它一直在我的腦海裡徘徊不去。」

16　revert to . . . 重新提起（某一話題）
17　spectral [ˈspektrəl] (a.) 幽靈的；鬼怪的
18　fain [feɪn] (adv.) 欣然地；樂意地
19　bas-relief [ˈbæsrɪliːf] (n.) 半浮雕（作品）
20　odious [ˈoʊdiəs] (a.) 可憎的；醜惡的
21　start [stɑːrt] (v.) 驚起；嚇一跳

2
胎記

"And you did dream of it?" continued Georgiana, hastily; for she dreaded lest a gush of tears should interrupt what she had to say. "A terrible dream! I wonder that you can forget it. Is it possible to forget this one expression?—'It is in her heart now; we must have it out!' Reflect, my husband; for by all means I would have you recall that dream."

The mind is in a sad state when Sleep, the all-involving, cannot confine her specters within the dim region of her sway[22], but suffers them to break forth, affrighting this actual life with secrets that perchance[23] belong to a deeper one.

Aylmer now remembered his dream. He had fancied himself with his servant Aminadab, attempting an operation for the removal of the birthmark; but the deeper went the knife, the deeper sank the hand, until at length its tiny grasp appeared to have caught hold of Georgiana's heart; whence, however, her husband was inexorably[24] resolved to cut or wrench it away.

When the dream had shaped itself perfectly in his memory, Aylmer sat in his wife's presence with a guilty feeling. Truth often finds its way to the mind close muffled[25] in robes of sleep, and then speaks with uncompromising directness of matters in regard to which we practice an unconscious self-deception during our waking moments. Until now he had not been aware of the tyrannizing influence acquired by one idea over his mind, and of the lengths which he might find in his heart to go for the sake of giving himself peace.

「那你是真的夢到了？」喬琪娜急忙說，深怕淚水一奪眶而出，就說不出要說的話了，「好可怕的夢！我不相信你會忘掉。難道你能忘掉這句話嗎？——『它已經長到她的心臟了，我們一定要把它挖掉！』老公，請你回想一下，無論如何，請你想起那個夢。」

　　人在入睡時，心智是無力而可悲的，因為無所不及的夢神無法將靈魂禁錮於渾沌的夢境之內，只能聽任它們破籠而出，以內心深藏的秘密來恐嚇眼前的現實生活。

　　艾墨現在想起那個夢了。他夢到自己跟助手阿迷一起在進行手術，想除去妻子的胎記。夢裡，手術刀切得越深，那隻小手就陷得越深，到最後他看到那隻小手緊緊抓住了喬琪娜的心臟，而他仍執意要把胎記切除或扯掉。

　　回想起這個夢境後，艾墨坐在妻子面前，滿心愧疚。真相，常趁著人們睡眠之際透露出實情，直言不諱地指出清醒時所做的自欺欺人。他現在才意識到，這個想法主宰了他的心智，而為了得到內心的平靜，他需要走上多長一段的心靈旅程。

22　sway [sweɪ] (n.) 支配；統治；勢力
23　perchance [pərˈtʃæns] (adv.) 也許
24　inexorably [ɪnˈeksərəbli] (adv.) 不為所動；無動於衷
25　muffle [ˈmʌfəl] (v.) 包著；裹著

❷
胎
記

"Aylmer," resumed Georgiana, solemnly, "I know not what may be the cost to both of us to rid me of this fatal birthmark. Perhaps its removal may cause cureless deformity; or it may be the stain goes as deep as life itself. Again: do we know that there is a possibility, on any terms, of unclasping the firm grip of this little hand which was laid upon me before I came into the world?"

"Dearest Georgiana, I have spent much thought upon the subject," hastily interrupted Aylmer. "I am convinced of the perfect practicability of its removal."

"If there be the remotest possibility of it," continued Georgiana, "let the attempt be made at whatever risk. Danger is nothing to me; for life, while this hateful mark makes me the object of your horror and disgust,—life is a burden which I would fling[26] down with joy. Either remove this dreadful hand, or take my wretched life! You have deep science. All the world bears witness of it. You have achieved great wonders. Cannot you remove this little, little mark, which I cover with the tips of two small fingers? Is this beyond your power, for the sake of your own peace, and to save your poor wife from madness?"

26 fling [flɪŋ] (v.) 丟；扔；拋

「艾墨，我不知道去掉這個不祥的胎記，需要我們付出多少的代價。切掉胎記，可能會造成永久性的傷害，甚至它本身就代表著生命。不過，不管要付出多大的代價，到底有沒有可能除掉這隻在我出生之前就緊緊抓著我的小手？」喬琪娜認真地說。

　　「親愛的喬琪娜，這件事我有想過，我覺得一定可以把它去掉的。」艾墨連忙打斷她。

　　「只要有一點點可能性，不管要冒多大的風險，我們都去試。我什麼危險都不怕。既然這個可憎的胎記會引起你對我的恐懼和反感，那麼生命對我來說就只是個負擔，我寧願不要苟活。要不就去掉這隻可怕的手，要不就取走我悲慘的生命！你是個大科學家，世人有目共睹。你創造了那麼多的奇蹟，那你能不能幫我去掉這個用兩隻小指指尖就能遮住的小小胎記？為了讓你的內心得到平靜，為了不讓你可憐的妻子發瘋，你能不能做到？」喬琪娜說。

Pygmalion

"Noblest, dearest, tenderest wife," cried Aylmer, rapturously[27], "doubt not my power. I have already given this matter the deepest thought—thought which might almost have enlightened me to create a being less perfect than yourself. Georgiana, you have led me deeper than ever into the heart of science. I feel myself fully competent to render this dear cheek as faultless as its fellow; and then, most beloved, what will be my triumph when I shall have corrected what Nature left imperfect in her fairest work! Even Pygmalion[28], when his sculptured woman assumed life, felt not greater ecstasy than mine will be."

"It is resolved, then," said Georgiana, faintly smiling. "And, Aylmer, spare me not, though you should find the birthmark take refuge in my heart at last."

「我最高貴、最親愛、最溫柔的妻子，」艾墨欣喜若狂地說：「不要懷疑我的能力，這件事情我已經仔細思考過。思考過程帶給我的啟發，都快要使我創造出一個跟你一樣完美的真人了。喬琪娜，你帶領我走進科學的奧秘深處。我想我一定能夠把這一半可愛的臉頰，變得跟另一邊的臉頰一樣完美無瑕。然後，我最心愛的妻子，等我矯正了大自然在其最美麗的傑作上所留下的缺憾後，我會有多快樂啊！就算是皮格梅隆的少女雕像獲得生命，他心中的狂喜也比不上我。」

「那就這麼決定了。」喬琪娜微微一笑地說：「還有，艾墨，不要捨不得我，就算最後你發現胎記已經長到我的心臟裡了。」

---

27 rapturously [ˈræptʃərəsli] (adv.) 欣喜若狂地
28 Pygmalion，皮格梅隆，希臘神話中的賽普勒斯國王，他愛上了自己所雕刻的少女雕像，於是對著雕像祈禱虔誠，後來女神為之感動，便賦予雕像生命。最後，他娶了雕像所化成的少女為妻。

Pygmalion and Galatea

Her husband tenderly kissed her cheek—her right cheek—not that which bore the impress of the crimson hand.

The next day Aylmer apprised his wife of[29] a plan that he had formed whereby he might have opportunity for the intense thought and constant watchfulness which the proposed operation would require; while Georgiana, likewise, would enjoy the perfect repose[30] essential to its success.

They were to seclude themselves in the extensive apartments occupied by Aylmer as a laboratory, and where, during his toilsome youth, he had made discoveries in the elemental powers of Nature that had roused the admiration of all the learned societies in Europe.

Seated calmly in this laboratory, the pale philosopher had investigated the secrets of the highest cloud region and of the profoundest mines; he had satisfied himself of the causes that kindled and kept alive the fires of the volcano; and had explained the mystery of fountains, and how it is that they gush forth, some so bright and pure, and others with such rich medicinal virtues, from the dark bosom of the earth.

Here, too, at an earlier period, he had studied the wonders of the human frame, and attempted to fathom[31] the very process by which Nature assimilates[32] all her precious influences from earth and air, and from the spiritual world, to create and foster[33] man, her masterpiece.

　　艾墨溫柔地親吻她的臉頰。他親的是右邊的臉頰，而不是印著緋紅小手的左側臉頰。

　　隔天，艾墨向妻子說明他的計畫，以便讓自己能夠進行縝密的思考和持續的觀察，這都是治療過程所需要的。而喬琪娜也能得到充分的休養，這事關成敗。

　　他們要住進艾墨當作實驗室的大房間裡。艾墨年輕時就是在這裡辛苦奮鬥，發現了大自然的種種奧秘，在歐洲學術界博得聲譽。

　　這個膚色白皙的科學家曾經靜靜地坐在這個實驗室裡，探索最高的雲層與最深的礦藏的秘密，找出火山烈焰燃起和不斷燃燒的原因，解開噴泉的秘密，說明噴泉如何從陰暗的地心噴出，而有些噴出的是純淨透明的水，有些噴出的則是富含醫療功效。

　　更早以前，他還在這裡研究過人類軀體的奧妙，試圖徹底弄清大自然如何從大地、天空和心靈世界汲取所有的精華，創造和滋養其偉大的傑作——人類。

29 apprise sb of . . . 告知某人……
30 repose [rɪˈpoʊz] (n.) 休息；安寧
31 fathom [ˈfæðəm] (v.) 搞懂；弄清楚
32 assimilate [əˈsɪmɪleɪt] (v.) 吸收；同化
33 foster [ˈfɑːstər] (v.) 養育

❷
胎記

The latter pursuit, however, Aylmer had long laid aside in unwilling recognition of the truth—against which all seekers sooner or later stumble—that our great creative Mother, while she amuses us with apparently working in the broadest sunshine, is yet severely careful to keep her own secrets, and, in spite of her pretended openness, shows us nothing but results. She permits us, indeed, to mar[34], but seldom to mend, and, like a jealous patentee[35], on no account to make.

Now, however, Aylmer resumed these half-forgotten investigations; not, of course, with such hopes or wishes as first suggested them; but because they involved much physiological truth and lay in the path of his proposed scheme for the treatment of Georgiana.

As he led her over the threshold of the laboratory, Georgiana was cold and tremulous. Aylmer looked cheerfully into her face, with intent to reassure her, but was so startled with the intense glow of the birthmark upon the whiteness of her cheek that he could not restrain a strong convulsive shudder. His wife fainted. "Aminadab! Aminadab!" shouted Aylmer, stamping violently on the floor. Forthwith there issued from an inner apartment a man of low stature, but bulky frame, with shaggy hair hanging about his visage, which was grimed with the vapors of the furnace.

This personage had been Aylmer's underworker during his whole scientific career, and was admirably fitted for that office by his great mechanical readiness, and the skill with which, while incapable of comprehending a single principle, he executed all the details of his master's experiments.

不過最後這項嘗試，艾墨早已擱置一旁，因為儘管他很不甘願，但他已經認清楚了——所有的探索者早晚都會向這個事實低頭——哺育萬物的自然之母雖然總在燦爛的陽光下運作，但極度小心不洩漏秘密。在假裝出來的開放坦然下，除了最後的結果，什麼也不讓我們看到。沒錯，她允許我們去「破壞」，卻極少讓我們去「修復」，而且她就像一個懷有戒心的專利權擁有人，決不允許我們去「創造」。

　　現在，艾墨要重拾這些早已遺忘的研究，他這次的目標跟以前不一樣。這些研究涉及到許多生理學方面的知識，在治療喬琪娜之前，他要先弄清楚這些知識。

　　當他帶著喬琪娜跨過實驗室的門檻時，喬琪娜渾身一陣冷顫。艾墨開心地看著她，想讓她放心，但是一看到胎記在她蒼白的臉頰上閃閃發光，就忍不住痙攣似地打了個大寒顫。喬琪娜頓時昏了過去。「阿迷！阿迷！」艾墨一邊大喊，一邊用力跺腳。實驗室裡立刻走出一個個子矮小的粗壯男人，他一頭蓬亂的頭髮，臉上沾滿了火爐的煤灰。

　　在艾墨的整個科學生涯中，這個人一直擔任艾墨的助手。他的表現非常稱職，因為他精通機械，技巧純熟，儘管他一條科學原理都不懂，但是實驗當中的細節，能都按照主人的指示完成。

---

34 mar [mɑːr] (v.) 毀壞
35 patentee [ˌpætənˈtiː] (n.) 專利權獲得者

With his vast strength, his shaggy hair, his smoky aspect, and the indescribable earthiness that incrusted him, he seemed to represent man's physical nature; while Aylmer's slender figure, and pale, intellectual face, were no less apt a type of the spiritual element.

"Throw open the door of the boudoir[36], Aminadab," said Aylmer, "and burn a pastil."

"Yes, master," answered Aminadab, looking intently at the lifeless form of Georgiana; and then he muttered to himself, "If she were my wife, I'd never part with that birthmark."

When Georgiana recovered consciousness she found herself breathing an atmosphere of penetrating fragrance, the gentle potency of which had recalled her from her deathlike faintness. The scene around her looked like enchantment. Aylmer had converted those smoky, dingy, somber rooms, where he had spent his brightest years in recondite[37] pursuits, into a series of beautiful apartments not unfit to be the secluded abode[38] of a lovely woman.

The walls were hung with gorgeous curtains, which imparted[39] the combination of grandeur and grace that no other species of adornment can achieve; and as they fell from the ceiling to the floor, their rich and ponderous folds, concealing all angles and straight lines, appeared to shut in the scene from infinite space.

　　阿迷的力氣很大，他頭髮蓬亂，滿身煙塵，渾身上下散發出一種難以形容的粗獷感，彷彿代表著人類肉體凡胎的本性。而艾墨身軀瘦長，膚色白皙，看起來很聰明，彷彿象徵著人類的心靈元素。

　　「阿迷，把寢室的門打開，然後點枝香膏。」艾墨說。

　　「遵命，主人。」阿迷回答。他看著喬琪娜癱倒的身體，自言自語地說：「如果她是我老婆，我才捨不得把胎記弄掉。」

　　喬琪娜醒來時，只覺得芳香撲鼻，就是這個溫和的香味將她從如死一般的昏厥中喚醒。她周圍的景象如夢似幻。艾墨年輕時從事深奧研究的房間一度都是骯髒昏暗、煙霧瀰漫的，如今都被他改裝成漂亮的居室，很適合當作美麗女子隱蔽的住所。

　　牆上掛著華麗的帷幔，既氣派又高雅，什麼裝飾都比不上。帷幔從天花板直落到地面上，厚沉的皺褶把其他各種形形色色的東西都遮掩住，這個地方好像被隔絕在無限的空間之外。

36 boudoir [ˈbuːdwɑːr] (n.) 女子閨房
37 recondite [ˈrekəndaɪt] (a.) 深奧的
38 abode [əˈboʊd] (n.) 住所
39 impart [ɪmˈpɑːrt] (v.) 透露

❷
胎記

95

For aught Georgiana knew, it might be a pavilion[40] among the clouds. And Aylmer, excluding the sunshine, which would have interfered with his chemical processes, had supplied its place with perfumed lamps, emitting flames of various hue, but all uniting in a soft, impurpled radiance. He now knelt by his wife's side, watching her earnestly, but without alarm; for he was confident in his science, and felt that he could draw a magic circle round her within which no evil might intrude.

"Where am I? Ah, I remember," said Georgiana, faintly; and she placed her hand over her cheek to hide the terrible mark from her husband's eyes.

"Fear not, dearest!" exclaimed he. "Do not shrink from me! Believe me, Georgiana, I even rejoice in this single imperfection, since it will be such a rapture to remove it."

"Oh, spare me!" sadly replied his wife. "Pray do not look at it again. I never can forget that convulsive shudder."

In order to soothe Georgiana, and, as it were, to release her mind from the burden of actual things, Aylmer now put in practice some of the light and playful secrets which science had taught him among its profounder lore[41].

Airy figures, absolutely bodiless ideas, and forms of unsubstantial beauty came and danced before her, imprinting their momentary footsteps on beams of light. Though she had some indistinct idea of the method of these optical phenomena, still the illusion was almost perfect enough to warrant the belief that her husband possessed sway over the spiritual world.

喬琪娜覺得這裡像一座雲中樓閣。這裡陽光照不進來，因為陽光會干擾艾墨的化學實驗，所以艾墨在這裡擺了許多芳香的燭燈，盞盞燃著不同顏色的火焰，然後融合成柔和的紫色光彩。他此刻跪在妻子身邊，很正經地看著她。他並不驚慌，因為他對自己的科學很有信心，覺得自己能夠在她身邊畫上一道保護的魔罩，不讓任何惡魔靠近。

　　「這是哪裡？啊，我想起來了。」喬琪娜虛弱地說，她伸手遮住臉上那塊可怕的胎記，不想讓丈夫看到。

　　「別怕，親愛的！別怕我！相信我，喬琪娜，我現在甚至為這塊缺陷感到高興，因為去掉它會帶給我無限的喜悅。」艾墨喊道。

　　「噢，饒了我吧！求你不要再看它了。我永遠也忘不了你那痙攣一般的寒顫。」喬琪娜傷心地說。

　　為了安撫喬琪娜，讓她忘卻現實的煩惱，艾墨開始採用深奧科學當中的一些小把戲。

　　飄忽的影子、無形的純粹意念、虛幻的美麗形象，一一來到喬琪娜眼前，翩翩起舞，在光束中留下轉瞬即逝的舞步。喬琪娜雖然對這些光學現象有些模糊的概念，但是這些幻覺是如此近乎完美，使她幾乎都快相信丈夫擁有操縱心靈世界的力量了。

40 pavilion [pə'vɪljən] (n.) 亭子；帳篷
41 lore [lɔ:r] (n.) 知識

Then again, when she felt a wish to look forth from her seclusion, immediately, as if her thoughts were answered, the procession of external existence flitted[42] across a screen. The scenery and the figures of actual life were perfectly represented, but with that bewitching, yet indescribable difference which always makes a picture, an image, or a shadow so much more attractive than the original.

When wearied of this, Aylmer bade her cast her eyes upon a vessel containing a quantity of earth. She did so, with little interest at first; but was soon startled to perceive the germ[43] of a plant shooting upward from the soil. Then came the slender stalk; the leaves gradually unfolded themselves; and amid them was a perfect and lovely flower.

"It is magical!" cried Georgiana. "I dare not touch it."

"Nay, pluck it," answered Aylmer,—"pluck it, and inhale its brief perfume while you may. The flower will wither in a few moments and leave nothing save its brown seed vessels; but thence may be perpetuated[44] a race as ephemeral[45] as itself."

But Georgiana had no sooner touched the flower than the whole plant suffered a blight[46], its leaves turning coal-black as if by the agency of fire.

"There was too powerful a stimulus," said Aylmer, thoughtfully.

To make up for this abortive experiment, he proposed to take her portrait by a scientific process of his own invention. It was to be effected by rays of light striking upon a polished plate of metal.

她突然想從這個與世隔絕的地方看看外面的世界，而這個念頭似乎立刻得到回應，一塊屏幕上現出一幕幕外界的景象，如實地呈現出真實世界的情景和人物，但又像繪畫、影像或投影那樣，具有令人心醉神迷、難以形容的魔力，比真實世界更加眩目。

　　等她看倦了之後，艾墨要她看一個裝著土的花盆。一開始她並不怎麼在意，但是她馬上吃驚地發現，一株幼芽正破土而出，接著長出纖細的莖，葉片緩緩展開，最後開出一朵細緻美麗的花朵。

　　「太神奇了！我不敢碰。」喬琪娜喊道。

　　「把花摘下來，快摘下來，聞它短暫的香味，它馬上就會枯萎，除了包著種子的褐色花托，什麼也不會留下。花托裡會留下一個和它一樣瞬息而逝的花種子。」艾墨說。

　　然而喬琪娜的手一碰到花，整株植物就枯萎，葉子像是被火烤焦一般，變成了黑色。

　　「刺激太大了。」艾墨若有所思地說。

　　為了彌補這個實驗的失敗，艾墨提議用他自己發明的一種科學方法，為她畫一張像。畫像的原理是讓光線照射到一塊平滑光亮的金屬板上。

42　flit [flɪt] (v.) 輕快地飛動

43　germ [dʒɜːrm] (n.) 幼芽；胚

44　perpetuate [pərˈpetʃueɪt] (v.) 保存

45　ephemeral [ɪˈfemərəl] (a.) 短暫的；瞬息的

46　blight [blaɪt] (n.)（植物）造成枯萎的病

Georgiana assented; but, on looking at the result, was affrighted to find the features of the portrait blurred and indefinable; while the minute figure of a hand appeared where the cheek should have been. Aylmer snatched the metallic plate and threw it into a jar of corrosive acid.

Soon, however, he forgot these mortifying[47] failures. In the intervals of study and chemical experiment he came to her flushed and exhausted, but seemed invigorated[48] by her presence, and spoke in glowing language of the resources of his art.

He gave a history of the long dynasty of the alchemists, who spent so many ages in quest of the universal solvent by which the golden principle might be elicited from all things vile and base.

Aylmer appeared to believe that, by the plainest scientific logic, it was altogether within the limits of possibility to discover this long-sought medium; "but," he added, "a philosopher who should go deep enough to acquire the power would attain too lofty[49] a wisdom to stoop to the exercise of it."

Not less singular were his opinions in regard to the elixir vitae[50]. He more than intimated that it was at his option to concoct a liquid that should prolong life for years, perhaps interminably; but that it would produce a discord in Nature which all the world, and chiefly the quaffer of the immortal nostrum[51], would find cause to curse.

"Aylmer, are you in earnest?" asked Georgiana, looking at him with amazement and fear. "It is terrible to possess such power, or even to dream of possessing it."

喬琪娜同意了，但是等到一看到結果，她嚇了一跳，畫像上的五官模糊不清，而且應該是臉頰的地方，卻只看得到一隻小手。艾墨把畫像搶過來，扔進一個裝有腐蝕性酸液的罈子裡。

　　艾墨很快把這些困窘的失敗拋到腦後。他在進行研究和化學實驗的空檔之際，不時過來找喬琪娜。他滿臉通紅、忙得焦頭爛額，可是當他一看到喬琪娜，就又精神百倍，興沖沖地大談他的科學。

　　他說起煉金術的歷史，說一代又一代的煉金術士們，自古以來都在尋找一種萬用劑，能夠從任何粗鄙的東西中提煉出黃金。

　　艾墨似乎很相信，人類可以透過最簡單的科學邏輯來找到這種萬用劑。「但是，能夠深入鑽研而獲得這種能力的科學家，一定是智慧超凡，才不屑把自己的本領用在這種事情上。」他補充說道。

　　艾墨對於長生不老藥也有與眾不同的看法。他言下之意，表示自己有能力調製出這樣的藥水，可以延長好幾年的壽命，甚至無限地延長。但如此一來就會擾亂大自然的秩序，全世界的人都會加以譴責，尤其是喝了長生不老藥的人。

　　「艾墨，你是說真的嗎？」喬琪娜又吃驚又害怕地看著他，說道：「擁有這種能力太可怕了，光是夢到就很可怕了。」

47 mortify ['mɔːrtɪfaɪ] (v.) 使受辱；傷害……的感情
48 invigorate [ɪn'vɪgəreɪt] (v.) 使精力充沛
49 lofty ['lɔːftɪ] (a.) 崇高的；高尚的
50 elixir vitae [ɪ'lɪksər 'viːtaɪ] (n.) 長生不老藥
51 nostrum ['nɑːstrəm] (n.) 靈丹；秘藥

❷
胎記

"Oh, do not tremble, my love," said her husband. "I would not wrong either you or myself by working such inharmonious effects upon our lives; but I would have you consider how trifling, in comparison, is the skill requisite to remove this little hand."

At the mention of the birthmark, Georgiana, as usual, shrank as if a red-hot iron had touched her cheek.

Again Aylmer applied himself to[52] his labors. She could hear his voice in the distant furnace room giving directions to Aminadab, whose harsh, uncouth, misshapen tones were audible in response, more like the grunt or growl of a brute than human speech.

After hours of absence, Aylmer reappeared and proposed that she should now examine his cabinet of chemical products and natural treasures of the earth.

Among the former he showed her a small vial[53], in which, he remarked, was contained a gentle yet most powerful fragrance, capable of impregnating[54] all the breezes that blow across a kingdom. They were of inestimable value, the contents of that little vial; and, as he said so, he threw some of the perfume into the air and filled the room with piercing and invigorating delight.

"And what is this?" asked Georgiana, pointing to a small crystal globe containing a gold-colored liquid. "It is so beautiful to the eye that I could imagine it the elixir of life."

「噢，不要擔心，親愛的，我不會拿這種破壞大自然和諧的藥來改變你，或改變我的生命。我只是想讓你知道，相形之下，去掉這隻小手的技術有多麼微不足道了。」艾墨説。

一提到胎記，喬琪娜立刻一如往常地往後一縮，彷彿一塊赤熱的鐵碰到了她的臉頰。

艾墨又走回實驗室工作。喬琪娜可以聽到他在遠遠的火爐間裡對阿迷下達命令，阿迷回答的聲音冷酷、粗野、古怪，不像是人在説話，反倒像是野獸在低吼。

幾個小時後，艾墨又回來了。他提議讓她看看他那放滿化學物品和天然寶物的櫃子。

他從化學物品堆中拿出一個小瓶子給她看，説裡面盛著一種氣味溫和但威力十足的香水，能使吹過一整個王國上空的微風都充滿香氣。這個小藥瓶裡的東西是無價之寶，他一邊説著，一邊往空中灑上幾滴，房間裡頓時充滿濃郁而提神的芬芳氣味。

「這又是什麼東西？」喬琪娜指著一個盛著金色液體的球狀小玻璃瓶，問道：「它好漂亮，就好像長生不老藥。」

52 apply oneself to . . . 專心於……；致力於……
53 vial ['vaɪəl] (n.) 小藥瓶
54 impregnate [ɪm'pregneɪt] (v.) 浸透；充滿

"In one sense it is," replied Aylmer; "or, rather, the elixir of immortality. It is the most precious poison that ever was concocted in this world. By its aid I could apportion[55] the lifetime of any mortal at whom you might point your finger. The strength of the dose would determine whether he were to linger[56] out years, or drop dead in the midst of a breath. No king on his guarded throne could keep his life if I, in my private station, should deem that the welfare of millions justified me in depriving him of it."

"Why do you keep such a terrific drug?" inquired Georgiana in horror. "

Do not mistrust me, dearest," said her husband, smiling; "its virtuous potency is yet greater than its harmful one. But see! here is a powerful cosmetic. With a few drops of this in a vase of water, freckles may be washed away as easily as the hands are cleansed. A stronger infusion would take the blood out of the cheek, and leave the rosiest beauty a pale ghost."

"Is it with this lotion that you intend to bathe my cheek?" asked Georgiana, anxiously.

"Oh, no," hastily replied her husband; "this is merely superficial. Your case demands a remedy that shall go deeper."

In his interviews with Georgiana, Aylmer generally made minute inquiries as to her sensations and whether the confinement of the rooms and the temperature of the atmosphere agreed with her. These questions had such a particular drift[57] that Georgiana began to conjecture[58] that she was already subjected to certain physical influences, either breathed in with the fragrant air or taken with her food.

「這可以説是一種長生不老藥沒錯，但説它是『生命之藥』就更貼切了。這是世界上最珍貴的毒藥。你隨便指一個人，我都可以用這個毒藥來控制他的壽命。劑量的多寡，會決定服藥者是會苟延殘喘多年，還是當場暴斃。如果我在實驗室裡做了決定，認為為了天下老百姓的幸福，應該剝奪國王的性命，那麼不管國王的戒備有多麼森嚴，他都無法保住自己的性命。」艾墨答道。

「你為什麼要放這麼可怕的毒藥？」喬琪娜嚇壞了。

「別誤會，親愛的，它的好處比壞處多。你再看看這個，這是一種強效保養品。只要在一瓶水裡滴上幾滴，臉上的雀斑就能像洗手一樣，輕輕鬆鬆地洗掉。濃度高一點的話，連臉頰上的血色都會被洗掉，臉頰最紅潤的美女都會變成蒼白的鬼魂。」艾墨笑著説道。

「你就是準備用這個藥水來洗我的臉頰嗎？」喬琪娜急了。

「不是，這只能用於表面治療，你的胎記需要能夠更深入作用的藥物。」艾墨急忙説道。

談話當中，艾墨總是會問些細枝末節的問題，像是她感覺如何、關在房間裡習不習慣、屋子裡的溫度適不適宜。他這樣問似乎別有用心，喬琪娜開始猜想自己是不是已經被藥物所影響，而藥物不是從芳香的空氣吸入，就是和食物一起吞進了肚子裡。

55 apportion [əˈpɔːrʃən] (v.) 分配
56 linger [ˈlɪŋgər] (v.)（久病）苟延殘喘
57 drift [drɪft] (n.) 主旨；要點
58 conjecture [kənˈdʒektʃər] (v.) 推測；猜想

She fancied likewise, but it might be altogether fancy, that there was a stirring up of her system—a strange, indefinite sensation creeping through her veins, and tingling, half painfully, half pleasurably, at her heart. Still, whenever she dared to look into the mirror, there she beheld herself pale as a white rose and with the crimson birthmark stamped upon her cheek. Not even Aylmer now hated it so much as she.

To dispel the tedium of the hours which her husband found it necessary to devote to the processes of combination and analysis, Georgiana turned over the volumes of his scientific library.

In many dark old tomes[59] she met with chapters full of romance and poetry. They were the works of philosophers of the middle ages, such as Albertus Magnus[60], Cornelius Agrippa[61], Paracelsus[62], and the famous friar who created the prophetic Brazen Head[63].

All these antique naturalists stood in advance of their centuries, yet were imbued with[64] some of their credulity, and therefore were believed, and perhaps imagined themselves to have acquired from the investigation of Nature a power above Nature, and from physics a sway over the spiritual world.

Hardly less curious and imaginative were the early volumes of the Transactions of the Royal Society, in which the members, knowing little of the limits of natural possibility, were continually recording wonders or proposing methods whereby wonders might be wrought.

她還覺得，她的體內在蠢蠢欲動，一種特殊而難以言喻的感覺，正隨著血管流遍全身，在她的心窩隱隱刺痛，有些疼，又有些舒服，不過這可能都只是她自己在幻想罷了。她只要往鏡子裡一看，就會看到自己臉色蒼白得像一朵白玫瑰，臉頰上赫然印著那塊緋紅色的胎記。這一刻，就連艾墨都沒有像她這麼痛恨這塊胎記。

艾墨需要長時間在實驗室裡進行物質的混合和分析，為了打發這些時間，喬琪娜開始翻起他卷帙浩繁的藏書。

在年久陳舊的大部頭書裡，她看到了浪漫詩意的篇章，那是一中古世紀哲學家的作品，像是大亞伯圖斯、阿格帕、帕拉塞蘇，還有創造出能未卜先知的黃銅頭像的著名修士。

這些古代的博物學家都是超越常時人代的人物，他們自信滿滿，受得到人們的信任。他們或許會想像，自己已經從探索大自然的過程中獲得了操控大自然的力量，在物理研究中得到了支配心靈世界的能力。

那一卷卷皇家學會的早期學報，它們的內容也同樣新奇、充滿想像力。對於自然界的極限了解尚少的會員們，他們不停地記下各種奇蹟，或是提出創造奇蹟的方法。

---

59 tome [toʊm] (n.) 冊；卷；大型書本
60 Albertus Magnus（1193?-1280），德國哲學家與神學家
61 Cornelius Agrippa（1486-1535），德國神秘哲學家，星相家，煉金術士
62 Paracelsus（1493-1541），瑞士的煉金術士、醫生、星相家、神秘學家
63 Brazen Head，指英國修士羅傑‧培根（Roger Bacon, 1214-1294）製做的黃銅頭像。據傳培根造了一隻銅頭，只要他聽到銅頭說話，他的計畫便會成功。反之，則會失敗。培根入睡，僕人奉命看守銅頭。銅頭一連說了三次話，第一次說「時辰到了」，半小時後說「時辰剛過」，再過半小時又說「時辰已過」。言畢，銅頭倒地，裂為碎片，再也沒有說過話。
64 be imbued with 滿懷（強烈的情感或想法）

But to Georgiana the most engrossing[65] volume was a large folio[66] from her husband's own hand, in which he had recorded every experiment of his scientific career, its original aim, the methods adopted for its development, and its final success or failure, with the circumstances to which either event was attributable.

The book, in truth, was both the history and emblem[67] of his ardent, ambitious, imaginative, yet practical and laborious life. He handled physical details as if there were nothing beyond them; yet spiritualized them all, and redeemed himself from materialism by his strong and eager aspiration towards the infinite. In his grasp the veriest clod of earth assumed a soul.

Georgiana, as she read, reverenced Aylmer and loved him more profoundly than ever, but with a less entire dependence on his judgment than heretofore. Much as he had accomplished, she could not but observe that his most splendid successes were almost invariably failures, if compared with the ideal at which he aimed. His brightest diamonds were the merest pebbles, and felt to be so by himself, in comparison with the inestimable gems[68] which lay hidden beyond his reach.

其中最吸引喬琪娜的一本書，就是丈夫的冊子。丈夫在冊子裡記錄了整個科學生涯中所做的每一項實驗，包括實驗的原訂目標、採取的做法、最後的結果，以及實驗成功或失敗的原因。

這本冊子不只是一種記錄，更是象徵著艾墨富於熱忱、野心、想像力卻又實際而辛勤的一生。他仔細地處理每一個物理細節，彷彿這是最至高無上的工作。這些東西都被昇華到精神層次，他熱切強烈地追求無限，覺得自己已經超脫了物質世界。在他手裡，泥土都會得到靈氣。

喬琪娜讀著艾墨的冊子，對他的崇敬和愛慕更甚於以往，但對他的判斷力卻不如以前那樣深信不疑。因為儘管他成就非凡，她卻無法不注意到，即使實驗結果輝煌，但如果用實驗最初訂定的目標來看，這些實驗可以說都是失敗的。和那些他無法觸及、深埋著的無價寶石比起來，他最耀眼的鑽石不過都是石頭，這也是他自己的感受。

65 engross [ɪnˈɡroʊs] (v.) 使全神貫注
66 folio [ˈfoʊlɪoʊ] (n.) 對開本
67 emblem [ˈɛmbləm] (n.) 象徵；標誌
68 gem [dʒɛm] (n.) 寶石；珠寶

The volume, rich with achievements that had won renown for its author, was yet as melancholy a record as ever mortal hand had penned. It was the sad confession and continual exemplification of the shortcomings of the composite man, the spirit burdened with clay and working in matter, and of the despair that assails[69] the higher nature at finding itself so miserably thwarted[70] by the earthly part. Perhaps every man of genius in whatever sphere might recognize the image of his own experience in Aylmer's journal.

So deeply did these reflections affect Georgiana that she laid her face upon the open volume and burst into tears. In this situation she was found by her husband.

"It is dangerous to read in a sorcerer's[71] books," said he with a smile, though his countenance was uneasy and displeased. "Georgiana, there are pages in that volume which I can scarcely glance over and keep my senses. Take heed lest it prove as detrimental[72] to you."

"It has made me worship you more than ever," said she.

"Ah, wait for this one success," rejoined he, "then worship me if you will. I shall deem myself hardly unworthy of it. But come, I have sought you for the luxury of your voice. Sing to me, dearest."

So she poured out the liquid music of her voice to quench the thirst of his spirit. He then took his leave with a boyish exuberance[73] of gayety, assuring her that her seclusion would endure but a little longer, and that the result was already certain.

艾墨的這本冊子，滿滿寫著他贏得聲望的各種成就，然而實際上，這卻是人世間一本可悲的箚記。它代表了一個感傷的表白，不斷以各種實例來揭示人類的脆弱，靈魂被泥土做成的肉體所累，卻又只能在物質世界中打滾，揭示了崇高的天性發現自己竟圍限於肉體的那股絕望。也許不管哪個領域的天才，都會在艾墨的旅程上看到自己的經歷。

　　這些想法深深衝擊著喬琪娜的心靈，她把頭埋在冊子裡，哭了起來。就在此時，艾墨撞見了這一幕。

　　「看術士的書是很危險的。」他笑著，露出不安與不悅的神情說道：「喬琪娜，這本冊子裡有許多地方我自己看了都很難保持理智，小心別讓它也害了你。」

　　「看了這本冊子，讓我更加崇拜你了。」她說。

　　「啊，先等這一次成功之後再說吧，到時候你再崇拜我也不遲，那時候我也會受之無愧。來吧，我來找你是想聽聽你美妙的歌聲，唱首歌給我聽吧，親愛的。」他說。

　　於是喬琪娜開口歌唱，她用流水般的悅耳歌聲，一解他心靈上的飢渴。之後，他像個孩子一樣歡喜雀躍地離開，在走之前還向她保證，她與世隔絕的生活很快就會結束，成功在望。

69　assail [əˈseɪl] (v.) 猛烈攻擊
70　thwart [θwɔːrt] (v.) 阻撓
71　sorcerer [ˈsɔːrsərər] (n.) 巫師；術士
72　detrimental [ˌdetriˈmentl] (a.) 有害的
73　exuberance [ɪgˈzuːbərəns] (n.) 充滿活力

Scarcely had he departed when Georgiana felt irresistibly impelled to follow him. She had forgotten to inform Aylmer of a symptom which for two or three hours past had begun to excite her attention. It was a sensation in the fatal birthmark, not painful, but which induced a restlessness throughout her system. Hastening after her husband, she intruded for the first time into the laboratory.

The first thing that struck her eye was the furnace, that hot and feverish worker, with the intense glow of its fire, which by the quantities of soot[74] clustered above it seemed to have been burning for ages. There was a distilling apparatus in full operation. Around the room were retorts[75], tubes, cylinders, crucibles[76], and other apparatus of chemical research. An electrical machine stood ready for immediate use.

The atmosphere felt oppressively close, and was tainted with gaseous odors which had been tormented forth by the processes of science. The severe and homely simplicity of the apartment, with its naked walls and brick pavement, looked strange, accustomed as Georgiana had become to the fantastic elegance of her boudoir. But what chiefly, indeed almost solely, drew her attention, was the aspect of Aylmer himself.

He was pale as death, anxious and absorbed, and hung over the furnace as if it depended upon his utmost watchfulness whether the liquid which it was distilling should be the draught of immortal happiness or misery. How different from the sanguine[77] and joyous mien that he had assumed for Georgiana's encouragement!

　　艾墨一離開，喬琪娜就忍不住跟上去。她忘了告訴艾墨，兩、三個小時前她的身體出現症狀，胎記開始有感覺，雖然不會痛，但她覺得全身焦躁不安。她快步追過去，第一次踏進了他的實驗室。

　　最先映入她眼簾的，是那座熾熱通紅的火爐。火爐裡閃著熊熊的火光，爐頂積滿煤灰，看起來像是已經燃燒了幾世紀之久。火爐上有個蒸餾的儀器正在進行蒸餾。實驗室裡滿是蒸餾瓶、試管、圓筒、坩堝等各種化學儀器。有一個電子機械已經在待命狀態，隨時可以使用。

　　實驗室裡的空氣很悶，瀰漫著實驗所發出的刺鼻氣味。裡頭的陳設很簡單、很樸素，牆壁或磚地上都沒有多餘的東西，這對於習慣華麗房間的喬琪娜來說，顯得很陌生。然而在其中，真正唯一吸引她注意的，是艾墨的模樣。

　　艾墨的臉色看起來就像死人一樣慘白，他專注、焦慮地彎著腰、看著火爐，彷彿蒸餾出來的液體到底會帶來永世的幸福還是悲慘，全賴於他嚴密的觀察。這和他為了寬慰喬琪娜而擺出的樂觀神態，完全不同！

---

74 soot [sʊt] (n.) 煤灰
75 retort [rɪˈtɔːrt] (n.) 蒸餾瓶
76 crucible [ˈkruːsɪbəl] (n.) 坩堝（化學容器，用來高溫加熱金屬等物質）
77 sanguine [ˈsæŋgwɪn] (a.) 滿懷希望的

"Carefully now, Aminadab; carefully, thou human machine; carefully, thou man of clay!" muttered Aylmer, more to himself than his assistant. "Now, if there be a thought too much or too little, it is all over."

"Ho! ho!" mumbled Aminadab. "Look, master! look!"

Aylmer raised his eyes hastily, and at first reddened, then grew paler than ever, on beholding Georgiana. He rushed towards her and seized her arm with a grip that left the print of his fingers upon it.

"Why do you come hither? Have you no trust in your husband?" cried he, impetuously[78]. "Would you throw the blight of that fatal birthmark over my labors? It is not well done. Go, prying[79] woman, go!"

"Nay, Aylmer," said Georgiana with the firmness of which she possessed no stinted[80] endowment, "it is not you that have a right to complain. You mistrust your wife; you have concealed the anxiety with which you watch the development of this experiment. Think not so unworthily of me, my husband. Tell me all the risk we run, and fear not that I shall shrink; for my share in it is far less than your own."

"No, no, Georgiana!" said Aylmer, impatiently; "it must not be."

"I submit," replied she calmly. "And, Aylmer, I shall quaff whatever draught you bring me; but it will be on the same principle that would induce me to take a dose of poison if offered by your hand."

「現在小心，阿迷。小心點，你這個人形機器。小心點，你這塊泥土！」艾墨喃喃道，他不像是在對助手説話，而是在自言自語：「現在，只要多一點或少一點，我們就前功盡棄了。」

「呵呵！你看，主人！你看！」阿迷咕噥道。

艾墨連忙抬頭一瞧，他看到了喬琪娜。他的臉上先是一陣通紅，接著變得更加蒼白。他快步走向喬琪娜，緊緊抓住她的手臂，在她的手臂上留下了指印。

「你為什麼跑進來？你不信任你的丈夫嗎？你想把那塊致命胎記的晦氣帶進我的實驗室嗎？你的藥水還沒釀好。回去，好奇的女人，回去！」他激動地説。

「不，艾墨，該抱怨的不是你。」做盡犧牲的喬琪娜用堅定的語氣説：「是你不信任你的妻子，這個實驗讓你很不安，你卻不敢跟我説。老公，不要看不起我，把我們要冒的風險都告訴我，不用擔心我會退縮，因為你所承受的風險，遠遠比我還大。」

「不，喬琪娜！我不説！」艾墨不耐煩地説。

「好吧，我屈服。還有，艾墨，不管你給我什麼藥水，我都會一飲而盡。就算你給我毒藥，我也會服下。」喬琪娜平靜地説。

---

78 impetuously [ɪmˈpetʃuəsli] (adv.) 激烈地；急躁地
79 pry [praɪ] (v.) 打探；探聽
80 stint [stɪnt] (v.) 吝惜；節制

"My noble wife," said Aylmer, deeply moved, "I knew not the height and depth of your nature until now. Nothing shall be concealed. Know, then, that this crimson hand, superficial as it seems, has clutched its grasp into your being with a strength of which I had no previous conception. I have already administered agents powerful enough to do aught except to change your entire physical system. Only one thing remains to be tried. If that fail us we are ruined."

"Why did you hesitate to tell me this?" asked she.

"Because, Georgiana," said Aylmer, in a low voice, "there is danger."

"Danger? There is but one danger—that this horrible stigma[81] shall be left upon my cheek!" cried Georgiana. "Remove it, remove it, whatever be the cost, or we shall both go mad!"

"Heaven knows your words are too true," said Aylmer, sadly. "And now, dearest, return to your boudoir. In a little while all will be tested."

He conducted her back and took leave of her with a solemn tenderness which spoke far more than his words how much was now at stake[82]. After his departure Georgiana became rapt[83] in musings[84]. She considered the character of Aylmer, and did it completer justice than at any previous moment.

Her heart exulted[85], while it trembled, at his honorable love—so pure and lofty that it would accept nothing less than perfection nor miserably make itself contented with an earthlier nature than he had dreamed of.

「我高貴的妻子，我到現在才看到你的崇高與深度。」艾墨深受感動地説：「我什麼也不用對你隱瞞了。我告訴你吧，這個紅色的手印雖然看起來是在表面，其實已經深深攫住你的軀體，其力量之大，超乎我的想像。我已經給你下了一些藥，這些藥的效果都很強，就差沒有改變你整個生理系統。現在就只剩一種藥劑要試了。如果這個藥劑失敗，我們就完了。」

「你之前為什麼都不告訴我？」她問。

艾墨聲音一沉，説道：「喬琪娜，因為這有危險。」

「危險？對我來説，唯一的危險就是讓這個可怕的印記留在我的臉頰上！」喬琪娜喊道：「把它弄掉！把它弄掉！不管要付出什麼代價，都要把它除掉！不然我們兩個人都會瘋掉的！」

「你説得完全沒有錯，親愛的，你現在回寢室去吧，我們等一下就可以知道結果了。」艾墨感慨地説。

他陪她走回寢室，在離開時，那份嚴肅與溫柔勝過一切言語，説明現在事情有多嚴重。在艾墨離開後，喬琪娜陷入沉思。她反覆琢磨艾墨的人格，態度比以往任何時候都更全面、更公正。

一想到他那崇高的愛，她的內心感到狂喜，卻又瑟瑟顫抖。他的愛是那麼純潔、那麼高尚，只容得下完美的事物，他夢寐以求的東西，不容一點點差池。

81　stigma [ˈstɪɡmə] (n.) 皮膚上的斑或疤
82　at stake 利害攸關；瀕於險境
83　rapt [ræpt] (a.) 全神貫注的
84　muse [mjuːz] (v.) 沉思
85　engross [ɪnˈɡroʊs] (v.) 使全神貫注

❷
胎記

She felt how much more precious was such a sentiment than that meaner kind which would have borne with the imperfection for her sake, and have been guilty of treason[86] to holy love by degrading its perfect idea to the level of the actual; and with her whole spirit she prayed that, for a single moment, she might satisfy his highest and deepest conception.

Longer than one moment she well knew it could not be; for his spirit was ever on the march, ever ascending, and each instant required something that was beyond the scope of the instant before.

The sound of her husband's footsteps aroused her. He bore a crystal goblet[87] containing a liquor colorless as water, but bright enough to be the draught of immortality. Aylmer was pale; but it seemed rather the consequence of a highly-wrought state of mind and tension of spirit than of fear or doubt.

"The concoction of the draught has been perfect," said he, in answer to Georgiana's look. "Unless all my science have deceived me, it cannot fail."

"Save on your account, my dearest Aylmer," observed his wife, "I might wish to put off this birthmark of mortality by relinquishing[88] mortality itself in preference to any other mode. Life is but a sad possession to those who have attained precisely the degree of moral advancement at which I stand. Were I weaker and blinder it might be happiness. Were I stronger, it might be endured hopefully. But, being what I find myself, methinks I am of all mortals the most fit to die."

她發覺艾墨的這種善感，比低劣的感情珍貴多了。低劣的感情，會為了她而忍受她的缺陷，讓完美的理想屈就於現實，因而背叛[86]神聖的愛。她全心全意地祈禱自己能夠實現他這份崇高而深邃的愛，哪怕只有短短的一刻也好。

她心裡清楚，要比短短一刻更久就不可能了，因為艾墨的精神不停地在前進，不停地在上升，每一刻都在追求超越前一刻。

丈夫的腳步聲驚醒了她。他端來一個水晶玻璃杯[87]，裡面盛著透明無色如水一般的液體，看起來晶瑩透亮，猶如長生不老藥。艾墨臉色蒼白，不過這應該是因為心情激動和精神緊張，而非由於恐懼或疑慮。

「藥水調製得非常理想。」艾墨回應喬琪娜詢問的表情說道：「它不可能失敗的，除非我一生的科學知識欺騙了我。」

「我心愛的艾墨，為了你，我寧願拋棄[88]生命，也不願用別的方式來去掉這塊凡人的胎記。對於到達我這般道德境界的人來說，生命不過是一份可悲的財產。如果我軟弱一點，盲目一點，生命可能是一種快樂。如果我堅強一點，我可能會樂觀地忍受這樣的生命。但就我現在所處的位置，我想世人當中沒有人比我更適合死去。」喬琪娜說。

86 treason ['triːzən] (n.) 背叛
87 goblet ['gɑːblɪt] (n.) 高腳酒杯
88 relinquish [rɪ'lɪŋkwɪʃ] (v.) 放棄

"You are fit for heaven without tasting death!" replied her husband "But why do we speak of dying? The draught cannot fail. Behold its effect upon this plant."

On the window seat there stood a geranium[89] diseased with yellow blotches[90], which had overspread all its leaves. Aylmer poured a small quantity of the liquid upon the soil in which it grew. In a little time, when the roots of the plant had taken up the moisture, the unsightly blotches began to be extinguished in a living verdure[91].

"There needed no proof," said Georgiana, quietly. "Give me the goblet I joyfully stake all upon[92] your word."

"Drink, then, thou lofty creature!" exclaimed Aylmer, with fervid admiration. "There is no taint of imperfection on thy spirit. Thy sensible frame, too, shall soon be all perfect."

She quaffed the liquid and returned the goblet to his hand.

"It is grateful," said she with a placid smile. "Methinks it is like water from a heavenly fountain; for it contains I know not what of unobtrusive[93] fragrance and deliciousness. It allays[94] a feverish thirst that had parched[95] me for many days. Now, dearest, let me sleep. My earthly senses are closing over my spirit like the leaves around the heart of a rose at sunset."

She spoke the last words with a gentle reluctance, as if it required almost more energy than she could command to pronounce the faint and lingering syllables.

Scarcely had they loitered[96] through her lips ere she was lost in slumber. Aylmer sat by her side, watching her aspect with the emotions proper to a man the whole value of whose existence was involved in the process now to be tested.

「你適合於天堂,卻不必嚐死亡的滋味!但是我們為什麼要說到死亡?這個藥水不可能失敗的,看看它對這棵植物的作用!」艾墨說。

在窗戶下面的椅子上,有一盆得了病的天竺葵,葉子上長滿了黃斑。艾墨往土壤裡倒進一點藥水,沒過多久,天竺葵的根部把水分吸收上來後,醜陋的黃斑便開始褪去,整棵植物頓時一片青翠,生意盎然。

「你不需要證明了,把杯子給我吧,我相信你說的話,我樂意賭上一切。」喬琪娜平靜地說。

「那麼,你就把它喝了吧,高貴的人!」艾墨滿心讚賞地喊道:「你的靈魂沒有絲毫瑕疵,你的軀體馬上也會變得完美無瑕。」

她大口喝盡,然後把杯子還給他。

「真爽口,就像是清泉裡冒出來的水。」她平靜地笑道:「我也說不清那裡面淡淡的香氣和滋味是什麼,但它解除了我多日來的焦渴。親愛的,現在讓我睡一覺吧。我的感官正在包攏我的靈魂,就像葉子在日落時分將玫瑰花心包裹起來。」

她最後幾個字說得有些勉強,彷彿吐出這一串微弱綿延的音節所需的力氣,已超出她所擁有的能量。

話一飄出她的芳唇,她就睡著了。艾墨坐在她身邊,看著她的臉,情緒激動,彷彿他存在的價值就取決於眼前這個實驗的成敗。

89 geranium [dʒə'reniəm] (n.) 天竺葵
90 blotch [blɑ:tʃ] (n.) 斑;疤
91 verdure ['vɜ:rdʒər] (n.) (草木的)青翠
92 stake something upon . . . 拿(生命、地位等)打賭
93 unobtrusive [ˌʌnəb'tru:sɪv] (a.) 不顯眼的
94 allay [ə'leɪ] (v.) 緩和;減輕
95 parch [pɑ:rtʃ] (v.) 使乾透;使焦乾
96 loiter ['lɔɪtər] (v.) 徘徊

❷
胎記

Mingled with this mood, however, was the philosophic investigation characteristic of the man of science. Not the minutest symptom escaped him. A heightened flush of the cheek, a slight irregularity of breath, a quiver of the eyelid, a hardly perceptible tremor through the frame,—such were the details which, as the moments passed, he wrote down in his folio volume. Intense thought had set its stamp upon every previous page of that volume, but the thoughts of years were all concentrated upon the last.

While thus employed, he failed not to gaze often at the fatal hand, and not without a shudder. Yet once, by a strange and unaccountable impulse he pressed it with his lips. His spirit recoiled, however, in the very act, and Georgiana, out of the midst of her deep sleep, moved uneasily and murmured as if in remonstrance[97]. Again Aylmer resumed his watch. Nor was it without avail[98]. The crimson hand, which at first had been strongly visible upon the marble paleness of Georgiana's cheek, now grew more faintly outlined.

She remained not less pale than ever; but the birthmark with every breath that came and went, lost somewhat of its former distinctness. Its presence had been awful; its departure was more awful still. Watch the stain of the rainbow fading out of the sky, and you will know how that mysterious symbol passed away.

"By Heaven! it is well-nigh[99] gone!" said Aylmer to himself, in almost irrepressible ecstasy. "I can scarcely trace it now. Success! success! And now it is like the faintest rose color. The lightest flush of blood across her cheek would overcome it. But she is so pale!"

和他的這種情緒摻雜在一起的，還有那種科學家特有的觀察精神。最細微的變化，都逃不過他的眼睛。臉頰的潮紅，呼吸的變化，眼瞼的輕顫，難以察覺的全身性顫抖——時間分分秒秒地過去，他將這些細節一一抄在他的那本大冊子裡。這本冊子的每一頁上都留下了他思緒的印記，而這多年的思慮現在全集中在這最後一頁。

他一邊忙著觀察、做記錄，一邊不忘隨時看著那致命的手印。他每次一看，都不由得打寒噤。這時，一陣莫名的衝動促使他湊上去親吻胎記，然而一碰到胎記時，他又畏縮了。沉睡中的喬琪娜不安地動了一下，嘴裡呢呢喃喃，彷彿在表示抗議。艾墨又繼續他的觀察，他觀察到了變化。在喬琪娜大理石般蒼白的臉頰上，緋紅色的小手本來還很清晰明顯，現在卻越來越模糊。

她的膚色還是跟之前一樣蒼白，但是隨著她的一呼一吸，胎記漸漸失去原先的輪廓。胎記存在時，令人觸目驚心；而現在當它要離去時，更令人生畏。只要看看彩虹如何在天空中漸漸消失，你就會知道那神秘的印記是如何消失的。

「天哪！胎記快消失了！」艾墨對自己說，他難以克制內心的狂喜，「現在幾乎不見了。成功了！成功了！只剩下很淡的玫瑰色了，只要她臉蛋微微一紅，就會蓋過去。只是，她好蒼白！」

97 remonstrance [rɪˈmɑːnstrəns] (n.) 抗議
98 avail [əˈveɪl] (n.) 效用
99 well-nigh [ˈwelnaɪ] (adv.) 幾乎

He drew aside the window curtain and suffered the light of natural day to fall into the room and rest upon her cheek. At the same time he heard a gross[100], hoarse chuckle[101], which he had long known as his servant Aminadab's expression of delight.

"Ah, clod! ah, earthly mass!" cried Aylmer, laughing in a sort of frenzy[102], "you have served me well! Matter and spirit—earth and heaven—have both done their part in this! Laugh, thing of the senses! You have earned the right to laugh."

These exclamations broke Georgiana's sleep. She slowly unclosed her eyes and gazed into the mirror which her husband had arranged for that purpose. A faint smile flitted over her lips when she recognized how barely perceptible was now that crimson hand which had once blazed forth with such disastrous brilliancy as to scare away all their happiness. But then her eyes sought Aylmer's face with a trouble and anxiety that he could by no means account for.

"My poor Aylmer!" murmured she.

"Poor? Nay, richest, happiest, most favored!" exclaimed he. "My peerless bride, it is successful! You are perfect!"

"My poor Aylmer," she repeated, with a more than human tenderness, "you have aimed loftily; you have done nobly. Do not repent[103] that with so high and pure a feeling, you have rejected the best the earth could offer. Aylmer, dearest Aylmer, I am dying!"

Alas! it was too true! The fatal hand had grappled with[104] the mystery of life, and was the bond by which an angelic spirit kept itself in union with a mortal frame.

艾墨拉開窗簾，讓陽光照進屋子，照在喬琪娜的臉頰上。這時他聽到一陣粗俗沙啞的輕笑，他知道那是助手阿迷高興時的笑聲。

　　「啊，你這個泥塊！這個凡物！」艾墨發狂似地大笑說道：「你做得真好啊！物質與精神，塵世與天堂，兩者都盡了該盡的本分！笑吧，你這個只有感官的東西！你有權利大笑！」

　　這些呼喊聲吵醒了喬琪娜。喬琪娜慢慢張開眼睛，望著丈夫為她準備好的鏡子。看到那塊過去醒目到足以嚇走他們所有幸福的緋紅色小手，如今已經幾乎消失不見，她的嘴角掠過一抹微笑，然後尋找艾墨的臉龐，眼中露出了艾墨所無法理解的擔憂與焦慮。

　　「我可憐的艾墨！」她喃喃地說。

　　「可憐？不，我是最富裕、最幸福的天之驕子艾墨！我舉世無雙的新娘，我們成功了！你現在完美無瑕了！」他喊道。

　　她用異常溫柔的聲音重覆道：「我可憐的艾墨，你目標崇高、行為高貴，千萬不要懊悔正因為這高尚純潔的感情，而推掉了這世間所能夠給你的最好的東西。艾墨，親愛的艾墨，我就要死了！」

　　啊！是的，沒錯！這個致命的手印已經緊緊攫住生命的秘密，是它把天國的靈魂和肉體結合在一起的。

❷
胎
記

As the last crimson tint of the birthmark—that sole token of human imperfection—faded from her cheek, the parting breath of the now perfect woman passed into the atmosphere, and her soul, lingering a moment near her husband, took its heavenward flight.

Then a hoarse, chuckling laugh was heard again! Thus ever does the gross fatality of earth exult in its invariable triumph over the immortal essence which, in this dim sphere of half development, demands the completeness of a higher state.

Yet, had Aylmer reached a profounder wisdom, he need not thus have flung away the happiness which would have woven his mortal life of the selfsame texture with the celestial. The momentary circumstance was too strong for him; he failed to look beyond the shadowy scope of time, and, living once for all in eternity, to find the perfect future in the present.

當這個胎記的最後一抹緋紅——人類缺陷的標誌——從她臉頰上消失時，這個如今完美無瑕的女子也吐出了最後一口氣。她的靈魂在丈夫身旁留連片刻之後，便往天國飛去。

這時屋裡又聽到沙啞的輕笑聲！不朽的精神在尚待開發的渾沌領域中，冀求更高境界的完美，而塵世無情的死亡，正為又一次戰勝這不朽的精神而歡呼！

然而，如果艾墨擁有更深刻的智慧，就毋須這樣拋棄這份幸福，這份幸福本可以將他的塵世生活變得如置天國。他不堪忍受塵世的短暫，他的目光未能超越時間的局限，也未能在永恆中盡力地活這一次，在當下找到完美的未來。

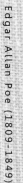

3

Edgar Allan Poe (1809-1849)

■ 愛倫・坡

The Cask of Amontillado

一桶白葡萄酒

The thousand injuries of Fortunato I had borne as I best could; but when he ventured upon insult, I vowed revenge. You, who so well know the nature of my soul, will not suppose, however, that I gave utterance to a threat. *At length* I would be avenged; this was a point definitively settled—but the very definitiveness with which it was resolved, precluded the idea of risk.

I must not only punish, but punish with impunity. A wrong is unredressed when retribution[1] overtakes its redresser. It is equally unredressed when the avenger fails to make himself felt as such to him who has done the wrong.

It must be understood, that neither by word nor deed had I given Fortunato cause to doubt my good will. I continued, as was my wont, to smile in his face, and he did not perceive that my smile *now* was at the thought of his immolation[2].

He had a weak point—this Fortunato—although in other regards he was a man to be respected and even feared. He prided himself on his connoisseurship in wine. Few Italians have the true virtuoso[3] spirit. For the most part their enthusiasm is adopted to suit the time and opportunity— to practice imposture[4] upon the British and Austrian *millionaires*.

In painting and gemmary, Fortunato, like his countrymen, was a quack[5]—but in the matter of old wines he was sincere. In this respect I did not differ from him materially: I was skilful in the Italian vintages myself, and bought largely whenever I could.

福度納多對我百般迫害，我都忍了下來，但他竟侮辱我，這個仇我非報不可。你早摸透了我的個性，不會當我只是說說嚇唬人。此仇非報不可，我是下定了決心，不容有什麼差池。

我不只要懲罰他，還要無後顧之憂地懲罰他。如果討回正義的人自己遭到報應，正義就不算被討回；如果復仇者無法讓惡人知道自己罪有應得，正義同樣不算被討回。

要知道，我的言行舉止都沒有讓福度納多起疑心。我依舊對他笑臉相迎，而他渾然不知，我之所以笑，是因為我正想著他會如何成為祭品。

福度納多這個人有個弱點，儘管他在其他方面算是令人敬重，甚至令人生畏。他自詡是品酒老手。沒有幾個義大利人是真正的藝術行家，大多數人都是為了迎合潮流和機會，才混入藝術這一行，好騙騙英國和奧地利的大富豪。

說到繪畫和珠寶，福度納多就跟他的同胞一樣，是個冒牌的專家，但是在陳酒這方面，他是真的識貨。這一點我跟他沒什麼差別，對於義大利酒，我也算內行，只要一有機會，我就會大量買進。

---

1 retribution [ˌretrɪˈbjuːʃən] (n.) 報應；應得的懲罰
2 immolation [ˌɪməˈleɪʃən] (n.) 祭品
3 virtuoso [ˌvɜːrtʃuˈoʊsoʊ] (n.) 藝術大師；美術家；古玩家
4 imposture [ɪmˈpɑːstʃər] (n.) 冒名頂替的欺騙行為
5 quack [kwæk] (n.) 冒牌者；裝內行的人

It was about dusk, one evening during the supreme madness of the carnival season, that I encountered my friend. He accosted[6] me with excessive warmth, for he had been drinking much.

The man wore motley[7]. He had on a tight-fitting parti-striped dress, and his head was surmounted by the conical cap and bells. I was so pleased to see him, that I thought I should never have done wringing his hand.

I said to him—"My dear Fortunato, you are luckily met. How remarkably well you are looking today! But I have received a pipe[8] of what passes for Amontillado, and I have my doubts."

"How?" said he. Amontillado? A pipe? Impossible! And in the middle of the carnival!"

"I have my doubts," I replied; "and I was silly enough to pay the full Amontillado price without consulting you in the matter. You were not to be found, and I was fearful of losing a bargain."

"Amontillado!"

"I have my doubts."

"Amontillado!"

"And I must satisfy them."

"Amontillado!"

"As you are engaged, I am on my way to Luchesi. If any one has a critical turn, it is he. He will tell me—"

6　accost [əˈkɑːst] (v.) 走上前與……說話
7　motley [ˈmɑːtli] (n.) 小丑穿的雜色彩衣
8　pipe [paɪp] (n.) 大酒桶（容量為 126 酒加侖）

在瘋狂的嘉年華會期間，一天傍晚，我遇到了這位老友。他喝多了，親熱地跟我打招呼。

這傢伙扮成了小丑的樣子，他穿著雜色條紋緊身衣，頭上戴了圓錐帽，上面繫著許多鈴鐺。看到他，我是這麼的高興，一直抓著他的手不放。

我對他說：「我親愛的福度納多，真高興碰到你。看看你今天氣色多好啊！我弄到了一大桶酒，對方說是雅夢白葡萄酒，不過我不太放心。」

「什麼？雅夢白葡萄酒？一大桶？不可能！在嘉年華會期間哪能弄得到！」他說。

「我不太放心，我居然笨到沒先找你鑑定一下，就照雅夢白葡萄酒的價格付了錢。我找不到你，但又怕錯失一筆好生意。」我說。

「雅夢白葡萄酒！」

「我不太放心。」

「雅夢白葡萄酒！」

「我得放下心來。」

「雅夢白葡萄酒！」

「你在忙吧，所以我正想去找魯可喜。他還有點鑑賞力，能告訴我——」

"Luchesi cannot tell Amontillado from Sherry."

"And yet some fools will have it that his taste is a match for your own."

"Come, let us go."

"Whither?"

"To your vaults[9]."

"My friend, no; I will not impose upon[10] your good nature. I perceive you have an engagement. Luchesi—"

"I have no engagement—come."

"My friend, no. It is not the engagement, but the severe cold with which I perceive you are afflicted. The vaults are insufferably damp. They are encrusted with nitre[11]."

"Let us go, nevertheless. The cold is merely nothing. Amontillado! You have been imposed upon. And as for Luchesi, he cannot distinguish Sherry from Amontillado."

Thus speaking, Fortunato possessed himself of my arm. Putting on a mask of black silk, and drawing a *roquelaure*[12] closely about my person, I suffered him to hurry me to my palazzo[13].

There were no attendants at home; they had absconded[14] to make merry in honor of the time. I had told them that I should not return until the morning, and had given them explicit orders not to stir from the house. These orders were sufficient, I well knew, to insure their immediate disappearance, one and all, as soon as my back was turned.

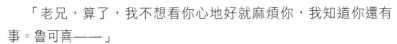

　　「魯可喜連雅夢白葡萄酒和雪利酒都分不清。」

　　「但有些傻子就說他的品味跟你不相上下。」

　　「我們走。」

　　「去哪兒？」

　　「你的酒窖。」

　　「老兄，算了，我不想看你心地好就麻煩你，我知道你還有事。魯可喜——」

　　「我沒事，走！」

　　「老兄，算了啦，這又不是什麼事，天氣這麼冷，我看你受不了的。酒窖裡潮濕得要命，牆上都結了一層硝石。」

　　「我們就走，冷天氣算什麼！雅夢白葡萄酒！你被騙啦！說到魯可喜，他分不清是雪利酒還是雅夢白葡萄酒的啦。」

　　福度納多一邊說道，一邊攙起我的手臂。我戴上黑綢面具，用披風把自己裹起來，任他一路催著我回我家。

　　我家裡沒有僕人在，他們都去嘉年華會上吃喝玩樂了。我跟他們說，我要到明天早上才會回家，還明確囑咐他們不要跑出去。我心裡有數，經過我這麼一吩咐，等我一踏出前門，他們就會立刻從後門溜走。

9　vault [vɑːlt] (n.) 地窖
10　impose upon 趁機利用；打擾；麻煩
11　nitre ['naɪtər] (n.) 硝石（自然界中的硝酸鹽物質）（= niter）
12　roquelaure ['rɔːkələːr] (n.) 及膝的披風（十八世紀歐洲男子常見的裝束）
13　palazzo [pə'læzə] (n.) 華麗的住所
14　abscond [æb'skɑːnd] (v.) 潛逃

I took from their sconces[15] two flambeaux[16], and giving one to Fortunato, bowed him through several suites of rooms to the archway that led into the vaults. I passed down a long and winding staircase, requesting him to be cautious as he followed. We came at length to the foot of the descent, and stood together on the damp ground of the catacombs[17] of the Montresors.

The gait of my friend was unsteady, and the bells upon his cap jingled as he strode.

"The pipe?" said he.

"It is farther on," said I; "but observe the white web-work which gleams from these cavern walls."

He turned towards me, and looked into my eyes with two filmy orbs that distilled the rheum[18] of intoxication .

"Nitre?" he asked, at length.

"Nitre," I replied. "How long have you had that cough?"

"Ugh! ugh! ugh!—ugh! ugh! ugh!—ugh! ugh! ugh!—ugh! ugh! ugh!—ugh! ugh! ugh!"

My poor friend found it impossible to reply for many minutes.

"It is nothing," he said, at last.

"Come," I said, with decision, "we will go back; your health is precious. You are rich, respected, admired, beloved; you are happy, as once I was. You are a man to be missed. For me it is no matter. We will go back; you will be ill, and I cannot be responsible. Besides, there is Luchesi—"

15 sconce [skɔːns] (n.) 固定於牆上的燭臺
16 flambeau ['flæmboʊ] (n.) 火把（flambeaux 是複數形）

我從牆上的燭臺取下兩支火把，一支交給福度納多，然後領他走過一間間的房間，來到通往地窖的拱廊。我走下一個長長的螺旋階梯，請他一路小心跟著。最後我們終於來到了樓梯底端，站在孟崔梭家族地下墓穴潮濕的地板上。

我的老朋友腳步搖搖晃晃，一邊走，帽子上的鈴鐺一邊鐺鐺作響。

「桶酒呢？」他說。

「在前面，不過你看，牆上有白色的網狀物在發光。」我說。

他轉過來，盯著我的眼睛，他的眼睛看起來濁濁的，流著過敏的分泌物。

「是硝石嗎？」他終於開口問道。

「是硝石。你是什麼時候開始對這個過敏的？」我問。

「咳！咳！咳！——咳！咳！咳！——咳！咳！咳！——咳！咳！咳！——咳！咳！咳！」

我可憐的老朋友半天答不出話來。

「這沒什麼。」他終於回答說。

我堅決地說：「來吧，我們回去，你的健康比較重要。你有錢，又備受敬重，大家都景仰你、喜愛你。你現在就跟我以前一樣快樂，你要是有什麼三長兩短，那可不得了。但如果換作是我，就無所謂了。我們回去吧，再待下去你會生病的，這責任我可擔當不起。再說，還有魯可喜——」

17 catacomb [ˈkætəkoʊm] (n.)（一般用複數）地下墓穴
18 rheum [ruːm] (n.) 黏液；分泌物

"Enough," he said; "the cough is a mere nothing; it will not kill me. I shall not die of a cough."

"True—true," I replied; "and, indeed, I had no intention of alarming you unnecessarily—but you should use all proper caution. A draught of this Medoc[19] will defend us from the damps."

Here I knocked off the neck of a bottle which I drew from a long row of its fellows that lay upon the mould.

"Drink," I said, presenting him the wine.

He raised it to his lips with a leer[20]. He paused and nodded to me familiarly, while his bells jingled.

"I drink," he said, "to the buried that repose around us."

"And I to your long life."

He again took my arm, and we proceeded.

"These vaults," he said, "are extensive."

"The Montresors," I replied, "were a great and numerous family."

"I forget your arms."

"A huge human foot d'or[21], in a field azure; the foot crushes a serpent rampant[22] whose fangs[23] are imbedded in the heel."

"And the motto?"

"*Nemo me impune lacessit*[24]."

"Good!" he said.

19 Medoc 梅鐸酒（法國西南部梅鐸省出產的紅酒）
20 leer [lɪr] (n.)（不懷好意的）斜眼看
21 d'or 金色的（golden）
22 rampant [ˈræmpənt] (a.)（紋章上的動物）躍立的

「別提這個了，這咳嗽沒什麼，死不了人的，又咳不死人。」他說。

「對，對，我也不想大驚小怪——不過該小心的時候還是要小心。喝口梅鐸酒，防防濕氣吧。」我說。

我從地上那一排葡萄酒中抽出一瓶，砸了瓶頸。

「喝吧！」我把酒遞給他。

他瞟了我一眼，把酒瓶舉到嘴邊。喝完後，他親熱地對我點頭，頭上的鈴鐺叮噹作響。

「為四周這些長眠地下的人，乾杯！」他說。

「我為你長命百歲乾杯。」

他又攙起我的手臂，我們繼續往前走。

「這地窖可真大。」他說。

「孟崔梭以前是個大家族。」我說。

「我忘了你們府上的家徽是什麼樣子的了。」

「上有一隻大大的人腳，金色的，背景是天藍色的。那隻腳把一隻騰起的大蛇踩爛了，大蛇的尖牙就咬著腳跟。」

「這有什麼寓意？」

「凡傷我者，必遭懲罰。」

「說的是！」他說。

---

23 fang [fæŋ] (n.) 尖銳的長牙（如蛇的毒牙）

24 *Nemo me impune lacessit.* 拉丁語，意為「攻擊我者，皆將受懲」（No one attacks me with impunity.）

The wine sparkled in his eyes and the bells jingled. My own fancy grew warm with the Medoc. We had passed through walls of piled bones, with casks and puncheons[25] intermingling, into the inmost recesses of the catacombs. I paused again, and this time I made bold to seize Fortunato by an arm above the elbow.

"The nitre!" I said: "see, it increases. It hangs like moss upon the vaults. We are below the river's bed. The drops of moisture trickle among the bones. Come, we will go back ere it is too late. Your cough—"

"It is nothing," he said; "let us go on. But first, another draught of the Medoc."

I broke and reached him a flacon[26] of De Grâve. He emptied it at a breath. His eyes flashed with a fierce light. He laughed and threw the bottle upwards with a gesticulation I did not understand.

I looked at him in surprise. He repeated the movement—a grotesque one.

"You do not comprehend?" he said.

"Not I," I replied.

"Then you are not of the brotherhood."

"How?"

"You are not of the masons[27]."

"Yes, yes," I said, "yes, yes."

"You? Impossible! A mason?"

"A mason," I replied.

"A sign," he said.

"It is this," I answered, producing a trowel[28] from beneath the folds of my *roquelaire*.

喝了酒後，他的眼睛閃閃發光，帽子上的鈴鐺不停地叮噹作響。梅鐸酒讓我也開始胡思亂想了。我們走過一個長長的走道，牆邊堆著人骨和大大小小的酒桶，來到墓穴的最深處。我停下來，放膽抓起福度納多的上臂。

我說：「你看，硝石！越來越多了，像苔蘚一樣掛在拱頂上。我們現在正在河床底下，水珠都滴在骨頭堆裡。來吧，我們趁早回去吧。你的咳嗽——」

「不礙事，繼續走。再讓我喝口梅鐸酒。」他說。

我砸破一瓶哥夫酒，遞給他。他一口氣喝光，眼裡閃著兇狠的目光。他開始大笑，用個奇怪的手勢把酒瓶往上一扔。

我吃驚地看著他。他又重複一遍這個怪異的動作。

「你不懂？」他說。

「我不懂。」我答。

「那你就不是同道。」

「什麼？」

「你不是共濟會的人。」

「我是共濟會的人沒錯。」我說道。

「你？不可能！你是共濟會的人？」

「我是共濟會的人。」我回道。

「證明給我看。」他說。

「這個。」我邊說，邊從披風裡面掏出一把抹子。

---

25 puncheon [ˈpʌntʃən] (n.) 大酒桶（能容 84 酒加侖）
26 flacon [ˈflækən] (n.) 有塞子的小瓶子
27 mason [ˈmeɪsən] (n.) 泥水工；共濟會會員（共濟會發源於中古時代，最初為泥水工組成的秘密團體，相遇時以暗號聯繫）
28 trowel [ˈtraʊəl] (n.) 泥水工用來塗灰泥的抹子

"You jest," he exclaimed, recoiling a few paces. "But let us proceed to the Amontillado."

"Be it so," I said, replacing the tool beneath the cloak, and again offering him my arm. He leaned upon it heavily. We continued our route in search of the Amontillado. We passed through a range of low arches, descended, passed on, and descending again, arrived at a deep crypt[29], in which the foulness of the air caused our flambeaux rather to glow than flame.

At the most remote end of the crypt there appeared another less spacious. Its walls had been lined with human remains, piled to the vault overhead, in the fashion of the great catacombs of Paris. Three sides of this interior crypt were still ornamented in this manner. From the fourth the bones had been thrown down, and lay promiscuously[30] upon the earth, forming at one point a mound of some size.

Within the wall thus exposed by the displacing of the bones, we perceived a still interior recess, in depth about four feet, in width three, in height six or seven. It seemed to have been constructed for no especial use within itself, but formed merely the interval between two of the colossal supports of the roof of the catacombs, and was backed by one of their circumscribing walls of solid granite[31].

It was in vain that Fortunato, uplifting his dull torch, endeavored to pry into the depths of the recess. Its termination the feeble light did not enable us to see.

「你真愛開玩笑。」他喊著，往後退了幾步，「我們還是繼續去找你那桶雅夢白葡萄酒吧。」

「那就走吧。」我說罷，便把抹子放回披風裡，伸出手臂攬著他，他沉沉靠著我的手，我們繼續往那桶雅夢白葡萄酒走去。我們走過一連串低矮的拱頂，然後下樓梯，繼續前進，又下樓梯，最後來到一個深幽的地窟，裡面空氣很混濁，火把的火光都變暗了。

地窟的盡頭，又出現一個更小的地窟，牆是骨骸堆成的，一直高高地堆到拱頂，就像巴黎那些大墓窖一樣。小地窟的三面牆都長個這個樣子，而第四面牆的骨頭被推倒，雜亂地堆在地上，形成一個偌大的人骨墩。

透過這面倒下的牆，可以看到一個壁龕，深約一公尺餘，寬近一公尺，高約兩公尺左右。看起來不是為了什麼特別的目的而挖出來的，不過是支持墓穴頂部兩根大柱之間的空隙罷了，背後就是墓穴的花崗石牆。

福度納多舉高昏暗的火把，努力想看清壁龕內部，但是什麼都看不到。在這麼微弱的光線下，根本看不到壁龕底。

29 crypt [krɪpt] (n.) 地窟
30 promiscuously [prəˈmɪskjuəsli] (adv.) 雜亂地
31 granite [ˈgrænɪt] (n.) 花崗石

"Proceed," I said; "herein is the Amontillado. As for Luchesi—"

"He is an ignoramus," interrupted my friend, as he stepped unsteadily forward, while I followed immediately at his heels. In an instant he had reached the extremity of the niche[32], and finding his progress arrested by the rock, stood stupidly bewildered.

A moment more and I had fettered him to the granite. In its surface were two iron staples[33], distant from each other about two feet, horizontally. From one of these depended a short chain, from the other a padlock. Throwing the links about his waist, it was but the work of a few seconds to secure it. He was too much astounded to resist. Withdrawing the key I stepped back from the recess.

"Pass your hand," I said, "over the wall; you cannot help feeling the nitre. Indeed it is very damp. Once more let me implore you to return. No? Then I must positively leave you. But I must first render you all the little attentions in my power."

"The Amontillado!" ejaculated my friend, not yet recovered from his astonishment.

"True," I replied; "the Amontillado."

As I said these words I busied myself among the pile of bones of which I have before spoken. Throwing them aside, I soon uncovered a quantity of building stone and mortar[34]. With these materials and with the aid of my trowel, I began vigorously to wall up the entrance of the niche.

我說：「往前走，雅夢白葡萄酒就在裡面。至於魯可喜——」

「他是個老千。」我的老朋友一面搖搖晃晃地往前走，一面打斷我，我緊緊跟在他身後。沒一下他就來到壁龕的盡頭，一見前面是石頭，沒路走了，他就停在原地。

沒一會兒功夫，我就把他鎖在花崗石牆上。牆上釘了兩個鐵環，左右相隔六十公分左右，其中一個鐵環掛著一條短鐵鏈，另外一個掛著一把大鎖。我把鐵鏈往他腰上繞，一眨眼功夫就把鏈子鎖上。福度納多很吃驚，根本沒想到要反抗。我拔掉鑰匙，走出壁龕。

我說：「伸手摸摸牆壁，都是硝石，是吧？這裡真的很潮濕。我再求你一次，回去吧。不要？那我只好留你一個人在這裡了。不過我還得先照顧你一下。」

「雅夢白葡萄酒！」我的老朋友喊道，他還沒清醒過來。

我答道：「對，雅夢白葡萄酒。」

我邊說著，邊在那堆骨骸裡開始忙起來。我把骨頭扔到一邊，找出藏在下面的磚頭和灰泥。我用這些材料，再靠那把抹子，開始一個勁地把壁龕的入口堵起來。

32 niche [nɪtʃ] (n.) 壁龕
33 staple [ˈsteɪpəl] (n.) U 字形釘
34 mortar [ˈmɔːrtər] (n.) 灰泥

I had scarcely laid the first tier[35] of the masonry[36] when I discovered that the intoxication of Fortunato had in a great measure worn off. The earliest indication I had of this was a low moaning cry from the depth of the recess. It was not the cry of a drunken man. There was then a long and obstinate silence. I laid the second tier, and the third, and the fourth; and then I heard the furious vibrations of the chain.

The noise lasted for several minutes, during which, that I might hearken to[37] it with the more satisfaction, I ceased my labors and sat down upon the bones. When at last the clanking subsided, I resumed the trowel, and finished without interruption the fifth, the sixth, and the seventh tier. The wall was now nearly upon a level with my breast. I again paused, and holding the flambeaux over the mason-work, threw a few feeble rays upon the figure within.

A succession of loud and shrill screams, bursting suddenly from the throat of the chained form, seemed to thrust me violently back. For a brief moment I hesitated—I trembled. Unsheathing my rapier[38], I began to grope[39] with it about the recess: but the thought of an instant reassured me.

I placed my hand upon the solid fabric of the catacombs, and felt satisfied. I reapproached the wall. I replied to the yells of him who clamored[40]. I re-echoed—I aided—I surpassed them in volume and in strength. I did this, and the clamorer grew still.

It was now midnight, and my task was drawing to a close. I had completed the eighth, the ninth, and the tenth tier. I had finished a portion of the last and the eleventh; there remained but a single stone to be fitted and plastered[41] in.

第一層磚頭剛砌完，我就知道福度納多的醉意醒了八成，因為壁龕深處傳來一聲幽幽的呻吟，那不是醉漢的叫聲。接著是一陣漫長的沉默。我砌完第二層、第三層、第四層之後，就聽到拚命搖晃鐵鏈的聲音，持續有好幾分鐘。

　　我索性停下手邊的工作，在骨頭堆上坐下，好聽個痛快。在噹啷聲終於停下來之後，我才又拿起抹子，一口氣砌完了第五層、第六層和第七層。這堵牆現在差不多跟我的胸部齊高了。我又停下來，把火把伸進石牆裡，微弱的火光就照在裡頭那人的身上。

　　這個被鐵鏈綁住的人，突然發出一連串尖銳響亮的叫喊，彷彿要把我猛力往後推似的。剎那間，我拿不定主意，瑟瑟直發抖。我拔出劍，在壁龕裡摸索起來，但轉念一想，又放下心了。

　　我把手貼在墓穴堅固的石牆上，安心了。我回到牆邊，回應他的吼叫：他叫一聲，我應一聲，叫得比他響、比他亮，最後他就安靜下來了。

　　這時已經半夜了，我也快弄完了。第八層、第九層、第十層已經砌上了。最後一層，也就是第十一層，我也快砌完了，就只消嵌進最後一塊磚頭，再抹上泥灰就行了。

---

35 tier [tɪr] (n.) 一層
36 masonry [ˈmeɪsənri] (n.)（用於建築的）石塊
37 hearken to 傾聽
38 rapier [ˈreɪpiər] (n.) 細長的輕劍
39 grope [groʊp] (v.) 摸索
40 clamor [ˈklæmər] (v.) 喧嚷
41 plaster [ˈplæstər] (v.) 塗上灰泥

❸
一桶白葡萄酒

I struggled with its weight; I placed it partially in its destined position. But now there came from out the niche a low laugh that erected the hairs upon my head. It was succeeded by a sad voice, which I had difficulty in recognizing as that of the noble Fortunato. The voice said—

"Ha! ha! ha!—he! he!—a very good joke indeed—an excellent jest. We will have many a rich laugh about it at the palazzo—he! he! he!—over our wine—he! he! he!"

"The Amontillado!" I said.

"He! he! he!—he! he! he!—yes, the Amontillado. But is it not getting late? Will not they be awaiting us at the palazzo, the Lady Fortunato and the rest? Let us be gone."

"Yes," I said, "let us be gone."

"*For the love of God, Montressor!*"

"Yes," I said, "for the love of God!"

But to these words I hearkened in vain for a reply. I grew impatient. I called aloud—

"Fortunato!"

No answer. I called again—

"Fortunato!"

磚頭不輕，我好不容易才把它舉上去。在我還沒完全塞進磚頭時，壁龕裡面傳出了一陣低沉的笑聲，嚇得我寒毛直豎。接下來是一個悲悽的聲音，一點都不像福度納多老爺的聲音。這個聲音說道——

「哈！哈！哈！——嘻！嘻！——真的是很讚的玩

笑——絕妙的玩笑。等我們回到大宅，就可有的笑了——嘻！嘻！嘻！——邊喝酒，邊大笑——嘻！嘻！嘻！」

「雅夢白葡萄酒！」我說。

「嘻！嘻！嘻！——嘻！嘻！嘻！——對，雅夢白葡萄酒。現在時間很晚了吧？福度納多夫人他們不是在大宅裡等我們嗎？我們走吧！」

我說：「對，我們走吧。」

「看在上帝的份上，走吧，孟崔梭！」

我說：「對，看在上帝的份上！」

我沒聽到他回話，便沉不住氣地喊——

「福度納多！」

沒有回應。我又喊——

「福度納多！」

No answer still. I thrust a torch through the remaining aperture[42] and let it fall within. There came forth in return only a jingling of the bells. My heart grew sick—on account of the dampness of the catacombs.

I hastened to make an end of my labor. I forced the last stone into its position; I plastered it up. Against the new masonry I re-erected the old rampart[43] of bones. For the half of a century no mortal has disturbed them. *In pace requiescat*[44]!

還是沒有回應。我把一根火把從縫隙裡丟進去，結果只聽到叮鈴噹啷的鈴鐺聲。我開始噁心起來，是墓穴裡的潮氣引起的。

我趕忙把牆砌完，塞進最後一塊磚頭，抹上灰泥，再把那堆骨頭沿著這堵新牆堆起來。半個世紀來，沒人動過這些骨骸。願死者安息！

---

42 aperture [ˈæpərtʃʊr] (n.) 縫隙
43 rampart [ˈræmpɑːrt] (n.)（通常指城堡周圍的堤狀）土牆或石牆
44 requiescat [ˌrekwɪˈeskæt] (n.) 祝福死者安息的禱文

4

Herman Melville (1819-1891)

避雷專家

■ 梅爾維爾

The Lightning-Rod Man

Whathat grand irregular thunder, thought I, standing on my hearth-stone among the Acroceraunian hills, as the scattered bolts boomed[1] overhead, and crashed down among the valleys, every bolt followed by zigzag irradiations, and swift slants of sharp rain, which audibly rang, like a charge of spear-points, on my low shingled roof. I suppose, though, that the mountains hereabouts break and churn up[2] the thunder, so that it is far more glorious here than on the plain.

Hark[3]!—someone at the door. Who is this that chooses a time of thunder for making calls? And why don't he, man-fashion, use the knocker, instead of making that doleful undertaker's clatter with his fist against the hollow panel? But let him in. Ah, here he comes.

"Good day, sir:" an entire stranger.

"Pray be seated." What is that strange-looking walking-stick he carries:

"A fine thunder-storm, sir."

"Fine?—Awful!"

"You are wet. Stand here on the hearth before the fire."

"Not for worlds!"

The stranger still stood in the exact middle of the cottage, where he had first planted himself. His singularity impelled a closer scrutiny.

---

1 boom [buːm] (v.) 隆隆作響
2 churn up 劇烈攪動；使劇烈翻騰
3 hark [hɑːrk] (v.) 聽

　　真壯觀的閃電，我心想。這裡是亞闊朗山區，我正站在壁爐邊的石階上，大大小小的閃電在天際隆隆作響，震徹山谷，枝狀的閃電此起彼落，挾帶著陣陣的急雨，如萬箭呼呼地射向我那低矮的瓦頂。想必是附近的山頂又穿破、攪動了帶電的雲層，所以這一帶的景觀比平地上壯麗許多。

　　聽！——門外有人。誰會選個雷電交加的時候來訪？而且這個人怎麼不規規矩矩地扣門環，卻像個葬儀社的人可憐兮兮地用拳頭亂敲一陣？先讓他進來吧。他進來了。

　　「您好，先生。」我並不認識他。

　　「請坐。」他手上拿著什麼怪手杖啊。

　　「很妙的雷雨吧，先生。」

　　「很妙？——是可怕吧！」

　　「您全身都濕透了，過來烤烤火。」

　　「萬萬不可！」

　　陌生人一進來就在屋子中央站定，現在仍站在原地。他舉止這麼奇特，我忍不住仔細打量他。

❹
避雷專家

A lean, gloomy figure. Hair dark and lank, mattedly streaked over his brow. His sunken pitfalls of eyes were ringed by indigo halos, and played with an innocuous[4] sort of lightning: the gleam without the bolt.

The whole man was dripping. He stood in a puddle on the bare oak floor: his strange walking-stick vertically resting at his side.

It was a polished copper rod, four feet long, lengthwise attached to a neat wooden staff, by insertion into two balls of greenish glass, ringed with copper bands. The metal rod terminated at the top tripodwise, in three keen tines[5], brightly gilt. He held the thing by the wooden part alone.

"Sir," said I, bowing politely, "have I the honor of a visit from that illustrious god, Jupiter Tonans[6]? So stood he in the Greek statue of old, grasping the lightning-bolt. If you be he, or his viceroy[7], I have to thank you for this noble storm you have brewed among our mountains. Listen: That was a glorious peal. Ah, to a lover of the majestic, it is a good thing to have the Thunderer himself in one's cottage. The thunder grows finer for that. But pray be seated. This old rush-bottomed arm-chair, I grant, is a poor substitute for your evergreen throne on Olympus; but, condescend to be seated."

---

4 innocuous [ɪˈnɑːkjuəs] (a.) 無害的
5 tine [taɪn] (n.) 分叉；尖齒
6 Jupiter Tonans 雷神（希臘神話中的天神宙斯，在羅馬神話中被分為雷神和雨神──Jupiter Pluvin──兩人）
7 viceroy [ˈvaɪsrɔɪ] (n.)（代表國王管理另一國家的）總督

他身材枯瘦，面帶愁容，細軟的黑髮散披在眉毛上。凹陷的眼窩周圍一道青色的眼圈，目光亮如閃電：只有閃光，沒有閃電，不會造成傷害。

他全身上下都在滴水，在橡木地板上滴出一個小水灘，他就站在水灘上，那支怪怪的手杖垂直地靠在身邊。

那是一根光亮的銅棒，長一公尺二十公分，用銅圈固定在一根精巧的木杖上，銅棒與木杖之間用兩顆綠色的玻璃球隔開。銅棒頂端分為三個分叉，都鍍得亮亮的。他只握著木頭的部分。

我禮貌地鞠了一個躬，說：「先生，我是否有這等榮幸，竟蒙偉大的雷神光臨寒舍？雷神的古老希臘雕像，就是像您這樣站著，手裡握著閃電。如果您就是雷神，或是雷神的使者，那我要謝謝您在這山區裡掀起壯觀的雷雨。您聽，多震撼的雷聲啊。對一個崇尚雄偉的大自然的人來說，能請到雷神來到家中作客，再榮幸不過了，雷聲也因此變得更動聽了。請您坐下吧，坐在這張舊扶手椅上，它當然比不上您在奧林帕斯山上永恆的寶座，但還是請您委屈委屈，坐下吧。」

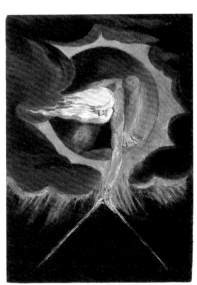

While I thus pleasantly spoke, the stranger eyed me, half in wonder, and half in a strange sort of horror; but did not move a foot.

"Do, sir, be seated; you need to be dried ere going forth again."

I planted the chair invitingly on the broad hearth, where a little fire had been kindled that afternoon to dissipate the dampness, not the cold; for it was early in the month of September.

But without heeding my solicitation, and still standing in the middle of the floor, the stranger gazed at me portentously[8] and spoke. "Sir," said he, "excuse me; but instead of my accepting your invitation to be seated on the hearth there, I solemnly warn you, that you had best accept mine, and stand with me in the middle of the room. Good heavens!" he cried, starting—"there is another of those awful crashes. I warn you, sir, quit the hearth."

"Mr. Jupiter Tonans," said I, quietly rolling my body on the stone, "I stand very well here."

"Are you so horridly ignorant, then," he cried, "as not to know, that by far the most dangerous part of a house, during such a terrific tempest as this, is the fire-place?"

"Nay, I did not know that," involuntarily stepping upon the first board next to the stone.

The stranger now assumed such an unpleasant air of successful admonition[9], that—quite involuntarily again—I stepped back upon the hearth, and threw myself into the erectest, proudest posture I could command. But I said nothing.

　　我客客氣氣說這話的同時，陌生人望著我，表情半是吃驚，半是莫名的恐懼，但他還是動也不動。

　　「先生，請坐下吧，您得烘乾衣服才能繼續趕路。」

　　我把扶手椅搬到壁爐前寬闊的石階上，壁爐裡從下午就燒著一小團火，倒不是為了取暖，而是為了去濕氣。現在才九月初。

　　陌生人並未理會我的話，仍佇立在屋子中央，用不祥的眼神望著我，說道：「先生，很抱歉，我不但不能接受您的邀請過去坐在壁爐邊，還要鄭重警告您，您最好聽我的話，過來跟我一起站在屋子中央。老天爺啊！」他嚇得大喊——「可怕的雷劈又來了。先生，我警告您，快離開壁爐。」

　　「雷神先生，我站在這裡很好啊。」我在石壁上安靜地轉了轉身體。

　　他喊道：「難道您這麼無知，不知道像這樣下大雷雨的時候，屋子裡最危險的地方就是壁爐？」

　　「這我倒是不知道。」我不自主地踏下石階。

　　陌生人此時露出得逞的表情，令我不悅，我不自覺又踏回石階上，擺出我所能擺出的最挺直、最驕傲的站姿，一言不發。

8　portentously [pɔːrˈtentəsli] (adv.) 徵兆不祥地
9　admonition [ˌædməˈnɪʃən] (n.) 告誡

❹
避雷專家

155

"For Heaven's sake," he cried, with a strange mixture of alarm and intimidation—"For Heaven's sake, get off the hearth! Know you not, that the heated air and soot are conductors;—to say nothing of those immense iron fire-dogs[10]? Quit the spot—I conjure—I command you."

"Mr. Jupiter Tonans, I am not accustomed to be commanded in my own house."

"Call me not by that pagan name. You are profane in this time of terror."

"Sir, will you be so good as to tell me your business? If you seek shelter from the storm, you are welcome, so long as you be civil; but if you come on business, open it forthwith. Who are you?"

"I am a dealer in lightning-rods," said the stranger, softening his tone; "my special business is—Merciful heaven! what a crash!—Have you ever been struck—your premises, I mean? No? It's best to be provided;"—significantly rattling his metallic staff on the floor;—"by nature, there are no castles in thunder-storms; yet, say but the word, and of this cottage I can make a Gibraltar[11] by a few waves of this wand. Hark, what Himalayas of concussions!"

"You interrupted yourself; your special business you were about to speak of."

"My special business is to travel the country for orders for lightning-rods. This is my specimen-rod;" tapping his staff; "I have the best of references"—fumbling in his pockets. "In Criggan last month, I put up three-and-twenty rods on only five buildings."

「看在老天爺的份上啊！」他喊道，語氣裡混合著驚慌與恐嚇，「看在老天爺的份上，別站在壁爐邊！難道你不知道熱空氣和煤灰會導電嗎？更別提壁爐裡那些放柴的大鐵架了！快走開——我請求你——我命令你。」

　「雷神先生，我不習慣在自己家還得聽從別人的命令。」

　「別那樣叫我，那是異教徒的神，在這麼可怕的時候，你還褻瀆神明。」

　「先生，您幫個忙，告訴我您的來意好嗎？如果您是來避雨的，那我歡迎您，只要您客氣點。但是如果您來是為了別的事，請直說吧。您到底是什麼人？」

　陌生人用比較和緩的口氣答道：「我是賣避雷針的，我的工作是——天啊！好響的雷聲！——你有沒被雷擊中過——我是說您的房子？沒有？那最好先預防一下。」他用銅棒敲敲地板，說：「照理說，天下沒有擋得住雷電的城堡，但話說回來，我只要揮一揮這根魔棒，就可以把您這個小房子變成一座堅強的堡壘。您聽，連喜馬拉雅山都震動啦！」

　「您把話岔開了，您剛正要說您的工作是？」

　「我的工作就是到各地推銷避雷針，這一支是樣品。」他敲敲銅棒，說：「我有顧客的推薦，上個月在葵岡，我在五棟房子上裝了二十三根避雷針。」他一邊說，一邊在口袋裡摸索。

10　fire-dog (n.)（壁爐裡）堆柴的架子
11　Gibraltar [dʒɪˈbrɔːltər] 直布羅陀（英國屬地，地中海的門戶，在此比喻「堅強的堡壘」）

"Let me see. Was it not at Criggan last week, about midnight on Saturday, that the steeple, the big elm, and the assembly-room cupola[12] were struck? Any of your rods there?"

"Not on the tree and cupola, but the steeple."

"Of what use is your rod, then?"

"Of life-and-death use. But my workman was heedless. In fitting the rod at top to the steeple, he allowed a part of the metal to graze[13] the tin sheeting. Hence the accident. Not my fault, but his. Hark!"

"Never mind. That clap burst quite loud enough to be heard without finger-pointing. Did you hear of the event at Montreal last year? A servant girl struck at her bed-side with a rosary[14] in her hand; the beads being metal. Does your beat extend into the Canadas?"

"No. And I hear that there, iron rods only are in use. They should have mine, which are copper. Iron is easily fused. Then they draw out the rod so slender, that it has not body enough to conduct the full electric current. The metal melts; the building is destroyed. My copper rods never act so. Those Canadians are fools. Some of them knob the rod at the top, which risks a deadly explosion, instead of imperceptibly carrying down the current into the earth, as this sort of rod does. Mine is the only true rod. Look at it. Only one dollar a foot."

"This abuse of your own calling in another might make one distrustful with respect to yourself."

「我想想，上星期六半夜，葵岡的教堂尖塔、大榆樹和圓頂會議廳，不是都被雷劈中了嗎？上面有您的避雷針嗎？」

「樹上和圓頂上沒有避雷針，但是教堂的尖塔上有。」

「那您的避雷針又有什麼用？」

「它有保命的作用。那次是我的工人粗心大意，在尖塔上裝避雷針的時候，讓避雷針接觸到錫片，所以才出事的。那是他的錯，不是我的。你聽！」

「別緊張，這一點雷聲不必大驚小怪。那您聽過去年蒙特婁那件事嗎？有個女傭坐在床邊，手裡握著一串念珠，結果被雷擊中了，那條念珠是金屬製的。您的推銷路線也經過加拿大嗎？」

「沒有。我聽說那裡只有鐵製的避雷針。他們應該用我的避雷針才對，我的避雷針是銅做的。鐵很容易熔化，而且他們把避雷針做得那麼細，根本不夠把電流傳導完。避雷針一熔化，建築物也就毀了。我的銅棒就不會這樣。那些加拿大人很笨，他們有些人還在針頭上裝球，這樣會炸死人的，而不是像我的銅棒是把電流導到地上。我的避雷針才是真正的避雷針。你看看，三十公分才一塊錢。」

「您閉口開口都在自吹自擂、貶人褒己，反而令人對您難以信任。」

12 cupola [ˈkjuːpələ] (n.) 圓屋頂
13 graze [ɡreɪz] (v.) 輕觸
14 rosary [ˈroʊzəri] (n.) （天主教徒用的）念珠

"Hark! The thunder becomes less muttering. It is nearing us, and nearing the earth, too. Hark! One crammed crash! All the vibrations made one by nearness. Another flash. Hold!"

"What do you?" I said, seeing him now, instantaneously relinquishing[15] his staff, lean intently forward towards the window, with his right fore and middle fingers on his left wrist. But ere the words had well escaped me, another exclamation escaped him.

"Crash! only three pulses—less than a third of a mile off—yonder, somewhere in that wood. I passed three stricken oaks there, ripped out new and glittering. The oak draws lightning more than other timber, having iron in solution in its sap[16]. Your floor here seems oak."

"Heart-of-oak. From the peculiar time of your call upon me, I suppose you purposely select stormy weather for your journeys. When the thunder is roaring, you deem it an hour peculiarly favorable for producing impressions favorable to your trade."

"Hark!—Awful!"

"For one who would arm others with fear you seem unbeseemingly[17] timorous yourself. Common men choose fair weather for their travels: you choose thunder-storms; and yet—"

"That I travel in thunder-storms, I grant; but not without particular precautions[18], such as only a lightning-rod man may know. Hark! Quick—look at my specimen rod. Only one dollar a foot."

「你聽！雷聲越來越清晰了，它離我們和地表都越來越近了。你聽！聲音都集中在一起！這麼近，雷聲都壓在一起了。又有閃電了，等等！」

「又怎麼了？」我問。只見他突然丟開手杖，把身體靠向窗口，右手的食指和中指搭在左手腕上，一副凝神專注的樣子。還沒等我把話問完，他又大喊一聲。

「砰！只響了三聲——不到五百公尺遠了——一定在那邊的樹林裡。我經過樹林的時候，看到三棵剛被劈倒的橡樹，樹心白亮亮的露在外面。橡木比其他木頭更容易遭到電擊，因為橡樹的汁液裡有溶解的鐵。你這裡的地板，好像就是橡木做的。」

「是橡木心做的。從您來訪的時間看來，我想您是故意選刮風下雨的天氣，出門做生意的吧。您覺得雷聲大作的時候，特別有利於推銷您的產品。」

「你聽！——多可怕啊！」

「您既然要利用別人的恐懼，自己就不應該這麼膽小。一般人都選好天氣出門，您卻專選雷雨天出門，但是又——」

「沒錯，我是專選雷雨天出門，但是有許多事情我必須特別注意，這些事情只有像我這樣的避雷專家才懂。你聽！快——看看我的樣品，三十公分只要一塊錢。」

15 relinquish [rɪˈlɪŋkwɪʃ] (v.) 放開
16 sap [sæp] (n.) 樹液；汁液
17 unbeseemingly (adv.) 與……不相稱地
18 precaution [prɪˈkɔːʃən] (n.) 預防措施

❹
避雷專家

"A very fine rod, I dare say. But what are these particular precautions of yours? Yet first let me close yonder shutters[19]; the slanting rain is beating through the sash[20]. I will bar up."

"Are you mad? Know you not that yon iron bar is a swift conductor? Desist[21]."

"I will simply close the shutters, then, and call my boy to bring me a wooden bar. Pray, touch the bell-pull there."

"Are you frantic? That bell-wire might blast you. Never touch bell-wire in a thunder-storm, nor ring a bell of any sort."

"Nor those in belfries[22]? Pray, will you tell me where and how one may be safe in a time like this? Is there any part of my house I may touch with hopes of my life?"

"There is; but not where you now stand. Come away from the wall. The current will sometimes run down a wall, and—a man being a better conductor than a wall—it would leave the wall and run into him. Swoop! That must have fallen very nigh. That must have been globular lightning."

"Very probably. Tell me at once, which is, in your opinion, the safest part of this house?

"This room, and this one spot in it where I stand. Come hither."

"The reasons first."

"Hark!—after the flash the gust[23]—the sashes shiver—the house, the house!—Come hither to me!"

「我敢說，這個避雷針一定不錯。但我要聽聽您有哪些事情要特別注意？不過先等我把那邊的窗戶關上，雨下得斜，都打進來了。我要把窗戶閂上。」

「你瘋了嗎？你不知道你的鐵閂會導電嗎？別碰它。」

「那我把窗戶關上就好了，然後叫男僕拿根木栓來。麻煩您，拉一下那邊的拉鈴。」

「你瘋了啊？拉鈴的繩子會讓你被雷劈到。雷雨天千萬不要碰拉鈴繩，什麼鈴啊、鐘啊，都不要碰。」

「那教堂鐘塔裡的大鐘也不行囉？那請您告訴我，這種天氣要待在哪裡才安全？我家裡有沒有什麼地方是我碰到還能活命的？」

「有，但不是你現在站的地方。別站在牆邊。電流有時候會沿著牆壁往下傳，然後——因為人體比牆壁更容易導電——電會離開牆壁，跑到人的身上。唉喲！這個雷一定很近，一定是落地雷。」

「很有可能。請您快告訴我，以您的看法，在這個屋子裡，哪裡最安全？」

「就這間房間，我現在站的這一點。快過來。」

「請先說理由。」

「你聽！——閃電之後是一陣狂風——窗格在震動——這間屋子，這間屋子！——快站過來！」

---

19 shutter [ˈʃʌtər] (n.)（窗戶玻璃外可關上的）窗板
20 sash [sæʃ] (n.) 窗框
21 desist [dɪˈsɪst] (v.) 停下（不再做⋯⋯）
22 belfry [ˈbelfri] (n.)（教堂的）鐘樓
23 gust [gʌst] (n.) 突然一陣強風

"The reasons, if you please."

"Come hither to me!"

"Thank you again, I think I will try my old stand—the hearth. And now, Mr. Lightning-rod-man, in the pauses of the thunder, be so good as to tell me your reasons for esteeming this one room of the house the safest, and your own one stand-point there the safest spot in it."

There was now a little cessation of the storm for a while. The Lightning-rod man seemed relieved, and replied:— "Your house is a one-storied house, with an attic and a cellar; this room is between. Hence its comparative[24] safety. Because lightning sometimes passes from the clouds to the earth, and sometimes from the earth to the clouds. Do you comprehend?—and I choose the middle of the room, because if the lightning should strike the house at all, it would come down the chimney or walls; so, obviously, the further you are from them, the better. Come hither to me, now."

"Presently. Something you just said, instead of alarming me, has strangely inspired confidence."

"What have I said?"

"You said that sometimes lightning flashes from the earth to the clouds."

"Aye, the returning-stroke, as it is called; when the earth, being overcharged with the fluid, flashes its surplus upward."

"The returning-stroke; that is, from earth to sky. Better and better. But come here on the hearth and dry yourself."

「請您先說理由。」

「快站過來！」

「謝謝您，不過我想我還是待在這裡，壁爐旁邊。現在，我的避雷專家，請您幫幫忙，趁雷聲停下的這會兒，告訴我為什麼這個房間是屋子裡最安全的房間，而您站的地方又是最安全的地點。」

雷雨暫時停下來了，避雷專家看樣子鬆了一口氣，回答道：「你的屋子只有一樓，外加一個閣樓和地下室，這個房間剛好在中間，相形之下就比較安全。因為閃電的電流有時候會從雲層傳到地面，有時候又會從地面傳到雲層。 ——你懂了沒？——我會選房間中間這一點站，是因為如果閃電真的打到了房子，電流會從煙囪或牆壁傳下來，所以啦，離這些地方越遠越好。現在站過來吧。」

「現在，您說的話不僅沒嚇到我，反而還讓我更放心了。」

「我說了什麼？」

「您說電流有時候會從地面傳到雲層。」

「對，那叫回天雷。如果地面的電流超過負荷，就會把多餘的電往上放。」

「回天雷，對了，從地面到天上。很好，很好。您過來壁爐邊把衣服烘乾吧。」

24 comparative [kəmˈperətɪv] (a.) 相比之下的

"I am better here, and better wet."

"How?"

"It is the safest thing you can do—Hark, again!—to get yourself thoroughly drenched in a thunder-storm. Wet clothes are better conductors than the body; and so, if the lightning strike, it might pass down the wet clothes without touching the body. The storm deepens again. Have you a rug in the house? Rugs are nonconductors. Get one, that I may stand on it here, and you, too. The skies blacken—it is dusk at noon. Hark!—the rug, the rug!"

I gave him one; while the hooded [25] mountains seemed closing and tumbling [26] into the cottage.

"And now, since our being dumb will not help us," said I, resuming my place, "let me hear your precautions in traveling during thunder-storms."

"Wait till this one is passed."

"Nay, proceed with the precautions. You stand in the safest possible place according to your own account. Go on."

"Briefly, then. I avoid pine-trees, high houses, lonely barns, upland pastures [27], running water, flocks of cattle and sheep, a crowd of men. If I travel on foot—as today— I do not walk fast; if in my buggy [28], I touch not its back or sides; if on horseback, I dismount and lead the horse. But of all things, I avoid tall men."

"Do I dream? Man avoid man? and in danger-time, too."

「我還是待在這裡比較好，而且衣服濕的比較好。」

「為什麼？」

「這樣最安全——你聽，又來了！——雷雨天的時候，就該把自己弄得全身溼透。濕掉的衣服比人體容易導電，所以如果被雷打中了，電流就會從濕衣服傳下去，而不會碰到身體。雨又變大了。你家裡有沒有小地毯？地毯不導電。拿一塊來，讓我站在上面，你也一起站在上面。天空暗下來了——大白天暗得像傍晚一樣。你聽！——地毯，地毯！」

我遞給了他一塊地毯，這時層層的雷雲，看似一路向我的小屋子翻騰過來。

「現在呢，沉默也無濟於事。跟我說說您在雷雨天出門時，還有哪些事情要特別注意的。」我邊說，邊走回原位。

「先等這陣雷雨過了吧。」

「不，現在就說吧。如您所說，您現在正站在屋子裡最安全的地方，所以說吧。」

「那我長話短說。我會避開松樹、高樓、獨棟的穀倉、高地上的牧場、流水、牛群、羊群和人群。如果我是步行，就像今天，我就不會走太快。如果我坐馬車，我就不靠車背，也不靠車邊。如果我騎馬，我就下來牽馬走。而最重要的是，我會避開高個子的人。」

「我不是在作夢吧？人在遇到危險的時候，也要避開人？」

25 hooded [ˈhʊdɪd] (a.) 帶風帽的

26 tumble [ˈtʌmbəl] (v.) 翻騰；翻滾

27 pasture [ˈpæstʃər] (n.) 牧場

28 buggy [ˈbʌgi] (n.)（一匹馬拉的）輕型馬車

"Tall men in a thunder-storm I avoid. Are you so grossly ignorant as not to know, that the height of a six-footer is sufficient to discharge an electric cloud upon him? Are not lonely Kentuckians, ploughing, smit in the unfinished furrow? Nay, if the six-footer stand by running water, the cloud will sometimes select him as its conductor to that running water. Hark! Sure, yon[29] black pinnacle[30] is split. Yes, a man is a good conductor. The lightning goes through and through a man, but only peels a tree. But sir, you have kept me so long answering your questions, that I have not yet come to business. Will you order one of my rods? Look at this specimen one? See: it is of the best of copper. Copper's the best conductor. Your house is low; but being upon the mountains, that lowness does not one whit[31] depress it. You mountaineers are most exposed. In mountainous countries the lightning-rod man should have most business. Look at the specimen, sir. One rod will answer for a house so small as this. Look over these recommendations. Only one rod, sir; cost, only twenty dollars. Hark! There go all the granite Taconics and Hoosics dashed together like pebbles. By the sound, that must have struck something. An elevation of five feet above the house, will protect twenty feet radius all about the rod. Only twenty dollars, sir—a dollar a foot. Hark!— Dreadful!—Will you order? Will you buy? Shall I put down your name? Think of being a heap of charred[32] offal[33], like a haltered horse burnt in his stall; and all in one flash!"

「雷雨天時要避開高個子。你太無知了，難道你不知道，一百八十公分的身高，就足以讓頭上的雲層放電？那些獨自在田裡犁田的肯塔基人，不就是這樣被雷打死的？而且如果一百八十公分的高個子站在流水旁邊，雲層有時候會選他當導體，通過他把電放到水裡去。你聽！黑色山峰上的石頭一定被打裂了。沒錯，人體是很好的導體。閃電能把人燒得精光，卻只會剝下一層樹皮。但是先生啊，你一直要我回答你的問題，我都沒機會跟你談生意了。你要不要訂我的避雷針？看看這一根樣品？你看，這是最好的銅做的，銅是最好的導體。你的屋子雖然不高，但是坐落在山上，所以也是枉然。你們這些住在山上的人最危險了，避雷專家在山區的生意應該是最好的。先生，看看這個樣品。像這樣的小屋子一根就夠了。看看這些推薦信。只要一根，先生，只花二十塊錢。你聽！這下把花崗石岩的泰康山和胡洗山都打成碎石了。聽這聲音，一定是打到了東西。裝一根超出屋頂一公尺半的避雷針，方圓六公尺內的東西就都安全了。只花二十塊錢，先生——一塊錢三十公分。你聽！——多可怕啊！——要不要訂？要不要買？可不可以讓我記下你的大名？你想想，變成一堆燒焦的內臟是什麼樣子？就像馬廄裡被燒死的馬匹那樣，而且只要一眨眼的工夫！」

29　yon [jɑːn] (a.) 那邊的
30　pinnacle [ˈpɪnəkəl] (n.) 山頂上的尖石
31　whit [wɪt] (n.) 絲毫；少量
32　char [tʃɑːr] (v.) 燒焦
33　offal [ˈɔːfəl] (n.) 內臟

"You pretended envoy[34] extraordinary and minister plenipotentiary[35] to and from Jupiter Tonans," laughed I; "you mere man who come here to put you and your pipestem between clay and sky, do you think that because you can strike a bit of green light from the Leyden jar [36], that you can thoroughly avert the supernal bolt? Your rod rusts, or breaks, and where are you? Who has empowered you, you Tetzel[37], to peddle round your indulgences from divine ordinations? The hairs of our heads are numbered, and the days of our lives. In thunder as in sunshine, I stand at ease in the hands of my God. False negotiator, away! See, the scroll of the storm is rolled back; the house is unharmed; and in the blue heavens I read in the rainbow, that the Deity will not, of purpose, make war on man's earth."

"Impious[38] wretch!" foamed the stranger, blackening in the face as the rainbow beamed, "I will publish your infidel[39] notions."

"Begone! move quickly! if quickly you can, you that shine forth into sight in moist times like the worm."

The scowl grew blacker on his face; the indigo-circles enlarged round his eyes as the storm-rings round the midnight moon. He sprang upon me; his tri-forked thing at my heart.

---

34 envoy [ˈenvɔɪ] (n.) 使節；使者
35 minister plenipotentiary 全權公使
36 Leyden jar 萊特電瓶（一種儲電裝置）

　　我笑著說：「我以為你是雷神派來的特派使節和全權欽差，沒想到你只不過是個在天地之間豎根銅叉的凡人，你以為在萊頓電瓶上打出一點綠光，就可以改變天雷的旨意？當你的避雷針生鏽了、斷了，你人又在哪裡？你這個狂妄的傢伙，誰授權你任意叫賣天神的奧秘？我們頭上的頭髮有限，我們的時日也有限。無論是打雷或是出太陽，我都安安心心地把命運交給上帝。你這個騙子，出去！看見沒有，雲層退回去了，我的房子安然無恙。只要看那藍天裡的彩虹，我就知道造物主是不會故意跟人類作對的。」

　　「你太邪門了！」他氣得大罵，天上的彩虹越亮，他的臉色就越黑，「我要向世人公布你的異教思想！」

　　「去！快去！越快越好！你只有在雨天時才會發亮，就像蟲一樣。」

　　他的眉頭變得更黑了，青色的眼圈顯得更大，活像午夜的月暈。他朝我撲過來，用三叉頭的棒子對著我的心臟。

37　Johann Tetzel（1465?-1519）德國修士，反對馬丁路德
38　impious ['ɪmpɪəs] (a.)（對宗教）不敬的
39　infidel ['ɪnfɪdəl] (n.) 異教徒

I seized it; I snapped it; I dashed it; I trod it; and dragging the dark lightning-king out of my door, flung his elbowed, copper scepter[40] after him.

But spite of my treatment, and spite of my dissuasive talk of him to my neighbors, the Lightning-rod man still dwells in the land; still travels in storm-time, and drives a brave trade with the fears of man.

我一把抓住，把避雷針搶過來折斷，摔到地上，猛踩一陣，然後把那邪惡的閃電國王拖出去，連同他那斷掉的銅製權杖一起丟出門外。

雖然他受到了我這番教訓，我也一再勸阻鄰人，但這位避雷專家仍然住在這一帶，而且一樣在雷雨天出門，利用人們的恐懼來做他大膽的生意。

---

40 scepter [ˈsɛptər] (n.) 國王的權杖

5

■ 馬克‧吐溫

The Celebrated Jumping Frog of Calaveras County

■ Mark Twain (1835-1910)

卡城名蛙

In compliance with the request of a friend of mine, who wrote me from the East, I called on good-natured, garrulous[1] old Simon Wheeler, and inquired after my friend's friend, Leonidas W. Smiley, as requested to do, and I hereunto append the result.

I have a lurking suspicion that Leonidas W. Smiley is a myth; that my friend never knew such a personage; and that he only conjectured that, if I asked old Wheeler about him, it would remind him of his infamous Jim Smiley, and he would go to work and bore me nearly to death with some infernal[2] reminiscence of him as long and tedious as it should be useless to me. If that was the design, it certainly succeeded.

I found Simon Wheeler dozing comfortably by the bar-room stove of the old, dilapidated[3] tavern in the ancient mining camp of Angel's, and I noticed that he was fat and bald-headed, and had an expression of winning gentleness and simplicity upon his tranquil countenance. He roused up and gave me good-day.

---

1 garrulous ['gærələs] (a.) 絮聒的
2 infernal [ɪn'fɜːrnl] (a.) 令人不愉快的
3 dilapidated [dɪ'læpɪdeɪtɪd] (a.) 破爛的；快倒塌的

　　一個朋友從東部寫信給我，應他的要求，我去拜訪了好脾氣、愛絮叨的西蒙‧惠勒老先生，跟他問起李尼達‧史買禮的近況，他是我朋友的朋友。以下就是這番拜訪的結果。

　　事後我開始懷疑，李尼達‧史買禮這個人是個幌子，我朋友可能根本不認識這樣一個人。我懷疑這個人是我朋友捏造出來的，如果我跟惠勒老先生問起這個人，就會讓他想起那個厚臉皮的吉姆‧史買禮，然後打開話匣子把那些又臭又長、跟我不相干的陳年舊事抖出來，把我煩死。如果這就是我朋友的目的，那他成功了。

　　我在安奇老礦山村那座破破爛爛的酒館見到西蒙‧惠勒時，他正靠在吧台的爐子邊，舒舒服服地打著盹。我注意到他很胖，童山濯濯，安詳的面容顯得溫和樸實。他醒過來，跟我打了聲招呼。

I told him a friend of mine had commissioned me to make some inquiries about a cherished companion of his boyhood named Leonidas W. Smiley Rev. Leonidas W. Smiley a young minister of the Gospel, who he had heard was at one time a resident of Angel's Camp. I added that, if Mr. Wheeler could tell me any thing about this Rev. Leonidas W. Smiley, I would feel under many obligations to him.

Simon Wheeler backed me into a corner and blockaded me there with his chair, and then sat me down and reeled off[4] the monotonous narrative which follows this paragraph.

He never smiled, he never frowned, he never changed his voice from the gentle-flowing key to which he tuned the initial sentence, he never betrayed the slightest suspicion of enthusiasm; but all through the interminable narrative there ran a vein of impressive earnestness and sincerity, which showed me plainly that, so far from his imagining that there was any thing ridiculous or funny about his story, he regarded it as a really important matter, and admired its two heroes as men of transcendent[5] genius in finesse[6].

To me, the spectacle of a man drifting serenely along through such a queer yarn without ever smiling, was exquisitely absurd. As I said before, I asked him to tell me what he knew of Rev. Leonidas W. Smiley, and he replied as follows. I let him go on in his own way, and never interrupted him once:

　　我告訴他，一個朋友託我來打聽兒時玩伴李尼達・史買禮牧師的下落，聽説這位年輕的福音傳教士在安奇礦山村住過一段時間。我還説，如果惠勒先生有任何消息能告訴我，我會感激不盡。

　　西蒙・惠勒把我逼到牆角，用他的椅子堵住我的出路，要我也坐下，然後一口氣説出下面這件枯燥乏味的事。

　　他從頭到尾沒笑過、沒皺過眉頭、沒改變過平和的語氣，也沒顯露過絲毫的熱情。在這沒完沒了的敘述當中，他從頭到尾都顯得認真嚴肅，顯然即使這件事情有任何可笑的成分，他也是把它看得很重要，而且對事件的兩位主角推崇備至，認為他們智慧過人。

　　對我來説，一個人能夠這麼平靜地述説這麼一個怪誕的故事，從頭到尾未發一噱，也真夠奇怪的了。我剛説了，我請他告訴我李尼達・史買禮牧師的消息，而下面就是他的回答。我任他一路説下去，沒有打斷他：

4 reel off 滔滔不絕地講
5 transcendent [træn'sendənt] (a.) 卓越的；出類拔萃的
6 finesse [fɪ'nes] (n.) 策略；手段

There was a feller here once by the name of Jim Smiley, in the winter of '49—or maybe it was the spring of '50—I don't recollect exactly, somehow, though what makes me think it was one or the other is because I remember the big flume wasn't finished when he first came to the camp; but any way, he was the curiousest man about always betting on any thing that turned up you ever see, if he could get any body to bet on the other side; and if he couldn't, he'd change sides. Any way that suited the other man would suit him any way just so's he got a bet, he was satisfied.

But still he was lucky, uncommon lucky; he most always come out winner. He was always ready and laying for a chance; there couldn't be no solittry thing mentioned but that feller'd offer to bet on it, and—take any side you please, as I was just telling you.

If there was a horse-race, you'd find him flush[7], or you'd find him busted at the end of it; if there was a dog-fight, he'd bet on it; if there was a cat-fight, he'd bet on it; if there was a chicken-fight, he'd bet on it; why, if there was two birds setting on a fence, he would bet you which one would fly first; or if there was a camp-meeting, he would be there reg'lar, to bet on Parson Walker, which he judged to be the best exhorter about here, and so he was, too, and a good man.

7 flush [flʌʃ] (a.)（撲克牌）同花的；清一色的

這裡以前有個叫做吉姆・史買禮的傢伙，那大概是在四九年的冬天，或五○年的春天吧，我記不太清楚了，總歸不是四九年就是五○年，因為我記得他剛來的時候，大引水槽還沒蓋好。別的不說，要比誰最古怪，他算得上是天下第一怪。這個人啊，只要能找得到人打賭，就一定要打賭。他碰上什麼，就賭什麼。要是別人不想下注，他就換押另外一邊賭。只要對方肯下注，他賭哪一邊都可以。他啊，只要能賭就萬事足。

　　而他的賭運，可好的了，出奇的好，十之八九都會贏。他隨時都準備好找機會跟人打賭，無論大事小事，只要有人提出來，他都賭，而且我剛說了，要押哪一邊隨你選。

　　要是有賽馬，他不是贏得滿載而歸，就是輸得一乾二淨。要是有鬥狗，他賭；要是有鬥貓，他賭；要是有鬥雞，他也賭。嘿，要是有兩隻小鳥落在籬笆上，他就跟你賭哪一隻會先飛走。要是村子裡有集會，他一定會到，到了就拿沃克牧師打賭，賭說沃克牧師的佈道在這一帶是最棒的，那還用說，沃克牧師本來就是個好人。

If he even seen a straddle-bug start to go anywheres, he would bet you how long it would take him to get wherever he was going to, and if you took him up[8], he would foller that straddle-bug to Mexico but what he would find out where he was bound for and how long he was on the road. Lots of the boys here has seen that Smiley, and can tell you about him. Why, it never made no difference to him he would bet on any thing the dangdest feller.

Parson Walker's wife laid very sick once, for a good while, and it seemed as if they warn't going to save her; but one morning he come in, and Smiley up and asked him how she was, and he said she was considerable better thank the Lord for his infinite mercy and coming on so smart that, with the blessing of Providence, she'd get well yet; and Smiley, before he thought, says, "Well, I'll risk two-and-a-half that she don't, any way."

Thish-yer Smiley had a mare[9] the boys called her the fifteen-minute nag[10], but that was only in fun, you know, because, of course, she was faster than that and he used to win money on that horse, for all she was so slow and always had the asthma, or the distemper[11], or the consumption[12], or something of that kind.

---

8 take sb up 接受……的建議
9 mare [mer] (n.) 母馬
10 nag [næg] (n.) 駑馬
11 distemper [dɪ'stempər] (n.)（動物）瘟熱病
12 consumption [kən'sʌmpʃən] (n.) 肺癆

要是他在地上看見一隻蟲子正朝某方向走，他就會跟你賭蟲子要花多久時間才會走到目的地，如果你答應跟他賭了，哪怕是蟲子要到墨西哥，他也會一路跟著，只為了弄清楚蟲子要去哪裡、花了多久時間。這裡的小男孩好多都見過史買禮，都能跟你說他的事。這個不可思議的傢伙什麼都賭，賭什麼對他來說都一樣。

　　有一回，沃克牧師的太太病得很重，有好一段時間誰也救不了。可是有天上午，沃克牧師走進來，史買禮站起身子，問候他太太，他說她好多了，感謝主的恩典，看樣子有主保佑，她會慢慢好起來。結果這史買禮想也不想就說：「我賭兩塊半她不會好起來。」

　　這個史買禮有一隻母馬，村裡的男孩管牠叫「一刻鐘老太太」，不過也是叫著好玩的，因為牠跑起來當然沒那麼慢，而且史買禮每次都靠牠贏錢。這隻母馬慢吞吞的，不是犯氣喘、生瘟病，就是有肺癆，反正就體弱多病。

They used to give her two or three hundred yards start, and then pass her under way; but always at the fag-end of the race she'd get excited and desperate-like, and come cavorting[13] and straddling up, and scattering her legs around limber, sometimes in the air, and sometimes out to one side amongst the fences, and kicking up m-o-r-e dust, and raising m-o-r-e racket[14] with her coughing and sneezing and blowing her nose and always fetch up at the stand just about a neck ahead, as near as you could cipher it down.

And he had a little small bull pup, that to look at him you'd think he wan't worth a cent, but to set around and look ornery[15], and lay for a chance to steal something. But as soon as money was up on him, he was a different dog; his underjaw'd begin to stick out like the fo'castle of a steamboat, and his teeth would uncover, and shine savage like the furnaces.

And a dog might tackle him, and bully-rag him, and bite him, and throw him over his shoulder two or three times, and Andrew Jackson which was the name of the pup Andrew Jackson would never let on but what he was satisfied, and hadn't expected nothing else and the bets being doubled and doubled on the other side all the time, till the money was all up; and then all of a sudden he would grab that other dog jest by the j'int of his hind leg and freeze on it not chew, you understand, but only jest grip and hang on till they thronged up the sponge, if it was a year.

每次賽馬他們都讓上牠兩、三百碼，然後中途輕輕鬆鬆超過牠，但只要比賽快結束時，牠就會亢奮起來，拚了老命往前蹦，四肢蹄子到處亂甩，甩空了的也有，甩偏了踢到籬笆上的也有，弄得塵土飛揚，還一邊咳嗽、打噴嚏、擤鼻涕的，弄得鬧哄哄，然後先馳得點，領先第二名一個頭，剛好讓大家能覷個清楚。

他還有一隻小鬥牛犬。看這小狗，你會以為牠啥都不值，就配在那兒拴著，一臉賊樣，等著找機會偷東西。但是，一旦有人在牠身上下注，牠轉眼就會變身。牠會把下巴伸出來，像大輪船的前甲板，牙齒都露了出來，像爐火一樣閃閃發光。

別的狗抓牠、咬牠、欺負牠，接二連三來給牠過肩摔，這安拙·傑森，牠就叫這名字，這安拙·傑森就逆來順受，毫不反抗。於是，押在另一條狗身上的賭注加倍再加倍，一直到沒錢再往上押了。這時候，牠就會一口咬住另一條狗的後腿，緊緊咬著，不哼，你明白嗎，光咬，咬著不動，直到狗投降，就算要等上一年牠也咬著不放。

13　cavort [kəˈvɔːrt] (v.) 亂蹦亂跳
14　racket [ˈrækɪt] (n.) 吵鬧聲
15　ornery [ˈɔːrnəri] (a.) 脾氣壞的

Smiley always come out winner on that pup, till he harnessed a dog once that didn't have no hind legs, because they'd been sawed off by a circular saw, and when the thing had gone along far enough, and the money was all up, and he come to make a snatch for his pet bolt, he saw in a minute how he'd been imposed on, and how the other dog had him in the door, so to speak, and he 'peared surprised, and then he looked sorter discouraged-like, and didn't try no more to win the fight, and so he got shucked out bad.

He give Smiley a look, as much as to say his heart was broke, and it was his fault, for putting up a dog that hadn't no hind legs for him to take bolt of, which was his main dependence in a fight, and then he limped off a piece and laid down and died.

It was a good pup, was that Andrew Jackson, and would have made a name for hisself if he'd lived, for the stuff was in him, and he had genius I know it, because he hadn't had no opportunities to speak of, and it don't stand to reason that a dog could make such a fight as he could under them circumstances, if he hadn't no talent. It always makes me feel sorry when I think of that last fight of his'n, and the way it turned out.

Well, thish-yer Smiley had rat-tarriers, and chicken cocks, and tom-cats, and all of them kind of things, till you couldn't rest, and you couldn't fetch nothing for him to bet on but he'd match you.

史買禮每次都靠這隻狗贏錢，直到在一條沒有後腿的狗身上吃了鱉，那條狗的後腿被鋸片給鋸掉了。那一次，兩條狗鬥了好一陣子，兩邊的錢都押上了，這時安拙・傑森照例跑上去要去咬對方的後腿，卻發現自己上當了。對方吃定牠，牠先是一臉吃驚，然後一陣心寒，無心贏賽，最後就輸得脫褲子囉。

　　當時牠看了史買禮一眼，好像是在說他傷透了牠的心，怎麼找了一條沒有腿的狗來讓牠咬，牠鬥狗靠的就是咬後腿啊，牠一瘸一瘸地走了幾步，然後就倒在地上，嗚呼哀哉了。

　　牠可是一條好狗，那個安拙・傑森，要是牠還活者，一定鬥出了名，因為牠有天分，又聰明，這點我很清楚，雖然牠沒辦法為自己發言。只有天才狗才能像牠這樣鬥。一想起牠的謝幕之作，一想起牠的下場，我鼻子就發酸。

　　這個史買禮啊，還養過抓老鼠的小獵狗，還養過小公雞、公貓，就這一類的玩意兒，不論你拿什麼動物去找他賭，他都可以跟你賭，讓你想罷休很難。

He ketched a frog one day, and took him home, and said he cal'klated to edercate him; and so he never done nothing for three months but set in his back yard and learn that frog to jump. And you bet you he did learn him, too. He'd give him a little punch behind, and the next minute you'd see that frog whirling in the air like a doughnut see him turn one summerset, or may be a couple, if he got a good start, and come down flat-footed and all right, like a cat.

He got him up so in the matter of catching flies, and kept him in practice so constant, that he'd nail a fly every time as far as he could see him. Smiley said all a frog wanted was education, and he could do most any thing and I believe him.

Why, I've seen him set Dan'l Webster down here on this floor Dan'l Webster was the name of the frog and sing out, "Flies, Dan'l, flies!" and quicker'n you could wink, he'd spring straight up, and snake a fly off'n the counter there, and flop down on the floor again as solid as a gob[16] of mud, and fall to scratching the side of his head with his hind foot as indifferent as if he hadn't no idea he'd been doin' any more'n any frog might do.

You never see a frog so modest and straightforward as he was, for all he was so gifted. And when it come to fair and square[17] jumping on a dead level, he could get over more ground at one straddle than any animal of his breed you ever see.

有一回，他抓了一隻青蛙帶回家，說是要訓練牠。接下來三個月，他什麼都不做，就只顧著在家裡的後院訓練那隻青蛙跳遠。果然，青蛙真給訓練成功了。他只要從後面點青蛙一下，你就看吧，青蛙馬上就像個甜甜圈一樣在空中打轉、翻筋斗。如果起跳跳得好，還可以翻兩下，然後四平八穩地落在地上，像隻貓一樣。

他還訓練青蛙抓蒼蠅，帶著牠苦練，練得青蛙只要看到蒼蠅，不論有多遠，就一定抓得到。史買禮說，青蛙要的就是訓練，只要你教牠，牠什麼都做得了。這話我相信。

你看，我就看過他把當兒‧偉德放在地板上，這隻青蛙就叫做當兒‧偉德。他大喊一聲：「蒼蠅，當兒，蒼蠅！」接著青蛙瞬間跳起來，把那邊櫃檯上的一隻蒼蠅吞下，然後像攤泥一樣噗搭一聲落回地板上，抬起後腳搔搔側腦勺，一副沒什麼了不起的樣子，好像覺得自己比別的青蛙也強不到哪裡去。

你再也找不到這麼謙虛、爽快的青蛙了，況且牠還這麼有能耐。只要是從平地上規規矩矩地往前跳，牠一跳絕對都比你見過的青蛙都跳得遠。

16　gob [gɑːb] (n.)（黏性物）一團；一塊
17　fare and square 光明正大地；遵守規則地

Jumping on a dead level was his strong suit, you understand; and when it come to that, Smiley would ante up[18] money on him as long as he had a red. Smiley was monstrous proud of his frog, and well he might be, for fellers that had traveled and been everywheres, all said he laid over any frog that ever they see.

Well, Smiley kept the beast in a little lattice[19] box, and he used to fetch him down town sometimes and lay for a bet. One day a feller a stranger in the camp, he was come across him with his box, and says: "What might it be that you've got in the box?"

And Smiley says, sorter indifferent like, "It might be a parrot, or it might be a canary, may be, but it an't it's only just a frog."

And the feller took it, and looked at it careful, and turned it round this way and that, and says, "H'm so 'tis. Well, what's he good for?"

"Well," Smiley says, easy and careless, "He's good enough for one thing, I should judge he can outjump any frog in Calaveras county."

The feller took the box again, and took another long, particular look, and give it back to Smiley, and says, very deliberate, "Well, I don't see no p'ints about that frog that's any better'n any other frog."

"May be you don't," Smiley says. "May be you understand frogs, and may be you don't understand 'em; may be you've had experience, and may be you an't only a amateur, as it were. Anyways, I've got my opinion, and I'll risk forty dollars that he can outjump any frog in Calaveras county."

從平地往前跳是牠最拿手的項目，你明白吧；只要比這一項，史買禮就一路把賭注押上去。這隻青蛙讓史買禮很自豪，可不嘛，那些見多識廣的老江湖都説，沒見過的這麼厲害的青蛙。

史買禮把這隻青蛙裝在一個小籠子裡，常帶牠去村子裡找人下注。有一天，村裡來了一個外地來的男人，碰見了史買禮正提著籠子，便問道：「你籠子裡裝了什麼啊？」

史買禮用一副滿不在乎的樣子説：「也許應該裝隻鸚鵡或是金絲雀，不過偏偏都不是，不過是一隻青蛙！」

男子把籠子接過來，轉過來轉過去，看個仔細，最後説：「果真是隻青蛙。這青蛙要幹麼用的？」

「這個嘛，牠就一個最大的本事，我敢説牠比卡城隨便一隻青蛙都跳得遠。」史買禮漫不經心地説。

男子又把籠子接過來，仔仔細細看了好半天，最後才還給史買禮，慢條斯理地説：「我可不覺得你這隻青蛙會比別的青蛙強到哪裡去。」

「或許你不覺得，或許你懂青蛙，也或許你不懂青蛙；或許你看多了，也或許你很外行。反正咧，我心裡有數，我就跟你賭四十塊錢，賭牠比卡城隨便一隻青蛙都跳得遠。」史買禮説。

18 ante up 付賭脹
19 lattice ['lætɪs] (n.) 格子框架

And the feller studied a minute, and then says, kinder sad like, "Well, I'm only a stranger here, and I an't got no frog; but if I had a frog, I'd bet you."

And then Smiley says, "That's all right that's all right if you'll hold my box a minute, I'll go and get you a frog." And so the feller took the box, and put up his forty dollars along with Smiley's, and set down to wait.

So he set there a good while thinking and thinking to hisself, and then he got the frog out and prized[20] his mouth open and took a tea-spoon and filled him full of quail shot[21] filled him pretty near up to his chin and set him on the floor. Smiley he went to the swamp and slopped around[22] in the mud for a long time, and finally he ketched a frog, and fetched him in, and give him to this feller, and says: "Now, if you're ready, set him alongside of Dan'l, with his fore-paws just even with Dan'l, and I'll give the word."

Then he says, "One—two—three—jump!" and him and the feller touched up the frogs from behind, and the new frog hopped off lively, but Dan'l give a heave, and hysted up his shoulders so like a Frenchman, but it wan't no use he couldn't budge[23]; he was planted as solid as an anvil, and he couldn't no more stir than if he was anchored out. Smiley was a good deal surprised, and he was disgusted too, but he didn't have no idea what the matter was, of course.

20　prize [praɪz] (v.) 撬開
21　quail shot 大小適於獵鵪鶉（quail）的小彈丸
22　slop around 懶散地踱來踱去
23　budge [bʌdʒ] (v.) 稍稍移動

　　男子想了一會兒，有些為難地說：「我嘛，是個外地人，也沒有青蛙。如果我有青蛙，我就跟你賭。」

　　史買禮說：「不要緊，不要緊，你幫我看著籠子，我這就去幫你抓隻青蛙來。」男子接過籠子，把他和史買禮各自的四十塊錢放在一起，坐下來等史買禮。

　　他坐在那等啊等，想啊想，接著把青蛙拿出來，扒開嘴巴，拿了一支小湯匙猛餵牠吃小彈丸，餵得都快滿到下巴了，然後再把青蛙放到地上。史買禮跑到泥塘裡，在爛泥巴裡轉了好一會兒，最後終於抓到一隻青蛙，帶回來交給男子，說道：「好啦，如果你準備好了，就把牠跟當兒並排擺著，把兩隻青蛙的前腳對齊，然後我來下口令。」

　　接著他下口令喊道：「一、二、三，跳！」他和男子從後面點一下自己的青蛙，只見那隻新來的青蛙跳起來了，當兒也作勢要跳，像個法國佬一樣肩膀都聳起來了，但卻怎麼樣也跳不起來，像塊鐵砧一樣沉在地上，怎麼也動不了，像船下了錨一樣。史買禮很吃驚，他氣壞了。當然啦，他根本不知道是怎麼一回事。

The feller took the money and started away; and when he was going out at the door, he sorter jerked his thumb over his shoulders this way at Dan'l, and says again, very deliberate, "Well, I don't see no p'ints about that frog that's any better'n any other frog."

Smiley he stood scratching his head and looking down at Dan'l a long time, and at last he says, "I do wonder what in the nation that frog throw'd off for I wonder if there an't something the matter with him he 'pears to look mighty baggy, somehow."

And he ketched Dan'l by the nap of the neck, and lifted him up and says, "Why, blame my cats, if he don't weigh five pound!" and turned him upside down, and he belched[24] out a double handful of shot. And then he see how it was, and he was the maddest man he set the frog down and took out after that feller, but he never ketchd him. And—

[Here Simon Wheeler heard his name called from the front yard, and got up to see what was wanted.] And turning to me as he moved away, he said: "Just set where you are, stranger, and rest easy I an't going to be gone a second."

24 belch [beltʃ] (v.) 打嗝

男子拿起錢離開。走出門的時候，他的大拇指越過肩頭、指指當兒，慢條斯理地又說了一次：「我可不覺得這青蛙比別的青蛙強到哪裡去。」

史買禮站在那裡抓耳搔頭，低頭看著當兒好一會兒，說道：「這隻青蛙是怎麼了，是不是出了什麼問題，牠肚子看起來很脹。」

他揪住當兒的後頸子，一把提起來，說：「牠要是沒五磅重才怪！」他把青蛙轉過來，頭下腳上地抓著，當兒馬上嗝出兩大把的小彈丸。他一見是這麼回事，可氣炸了。他放下青蛙，出門去追男子，但男子已經消失了。後來啊——

（這時西蒙·惠勒聽到前院有人叫他，便起身去看是誰找他）他一邊走，一邊轉頭對我說：「先生，你在這裡坐著，休息一下，我等一下就回來。」

But, by your leave, I did not think that a continuation of the history of the enterprising vagabond[25] Jim Smiley would be likely to afford me much information concerning the Rev. Leonidas W. Smiley, and so I started away.

At the door I met the sociable Wheeler returning, and he button-holed[26] me and recommenced: "Well, thish-yer Smiley had a yeller one-eyed cow that didn't have no tail, only jest a short stump like a bannanner, and—"

"Oh! hang Smiley and his afflicted cow!" I muttered, good-naturedly, and bidding the old gentleman good-day, I departed.

　　請您見諒了。我想，再往下聽這賭膽包天的閒人吉姆・史買禮的事，也打聽不到李尼達・史買禮牧師的消息，於是我起身離開。

　　我一到門口，愛交際的惠勒老先生就回來了。他留住我，又開始說：「這個史買禮啊，他養過一隻獨眼的黃母牛，沒有尾巴，就短短的一截，像跟香蕉，還有啊——」

　　「唉，誰管那個史買禮和他的病母牛！」我親切地嘟囔道，然後跟老先生道別，就此告辭。

25　vagabond [ˈvæɡəbɑːnd] (n.) 遊手好閒的懶漢
26　button-hole [ˈbʌtnhoʊl] (v.) 強留某人談話

6

O. Henry (1862-1910)

歐・亨利

愛的犧牲

A Service of Love

When one loves one's Art no service seems too hard.

That is our premise[1]. This story shall draw a conclusion from it, and show at the same time that the premise is incorrect. That will be a new thing in logic, and a feat in story-telling somewhat older than the great wall of China.

Joe Larrabee came out of the post-oak flats of the Middle West pulsing with a genius for pictorial art. At six he drew a picture of the town pump with a prominent citizen passing it hastily. This effort was framed and hung in the drug store window by the side of the ear of corn with an uneven number of rows. At twenty he left for New York with a flowing necktie and a capital tied up somewhat closer.

Delia Caruthers did things in six octaves[2] so promisingly in a pine-tree village in the South that her relatives chipped in[3] enough in her chip hat[4] for her to go "North" and "finish." They could not see her f—, but that is our story.

Joe and Delia met in an atelier[5] where a number of art and music students had gathered to discuss chiaroscuro[6], Wagner, music, Rembrandt's works, pictures, Waldteufel[7], wall paper, Chopin and Oolong.

---

1 premise [ˈpremɪs] (n.) 前提
2 octave [ˈɔːkteɪv] (n.) 八度音（six octaves 在此指鋼琴）
3 chip in 湊錢
4 chip hat 以棕櫚葉條或稻草編成的帽子

一個人深愛其藝術時，什麼樣的犧牲都不會為難。

上面這一句是我們的前提，這篇故事會從中得到一個結論，最後證明這個前提是錯誤的。從邏輯學上看來，這會是個新發現，但是從文學的觀點看來，這個前提千古不渝。

喬‧雷若比出身美國中西部橡樹參天的平原，渾身充滿繪畫藝術的天才。六歲的時候，他就畫了一幅畫，畫的是鎮上的抽水機，前面匆匆走過一個鎮上的大人物。這幅畫被框起來，掛在藥房的櫥窗裡，旁邊掛著一個玉米穗，玉米穗上帶著幾排參差不齊的玉米粒。二十歲的時候，他離鄉背井，前往紐約，打著一條飄拂的領帶，帶著一個比領帶還輕盈的荷包。

黛莉亞‧卡魯特出身美國南方一個松林小村，她的琴藝過人，親人為她湊足錢，讓她去「北方深造」。他們無法看到她……這就是我們接下來要講的故事。

喬和黛莉亞在一間藝術家的工作室相識，不少學藝術和音樂的學生都會聚在這裡，討論明暗對照法、華格納、音樂、林布蘭的作品、繪畫、華杜飛、壁紙、蕭邦和烏龍茶。

5　atelier [ˌætəlˈjeɪ] (n.) 藝術家的工作室
6　chiaroscuro [kɪˌɑːrəsˈkuːroʊ] (n.)（繪畫的）明暗對照法
7　Waldteufel 華杜飛（法國作曲家）

Joe and Delia became enamored one of the other, or each of the other, as you please, and in a short time were married—for (see above), *when one loves one's Art no service seems too hard.*

Mr. and Mrs. Larrabee began housekeeping in a flat. It was a lonesome flat—something like the A sharp[8] way down at the left-hand end of the keyboard. And they were happy; for they had their Art, and they had each other. And my advice to the rich young man would be—sell all thou hast, and give it to the poor—janitor for the privilege of living in a flat with your Art and your Delia.

Flat-dwellers shall indorse my dictum that theirs is the only true happiness. If a home is happy it cannot fit too close—let the dresser collapse and become a billiard table; let the mantel turn to a rowing machine, the escritoire[9] to a spare bedchamber, the washstand to an upright piano; let the four walls come together, if they will, so you and your Delia are between.

But if home be the other kind, let it be wide and long— enter you at the Golden Gate, hang your hat on Hatteras, your cape on Cape Horn and go out by the Labrador[10].

---

8 sharp [ʃɑːrp] (n.) 高半音
9 escritoire [ˌeskrɪˈtwɑːr] (n.) 寫字檯
10 Golden Gate，金門海峽，位美國西岸舊金山灣口。Hatteras，美國東岸 北卡羅來納州海岸小島。Cape Horn，合恩角，位於南美南端。Labrador ，加拿大東岸一區。

　喬和黛莉亞互相 —— 或說彼此 —— 看你喜歡怎麼說，一見傾心。他們很快就結了婚 —— 因為（請見一開始所提及的前提），一個人深愛其藝術時，什麼樣的犧牲都不會為難。

　雷若比夫婦租了一間公寓，開始組織家庭。那是一間冷冷清清的公寓，冷清得像鋼琴鍵盤最左端的升 A 低音。但是他們很幸福，因為他們有自己的藝術，還有彼此。我會建議這個富有的年輕人——為了能夠跟你的藝術和你的黛莉亞住在公寓裡，趕快把你所有的東西都賣掉，施捨給窮苦的門房吧。

　住公寓的人都會贊同我的看法，認為公寓生活才是唯一真正的幸福。只要兩人幸福，屋子小一點也無妨——就讓梳妝檯坍下來成為撞球桌，讓壁爐架變為練習划船的器材，讓書桌充當臨時的臥榻，讓盥洗台充當豎式鋼琴。如果可能的話，讓四壁靠攏，把你和你的黛莉亞圍起來。

　如果家庭不幸福，任憑屋子再怎麼寬敞——從美國西岸的金門進去，把帽子掛在美國東岸的哈德拉斯，把披風掛在南美南端的合恩角，再從加拿大東岸的拉布拉多走出門——也是枉然的。

Joe was painting in the class of the great Magister—you know his fame. His fees are high; his lessons are light—his high-lights have brought him renown. Delia was studying under Rosenstock—you know his repute as a disturber of the piano keys.

They were mighty happy as long as their money lasted. So is every—but I will not be cynical. Their aims were very clear and defined.

Joe was to become capable very soon of turning out pictures that old gentlemen with thin side-whiskers and thick pocketbooks would sandbag one another in his studio for the privilege of buying. Delia was to become familiar and then contemptuous with Music, so that when she saw the orchestra seats and boxes unsold she could have sore throat and lobster in a private dining-room and refuse to go on the stage.

But the best, in my opinion, was the home life in the little flat—the ardent, voluble[11] chats after the day's study; the cozy dinners and fresh, light breakfasts; the interchange of ambitions—ambitions interwoven each with the other's or else inconsiderable—the mutual help and inspiration; and—overlook my artlessness—stuffed olives and cheese sandwiches at 11 p.m.

---

11 voluble ['vɑːljʊbəl] (a.) 滔滔不絕的

　　喬在偉大的馬基特門下學畫——各位都知道他的名氣。他的學費昂貴、課程基礎——他憑藉這高超的秀技贏得聲望。黛莉亞在羅森朵門下習琴——各位也知道他以擾亂鋼琴鍵盤聞名。

　　只要錢還沒用完，他們就非常幸福，每個人都是如此——不過我不想在這裡說那些憤世嫉俗的話。他們的目標清楚而明確。

　　喬很快就要有畫作問世，那些鬢鬚稀疏、荷包厚實的老先生會爭先恐後地擠到他的畫室裡搶購。黛莉亞要成為音樂家，然後大擺架子，如果看到音樂廳裡的座位和包廂沒坐滿，就推託說喉嚨不舒服，拒絕登臺，然後在私人專用的餐室裡享用龍蝦大餐。

　　但是依我看來，最美滿的，還是這小公寓裡的家庭生活——上了整天課之後的情話絮語，舒適的晚餐和清新簡單的早餐，談著彼此的志向——他們關心彼此的志向，這樣他們的志向才會顯得有意義——他們互相加油打氣，還有——恕我用語平凡——晚上十一點鐘的夾心橄欖和乳酪三明治。

But after a while Art flagged. It sometimes does, even if some switchman doesn't flag it. Everything going out and nothing coming in, as the vulgarians[12] say. Money was lacking to pay Mr. Magister and Herr Rosenstock their prices. *When one loves one's Art no service seems too hard.* So, Delia said she must give music lessons to keep the chafing dish[13] bubbling.

For two or three days she went out canvassing[14] for pupils. One evening she came home elated.

"Joe, dear," she said, gleefully, "I've a pupil. And, oh, the loveliest people! General—General A. B. Pinkney's daughter—on Seventy-first street. Such a splendid house, Joe—you ought to see the front door! Byzantine I think you would call it. And inside! Oh, Joe, I never saw anything like it before."

"My pupil is his daughter Clementina. I dearly love her already. She's a delicate thing-dresses always in white; and the sweetest, simplest manners! Only eighteen years old. I'm to give three lessons a week; and, just think, Joe! $5 a lesson. I don't mind it a bit; for when I get two or three more pupils I can resume my lessons with Herr Rosenstock. Now, smooth out that wrinkle between your brows, dear, and let's have a nice supper."

"That's all right for you, Dele," said Joe, attacking a can of peas with a carving knife and a hatchet, "but how about me? Do you think I'm going to let you hustle for wages while I philander[15] in the regions of high art? Not by the bones of Benvenuto Cellini[16]! I guess I can sell papers or lay cobblestones, and bring in a dollar or two."

但沒多久，藝術動搖了。藝術本來有時就會動搖，即使沒有人去搖動它。俗語說得好，坐吃山空。他們沒有錢付給馬基特先生和羅森朵老師。一個人深愛其藝術時，什麼樣的犧牲都不會為難。於是，黛莉亞說，她要收學生上音樂課，家裡才不會斷炊。

　　她在外面奔走了兩、三天，招攬學生。一天傍晚，她興高采烈地回到家。

　　「喬，親愛的，我有一個學生了。」她開心地說：「那是個好人家，是一個將軍——品尼將軍的女兒，就住在七十一街。他們家好漂亮，喬，你應該看看他們家的大門！應該是拜占庭式的吧。還有屋子裡面！噢，喬，這是我看過最漂亮的房子了。」

　　「我的學生是他的女兒可蕾曼。我一見她就好喜歡。她是個嬌弱的孩子，都穿著一身白色的衣服，氣質甜美又大方！她才十八歲。我一星期上三堂課，你想想看，喬！一堂課五塊錢。我一點都不在意，等我再多收兩、三個學生，我就可以繼續跟羅森朵老師上課了。別再皺眉頭了，親愛的，我們現在好好享受我們的晚餐吧。」

　　「黛兒，你覺得沒關係，但我呢？」喬一邊說，一邊用切肉刀和小斧頭打開一罐豆子，「你想，我會讓你在外面奔波賺錢，自己卻在藝術的殿堂裡享受嗎？切利尼在上，我做不到！我想我可以去賣報紙或鋪馬路，多少也賺個一、兩塊錢回來。」

12　vulgarian [vʌlˈgɛərɪən] (n.) 俗人（尤指有錢而無品味的人）

13　chafing dish 火鍋（下有加熱裝置，通常放在餐桌上的鍋子）

14　canvass [ˈkænvəs] (v.) 遊說；推銷

15　philander [fɪˈlændər] (v.) 追逐

16　Benvenuto Cellini 義大利文藝復興時期雕刻家與版畫家

Delia came and hung about his neck.

"Joe, dear, you are silly. You must keep on at your studies. It is not as if I had quit my music and gone to work at something else. While I teach I learn. I am always with my music. And we can live as happily as millionaires on $15 a week. You mustn't think of leaving Mr. Magister."

"All right," said Joe, reaching for the blue scalloped vegetable dish. "But I hate for you to be giving lessons. It isn't Art. But you're a trump[17] and a dear to do it."

"When one loves one's Art no service seems too hard," said Delia.

"Magister praised the sky in that sketch I made in the park," said Joe. "And Tinkle gave me permission to hang two of them in his window. I may sell one if the right kind of a moneyed idiot sees them."

"I'm sure you will," said Delia, sweetly. "And now let's be thankful for Gen. Pinkney and this veal roast."

During all of the next week the Larrabees had an early breakfast. Joe was enthusiastic about some morning-effect sketches he was doing in Central Park, and Delia packed him off[18] breakfasted, coddled, praised and kissed at 7 o'clock. Art is an engaging mistress. It was most times 7 o'clock when he returned in the evening.

At the end of the week Delia, sweetly proud but languid[19], triumphantly tossed three five-dollar bills on the 8x10 (inches) centre table of the 8x10 (feet) flat parlor.

黛莉亞走過來，用雙手環住喬的脖子。

「喬，親愛的，你真傻，你一定要繼續你的學業。我又不是放棄了我的音樂、跑去做別的工作。我這是教學相長，我永遠都跟我的音樂在一起。而且一星期有十五塊錢，我們就可以過得跟百萬富翁一樣快樂。你一定不可以有離開馬基特老師的想法。」

喬一邊伸手去拿那個貝殼形的藍色盤子，一邊說道：「好吧，我是不喜歡你去教課，教課不是藝術。但是，你這麼做令我欽佩，令我感動。」

「一個人深愛其藝術時，什麼樣的犧牲都不算為難。」黛莉亞說。

「我在公園裡畫的那張素描，馬基特稱讚我的天空畫得很好。丁克還讓我掛兩張在他的櫥窗裡，如果哪個有錢的外行人看到了，可能就可以賣掉一張。」喬說。

「一定可以的。現在，讓我們感謝品尼將軍和這盤烤牛肉吧。」黛莉亞溫柔地說。

接下來一整個星期，他們夫妻都早早就用過早餐。喬一心想捕捉早晨的光線，在中央公園畫幾張速寫，於是黛莉亞早早就讓他吃完早餐，給他擁抱、讚美和親吻，七點鐘就把他送出門。藝術是一個迷人的情婦。等到喬回到家時，多半已經晚上七點了。

週末的時候，黛莉亞一臉自豪卻又疲倦不堪，得意地把三張五塊錢的紙鈔，扔在二點五乘三（公尺）大小公寓客廳裡的那張二十乘二十五（公分）大小的桌子上。

---

17 trump [trʌmp] (n.) 值得欽佩的人
18 pack somebody off 把……打發走
19 languid [ˈlæŋgwɪd] (a.) 疲倦的

"Sometimes," she said, a little wearily, "Clementina tries me. I'm afraid she doesn't practice enough, and I have to tell her the same things so often. And then she always dresses entirely in white, and that does get monotonous. But Gen. Pinkney is the dearest old man! I wish you could know him, Joe. He comes in sometimes when I am with Clementina at the piano—he is a widower, you know—and stands there pulling his white goatee. 'And how are the semiquavers[20] and the demisemiquavers[21] progressing?' he always asks."

"I wish you could see the wainscoting[22] in that drawing-room, Joe! And those Astrakhan[23] rug portieres[24]. And Clementina has such a funny little cough. I hope she is stronger than she looks. Oh, I really am getting attached to her, she is so gentle and high bred. Gen. Pinkney's brother was once Minister to Bolivia."

And then Joe, with the air of a Monte Cristo[25], drew forth a ten, a five, a two and a one—all legal tender notes—and laid them beside Delia's earnings.

"Sold that watercolor of the obelisk[26] to a man from Peoria," he announced overwhelmingly.

"Don't joke with me," said Delia, "not from Peoria!"

---

20 semiquaver ['semɪˌkweɪvər] (n.) 十六分音符
21 demisemiquaver ['demɪsemɪˌkeɪvər] (n.) 三十二分音符
22 wainscoting ['weɪnkskətɪŋ] (n.) （牆壁下半部的）護壁板
23 Astrakhan 阿斯特拉罕（位於俄羅斯南部，出產小羊毛）
24 portiere [pɔːtjˈɛər] (n.) 門簾

她面帶倦容說：「有時候，可
蕾曼不太好教。我覺得她練習得不
夠，同樣的事情要叮嚀好幾遍。而
且她老是一身白色的衣服，看久了
會令人覺得單調。不過品尼將軍是
個很可愛的老先生！喬，真希望你
有機會認識他。我教可蕾曼練琴的
時候，他偶爾會走進來——他是個
鰥夫，你知道——他會站在那裡，
摸著他的山羊鬍子，然後問：『十六
分音符和三十二分音符，教得怎麼
樣啦？』」

「喬，我真希望你能看看他們家客廳裡的護壁板，還有那些南
俄的小羊毛門簾。可蕾曼老是有點咳嗽，我希望她的身體不會像她
看起來那樣的差。噢，我真的越來越喜歡她了，她又溫柔又有禮
教。品尼將軍的哥哥以前還是派駐玻利維亞的公使呢。」

這時，喬也神氣得像基度山伯爵一樣，從口袋裡掏出一張十
元、一張五元、一張兩塊和一張一塊的紙鈔——全都是實實在在
的真鈔——擺在黛莉亞賺來的錢旁邊。

「方尖碑那幅水彩畫，賣給了一個培瑞來的人。」他得意地宣
布。

「別跟我開玩笑了，培瑞來的！」黛莉亞說道。

---

25 Monte Cristo，基度山伯爵，為法國小說家大仲馬作品中的人物。年輕
　　時遭好友忌妒，被陷害入獄，逃脫後在基度山島掘獲寶藏，改稱基度山
　　伯爵，逐一報復仇人。
26 obelisk [ˈɔːbəlɪsk] (n.)（紀念人或事的）方尖碑

"All the way. I wish you could see him, Dele. Fat man with a woolen muffler[27] and a quill toothpick. He saw the sketch in Tinkle's window and thought it was a windmill at first, he was game, though, and bought it anyhow. He ordered another—an oil sketch of the Lackawanna freight depot—to take back with him. Music lessons! Oh, I guess Art is still in it."

"I'm so glad you've kept on," said Delia, heartily. "You're bound to win, dear. Thirty-three dollars! We never had so much to spend before. We'll have oysters tonight."

"And filet mignon[28] with champignons," said Joe. "Were is the olive fork?"

On the next Saturday evening Joe reached home first. He spread his $18 on the parlor table and washed what seemed to be a great deal of dark paint from his hands.

Half an hour later Delia arrived, her right hand tied up in a shapeless bundle of wraps and bandages.

"How is this?" asked Joe after the usual greetings. Delia laughed, but not very joyously.

---

27 muffler ['mʌflər] (n.) 厚圍巾
28 filet mignon 菲力牛排（取於腰間肉，是最上等的牛排）

「是啊,是從培瑞來的人。黛兒,真希望你能見見他。一個胖男人,圍著羊毛圍巾,叼著一根翹管牙籤。他在丁克的櫥窗看到我的素描,起先還以為是一座風車,不過他出手大方,二話不說就買下來了。他還另外預訂了一幅油畫,要我畫拉瓦那的貨運車站,想一起帶回去。音樂課!噢,我想教音樂還算是藝術吧。」

「我真高興你沒有放棄,你一定會成功的,親愛的。」黛莉亞開心地說:「三十三塊錢!我們從來沒有過這麼多錢可以花!今天晚上我們吃牡蠣。」

「還有牛排加蘑菇。橄欖叉在哪裡?」喬說。

第二個星期六傍晚,喬先回到家。他把賺來的十八塊錢攤在客廳的桌子上,然後洗掉滿手上看來像是深色顏料的東西。

半個小時後,黛莉亞也到家了,右手用繃帶亂七八糟地包成一團。

「怎麼了?」一如往常打過招呼後,喬問。黛莉亞笑了,但是笑得不怎麼開懷。

"Clementina," she explained, "insisted upon a Welsh rabbit[29] after her lesson. She is such a queer girl. Welsh rabbits at 5 in the afternoon. The General was there. You should have seen him run for the chafing dish, Joe, just as if there wasn't a servant in the house. I know Clementina isn't in good health; she is so nervous. In serving the rabbit she spilled a great lot of it, boiling hot, over my hand and wrist. It hurt awfully, Joe. And the dear girl was so sorry! But Gen. Pinkney!—Joe, that old man nearly went distracted. He rushed downstairs and sent somebody—they said the furnace man or somebody in the basement—out to a drug store for some oil and things to bind it up with. It doesn't hurt so much now."

"What's this?" asked Joe, taking the hand tenderly and pulling at some white strands beneath the bandages.

"It's something soft," said Delia, "that had oil on it. Oh, Joe, did you sell another sketch?" She had seen the money on the table.

"Did I?" said Joe; "just ask the man from Peoria. He got his depot today, and he isn't sure but he thinks he wants another parkscape and a view on the Hudson. What time this afternoon did you burn your hand, Dele?"

"Five o'clock, I think," said Dele, plaintively[30]. "The iron—I mean the rabbit came off the fire about that time. You ought to have seen Gen. Pinkney, Joe, when—"

"Sit down here a moment, Dele," said Joe. He drew her to the couch, sat beside her and put his arm across her shoulders.

她解釋説：「可蕾曼上完課後，執意要吃威爾斯乳酪。她真是個奇怪的女孩，下午五點鐘吃威爾斯乳酪。將軍也在。你真該看看他跑去拿鍋子的樣子，喬，好像家裡沒僕人似的。我知道可蕾曼的身體不太好，而且很神經質。她澆乳酪的時候，把乳酪潑出來了一大半，還滾燙的，就潑到我的手和手腕上。痛得要命呢，喬。那可憐的女孩很過意不去！還有品尼將軍！——喬，那位老先生簡直都慌了，他馬上衝下樓派人——他們説是在地下室看火爐之類的人——去藥房買了些油和包紮的東西回來。現在，沒那麼痛了。」

　　「這是什麼？」喬溫柔地捧起黛莉亞的手，拉拉從繃帶下面露出的白線。

　　黛莉亞説：「這是軟紗，上面有油。噢，喬，你是不是又賣掉一幅畫了？」她看到桌上的錢。

　　「我是不是又賣掉一幅畫？問培瑞來的那個人就知道啦，他今天拿到車站那張油畫了。他還不確定，不過他説他可能還想要一張公園的風景畫，還有一張哈德遜河的河景。黛兒，你今天下午什麼時候燙傷手的？」喬説。

　　「五點的時候吧，我想。」黛莉亞説，聲音有些委屈。「熨斗——乳酪大概就是那個時候煮好的。你真該見見品尼將軍，喬，他——」

　　「先坐下來吧，黛兒。」喬一邊説著，一邊把她拉到沙發前，在她身旁坐下，伸手摟住她的肩。

---

29 Welsh rabbit 威爾斯乳酪（將乳酪加熱熔化後塗於麵包上吃，有時乳酪裡還加牛奶或啤酒）
30 plaintively ['pleɪntɪvli] (adv.)（聲音）委屈地；哭訴地

"What have you been doing for the last two weeks, Dele?" he asked.

She braved it for a moment or two with an eye full of love and stubbornness, and murmured a phrase or two vaguely of Gen. Pinkney; but at length down went her head and out came the truth and tears.

"I couldn't get any pupils," she confessed. "And I couldn't bear to have you give up your lessons; and I got a place ironing shirts in that big Twenty-fourth street laundry. And I think I did very well to make up both General Pinkney and Clementina, don't you, Joe? And when a girl in the laundry set down a hot iron on my hand this afternoon I was all the way home making up that story about the Welsh rabbit. You're not angry, are you, Joe? And if I hadn't got the work you mightn't have sold your sketches to that man from Peoria."

"He wasn't from Peoria," said Joe, slowly.

"Well, it doesn't matter where he was from. How clever you are, Joe—and—kiss me, Joe—and what made you ever suspect that I wasn't giving music lessons to Clementina?"

"I didn't," said Joe, "until tonight. And I wouldn't have then, only I sent up this cotton waste and oil from the engine-room this afternoon for a girl upstairs who had her hand burned with a smoothing-iron. I've been firing the engine in that laundry for the last two weeks."

"And then you didn't—"

「這兩個星期，你到底在做什麼，黛兒？」他問。

她帶著充滿愛意和固執的眼神，撐了那麼一會兒，嘴裡含含糊糊地說著品尼將軍，但最後她還是低下頭，流下眼淚，說出實情。

她坦言說：「我找不到學生，但是又不忍心看你放棄學業，最後我在二十四街那間大洗衣店找到燙衣服的工作。喬，品尼將軍和可蕾曼的故事我編得還不錯吧？今天下午，洗衣店裡一個女孩拿熨斗燙到我，回家路上我就在編這個乳酪的故事。你不生氣吧，喬？我要是沒有這份工作，你的畫可能就不會賣給那個培瑞來的人了。」

「那個人不是培瑞來的。」喬慢慢地說。

「他是從哪裡來的都無所謂，喬，你很有天分——親我一下，喬——你怎麼會想到我不是在給可蕾曼上音樂課？」

喬說：「我一直到今天晚上才起疑，而且要不是今天下午我把機器間這團廢紗頭和油送到樓上，給一個被熨斗燙傷手的女孩，我也不會起疑。我這兩個星期都在那間洗衣店的爐子間看火。」

「那你沒有——」

"My purchaser from Peoria," said Joe, "and Gen. Pinkney are both creations of the same art—but you wouldn't call it either painting or music."

And then they both laughed, and Joe began:

"When one loves one's Art no service seems—"

But Delia stopped him with her hand on his lips. "No," she said—"just '*When one loves.*'"

喬說：「那個從培瑞來的買主，還有品尼將軍，都是同一種藝術的產物——不過這種藝術不叫繪畫，也不叫音樂。」

兩人都笑了，喬開口說：

「一個人深愛其藝術時，什麼樣的犧牲——」

黛莉亞用手輕輕遮住喬的嘴唇，不讓他說下去。她說：「別說了，——說『一個人深愛的時候』，就夠了。」

7

Stephen Crane (1871-1900)

風雪淪落人

■ 史蒂芬・克恩

The Men in the Storm

The blizzard[1] began to swirl great clouds of snow along the streets, sweeping it down from the roofs and up from the pavements until the faces of pedestrians tingled and burned as from a thousand needle-prickings. Those on the walks huddled their necks closely in the collars of their coats and went along stooping[2] like a race of aged people. The drivers of vehicles hurried their horses furiously on their way. They were made more cruel by the exposure of their positions, aloft on high seats.

The street cars, bound up-town, went slowly, the horses slipping and straining in the spongy brown mass that lay between the rails. The drivers, muffled to the eyes, stood erect and facing the wind, models of grim philosophy. Overhead the trains rumbled and roared, and the dark structure of the elevated railroad, stretching over the avenue, dripped little streams and drops of water upon the mud and snow beneath it.

All the clatter[3] of the street was softened by the masses that lay upon the cobbles until, even to one who looked from a window, it became important music, a melody of life made necessary to the ear by the dreariness of the pitiless beat and sweep of the storm.

1 blizzard ['blɪzərd] (n.) 暴風雪
2 stoop [stuːp] (v.) 彎腰駝背
3 clatter ['klætər] (n.) 吵嚷；喧鬧

　　暴風雪開始在街上捲起濃密的白雪，屋頂上的積雪被颳下，人行道上的雪堆被吹起，刮得行人的臉痛得像千萬根針在刺一般。走在路上的行人把頸子縮在大衣的領子下，蜷縮著身子快步前進，看起來就像是在進行長青組的賽跑一樣。馬車夫發狂似地趨馬前進，他們坐在高高的椅子上，畫面看起來愈顯殘酷。

　　駛往城北的街車緩緩前進，拉車的馬匹在軌道間稀軟的爛泥裡滑跌掙扎。駕車的車夫全身裹得只露出一雙眼睛，迎著風直挺挺地站著，看起來就像是一個堅忍人生的典範。頭頂上方的火車轟隆隆地駛過，橫跨在街道上空的灰暗鐵道高橋，滴流著雪水落到橋下的泥巴雪地上。

　　鵝卵石上的積雪，讓街上的喧囂聲聽起來不那麼刺耳。在這種無情的風雪下，街上的喧囂聲是不可少的樂聲，是人們耳裡不可或缺的生命旋律，即使是對從窗裡向外望的人來說，也是如此。

Occasionally one could see black figures of men busily shoveling the white drifts[4] from the walks. The sounds from their labor created new recollections of rural experiences which every man manages to have in a measure[5]. Later, the immense windows of the shops became aglow with light, throwing great beams of orange and yellow upon the pavement.

They were infinitely cheerful, yet in a way they accented the force and discomfort of the storm, and gave a meaning to the pace of the people and the vehicles, scores of pedestrians and drivers, wretched with cold faces, necks and feet, speeding for scores of unknown doors and entrances, scattering to an infinite variety of shelters, to places which the imagination made warm with the familiar colors of home.

There was an absolute expression of hot dinners in the pace of the people. If one dared to speculate upon the destination of those who came trooping, he lost himself in a maze of social calculations; he might fling a handful of sand and attempt to follow the flight of each particular grain.

But as to the suggestion of hot dinners, he was in firm lines of thought, for it was upon every hurrying face. It is a matter of tradition; it is from the tales of childhood. It comes forth with every storm.

4 drift [drɪft] (n.) 堆積物
5 in a measure 多多少少；到某種程度

　　偶爾可以看到幾個黑色的人影，在人行道上的忙著鏟雪。鏟雪的聲音形成了另類的田園感受，那是人們多多少少都嚮往的。稍後，商店的大櫥窗一一亮起燈，在人行道上投下橙黃色的光。

　　這些燈光襯托出風雪的兇猛無情，卻也令人感到愉悅，讓人們和馬車的行進變得有意義，讓行人和車夫感到有所目標。人們冰冷的臉頰、脖子和雙腳都凍僵了，他們急急地躲進四周的房子門口，到處找各種地方躲風雪，每個躲藏的角落儼然都有了家的味道，顯得暖暖的。

　　人們為著熱騰騰的晚餐而加快腳步。如果你想知道這些人會各奔何處，那你會被搞得錯亂，那好比是把手中的一把沙子灑出去，然後去追蹤每一粒沙子的去向。

　　但是若說是為了熱騰騰的晚餐而趕路，那是錯不了的，因為在每一個匆匆的神色上都可以看到這一點。這像是一種傳統，始自孩提時代的故事，只要一颳起風雪，就會顯現出來。

However, in a certain part of a dark West-side street, there was a collection of men to whom these things were as if they were not. In this street was located a charitable house where for five cents the homeless of the city could get a bed at night and, in the morning, coffee and bread.

During the afternoon of the storm, the whirling snows acted as drivers, as men with whips, and at half-past three, the walk before the closed doors of the house was covered with wanderers of the street, waiting. For some distance on either side of the place they could be seen lurking[6] in doorways and behind projecting parts of buildings, gathering in close bunches in an effort to get warm.

A covered wagon drawn up near the curb sheltered a dozen of them. Under the stairs that led to the elevated railway station, there were six or eight, their hands stuffed deep in their pockets, their shoulders stooped, jiggling[7] their feet.

Others always could be seen coming, a strange procession, some slouching[8] along with the characteristic hopeless gait of professional strays, some coming with hesitating steps wearing the air of men to whom this sort of thing was new.

---

6 lurk [lɜːrk] (v.) 躲藏
7 jiggle [ˈdʒɪgəl] (v.) 左右擺動
8 slouch [slautʃ] (v.) 無精打采地走

　　然而，在西城一條昏暗的街上，聚集了一群人，對他們來說，這一切就顯得不具意義了。街上有一間收容所，城裡的遊民花五分錢，就可以分到一張床過夜，早上還有咖啡和麵包。

　　這天下午，狂風飛雪像一個執著鞭子的車夫，把這些遊民趕到一棟大門緊閉的屋子前，到了三點半，這裡已經站滿了等待的遊民。從收容所的兩側一路延伸開來，可以看到他們成群地躲在一扇扇的門前和一道道的屋簷下，擠在一起取暖。

　　一輛停在路邊的有篷馬車，為十幾個遊民提供了避風躲雪的地方。在鐵橋的樓梯下方，站了六到八個遊民，他們兩手深深插在口袋裡，縮著脖子，抖著雙腳。

　　不停地有人陸陸續續走過來，形成一個奇怪的隊伍，有些人無精打采，拖著專業遊民典型的絕望腳步，有些人遲疑不決，顯然是第一次來到這種地方。

It was an afternoon of incredible length. The snow, blowing in twisting clouds, sought out the men in their meager hiding-places and skillfully beat in among them, drenching their persons with showers of fine, stinging flakes.

They crowded together, muttering, and fumbling in their pockets to get their red, inflamed wrists covered by the cloth.

Newcomers usually halted at one end of the groups and addressed a question, perhaps much as a matter of form, "Is it open yet?"

Those who had been waiting inclined to take the questioner seriously and become contemptuous. "No; do yeh think we'd be standin' here?"

The gathering swelled in numbers steadily and persistently. One could always see them coming, trudging slowly through the storm. Finally, the little snow plains in the street began to assume a leaden hue from the shadows of evening.

The buildings upreared gloomily save where various windows became brilliant figures of light that made shimmers and splashes of yellow on the snow. A street lamp on the curb struggled to illuminate, but it was reduced to impotent blindness by the swift gusts of sleet[9] crusting its panes.

In this half-darkness, the men began to come from their shelter places and mass in front of the doors of charity. They were of all types, but the nationalities were mostly American, German and Irish.

這是一個無比漫長的下午。盤旋飛舞的白雪找出這些無處可躲的遊民，靈巧地撲向他們，用刺人的細緻雪花包圍他們。

他們擠在一起，嘴裡嘀嘀咕咕，凍得發紅的雙手在口袋裡亂鑽，尋求遮蔽。

新來的人通常會在其中一群這樣的人面前停下腳步，問起一個同樣的問題，就像是例行公事一樣：「門開了沒？」

早等在那裡的人會很認真地看待這個問題，不耐煩地答道：「沒啦！要是開了，我們幹嘛還站在這裡？」

人群穩定而持續地擴大，你可以看到風雪中一直有人拖著沉重的腳步走過來。最後，街上一堆堆的雪，開始在黃昏的陰影下，染上一層灰暗的色調。

一棟棟樓房陰鬱地聳立著，大大小小的窗戶變成一塊塊的亮片，透出的黃色光芒照得飛雪閃閃爍爍。路邊一盞街燈吃力地發出亮光，放出微弱的光暈，一陣陣猛烈的雪雨在燈罩上結了一層薄冰。

在這昏暗的暮色下，遊民開始走出避風的地方，聚集在收容所的大門前。其中形形色色的人都有，但絕大部分是美國人、德國人和愛爾蘭人。

9 sleet [sliːt] (n.) 夾雜著冰的雨

Many were strong, healthy, clear-skinned fellows with that stamp of countenance which is not frequently seen upon seekers after charity. There were men of undoubted patience, industry and temperance, who in time of ill-fortune, do not habitually turn to rail at[10] the state of society, snarling at the arrogance of the rich and bemoaning the cowardice of the poor, but who at these times are apt to wear a sudden and singular meekness, as if they saw the world's progress marching from them and were trying to perceive where they had failed, what they had lacked, to be thus vanquished[11] in the race.

Then there were others of the shifting, Bowery[12] lodging house[13] element who were used to paying ten cents for a place to sleep, but who now came here because it was cheaper.

But they were all mixed in one mass so thoroughly that one could not have discerned the different elements but for the fact that the laboring men, for the most part, remained silent and impassive[14] in the blizzard, their eyes fixed on the windows of the house, statues of patience.

The sidewalk soon became completely blocked by the bodies of the men. They pressed close to one another like sheep in a winter's gale[15], keeping one another warm by the heat of their bodies. The snow came down upon this compressed group of men until, directly from above, it might have appeared like a heap of snow-covered merchandise, if it were not for the fact that the crowd swayed gently with a unanimous[16], rhythmical motion.

在這些人裡頭，也可以看健康、強壯、皮膚乾淨的傢伙，這在尋求慈善機構幫助的人當中，並不常見。裡頭也有吃苦耐勞、勤奮節制的男人，他們落魄了，但還不習慣去埋怨社會現實，或是罵富人太臭屁、哀嘆窮人太怯懦，在這種時候他們反而會變得異常溫順。他們彷彿看到了世界前進的腳步正在遠離他們，他們急欲了解自己是哪裡失敗了，缺少什麼了，才會在競爭中被擊垮。

此外，還有四處為家、從廉價出租屋來的人，那裡睡一晚要十分錢，但這裡更便宜，所以他們現在也跑來了。

不過因為他們這些人都混在這一大群人裡，所以也看不出有什麼不同。你只會看到這些爭先恐後的人，大多時候都默默不語、面無表情，眼睛直望著收容所的窗戶，在風雪中耐心地等待。

人行道不久就擠滿了人。他們像冬天寒風中的羊群，緊緊挨在一起，用彼此的體溫取暖。大雪不斷飄落在擁擠的人群上，如果不是他們一致而有節奏地慢慢向前移動，由上往下看，看起來就像是覆蓋著白雪的貨物。

10 rail at 抱怨；對……不滿
11 vanquish [ˈvæŋkwɪʃ] (v.) 徹底擊敗
12 Bowery 鮑爾瑞（紐約市街名，以廉價旅館、遊民、犯罪而聞名）
13 lodging house 按日或按星期出租房間的房子
14 impassive [ɪmˈpæsɪv] (a.) 面無表情；無動於衷
15 gale [geɪl] (n.) 大風
16 unanimous [juˈnænɪməs] (a.) 一致的

❼
風雪淪落人

It was wonderful to see how the snow lay upon the heads and shoulders of these men, in little ridges an inch thick perhaps in places, the flakes steadily adding drop and drop, precisely as they fall upon the unresisting grass of the fields.

The feet of the men were all wet and cold and the wish to warm them accounted for the slow, gentle, rhythmical motion. Occasionally some man whose ears or nose tingled acutely from the cold winds would wriggle[17] down until his head was protected by the shoulders of his companions.

There was a continuous murmuring discussion as to the probability of the doors being speedily opened. They persistently lifted their eyes toward the windows. One could hear little combats of opinion.

"There's a light in th' winder!"

"Naw; it's a reflection f'm across th' way."

"Well, didn't I see 'em lite it?"

"You did?"

"I did!"

"Well, then, that settles it!"

As the time approached when they expected to be allowed to enter, the men crowded to the doors in an unspeakable crush, jamming and wedging[18] in a way that it seemed would crack bones. They surged heavily against the building in a powerful wave of pushing shoulders. Once a rumor flitted among all the tossing heads.

　雪花落在這些人的頭上、肩膀上，甚至積成了幾公分厚的小雪堆。雪花不斷地飄落在人們的身上，就像飄落在原野上毫無反抗之力的小草上。看著這樣的畫面，令人稱奇。

　人們的腳又濕又凍，想暖和雙腳的渴望，推動著他們緩慢、溫和、有節奏地向前移動。偶爾有人的耳朵或鼻子被寒風刺痛了，就會扭動著縮起身子，直到旁邊的人的肩膀為他擋住了冷風。

　人群裡一直在低聲討論門是不是快要開了。他們不斷望向收容所的窗戶。你可以聽到他們有一句沒一句地爭執。

　「窗戶裡的燈亮了！」

　「才不是咧，那是對面的反光。」

　「奇怪了，我明明看到他們點燈啦。」

　「真的？」

　「真的！」

　「那就是啦！」

　算算開門的時間快要到了，他們開始湧向大門，不停地向前推啊、擠啊，簡直都快要把骨頭擠碎了。他們推擠的肩膀形成一股巨浪，重重地湧向收容所。突然，一股謠言在攢動的人頭中傳開。

17　wriggle [ˈrɪgəl] (v.) 蠕動
18　wedge [wɛdʒ] (v.) 擠入

"They can't open th' doors! Th' fellers er smack up ag'in 'em."

Then a dull roar of rage came from the men on the outskirts; but all the time they strained and pushed until it appeared to be impossible for those that they cried out against to do anything but be crushed to pulp[19].

"Ah, git away f'm th' door!"

"Git outa that!"

"Throw 'em out!"

"Kill 'em!"

"Say, fellers, now, what th' 'ell? Give 'em a chanct t' open th' door!"

"Yeh damned pigs, give 'em a chanct t' open th' door!"

Men in the outskirts of the crowd occasionally yelled when a boot-heel of one of frantic trampling feet crushed on their freezing extremities.

"Git off me feet, yeh clumsy tarrier!"

"Say, don't stand on me feet! Walk on th' ground!"

A man near the doors suddenly shouted: "O-o-oh! Le' me out—le' me out!" And another, a man of infinite valor, once twisted his head so as to half face those who were pushing behind him.

"Quit yer shovin', yeh"—and he delivered a volley[20] of the most powerful and singular invective[21] straight into the faces of the men behind him. It was as if he was hammering the noses of them with curses of triple brass.

「他們開不了門啦！前面的
人把門擋住啦。」

　　人群外圍傳來憤怒的抗議
聲。他們不斷向前推擠，前面的
人擋不住，只能等著被擠成肉
醬。

　　「喂，別擋著門！」

　　「門邊的人滾開！」

　　「把他們趕出去！」

　　「打死他們！」

　　「喂，你們怎麼搞的？讓
開，讓他們開門啊！」

　　「對啊，你們這些死豬，讓開，讓他們開門！」

　　外圍偶爾有人凍僵的腳被瘋狂踐踏的靴跟踩到，痛得大叫。

　　「你踩到我的腳啦，你這個笨蛋！」

　　「喂，別站在我的腳上！把你的腳放在地上！」

　　門邊突然有人大叫：「噢——噢——唉喲！讓我出去——讓
我出去！」還有一個人，勇氣十足，扭過頭來，側著臉瞪著後面擠
他的人。

　　「別擠了，你！」——他對著後面的臉一頓痛罵，就好像吹著
三管的銅管樂器，對著後面人的鼻子猛轟。

19　pulp [pʌlp] (n.) 糊狀物
20　volley [ˈvɑːli] (n.) 一頓；一陣
21　invective [ɪnˈvektɪv] (n.) 痛罵

❼
風
雪
淪
落
人

His face, red with rage, could be seen; upon it, an expression of sublime disregard of consequences. But nobody cared to reply to his imprecations[22]; it was too cold. Many of them snickered[23] and all continued to push.

In occasional pauses of the crowd's movement the men had opportunity to make jokes; usually grim things, and no doubt very uncouth. Nevertheless, they are notable—one does not expect to find the quality of humor in a heap of old clothes under a snowdrift.

The winds seemed to grow fiercer as time wore on. Some of the gusts of snow that came down on the close collection of heads cut like knives and needles, and the men huddled, and swore, not like dark assassins, but in a sort of American fashion, grimly and desperately, it is true, but yet with a wondrous under-effect, indefinable and mystic, as if there was some kind of humor in this catastrophe, in this situation in a night of snow-laden winds.

Once, the window of the huge dry goods[24] shop across the street furnished material for a few moments of forgetfulness. In the brilliantly-lighted space appeared the figure of a man. He was rather stout and very well clothed. His whiskers were fashioned charmingly after those of the Prince of Wales.

---

22 imprecation [ˌɪmprɪˈkeɪʃən] (n.) 罵人的話
23 snicker [ˈsnɪkər] (v.) 偷笑；竊笑
24 dry goods 布料；紡織品

他的臉漲得血紅，一副豁出去了的表情，但是沒有人理會他。天氣太冷了。不少人在偷笑，而整個人群還是不停地向前擠。

推擠偶爾會停下來，有人會趁機說說笑話，多半是悽慘殘酷的笑話，而且想當然耳是粗俗不堪的，但也算是很難得啦——一堆窮人在寒風雪地裡，能有這樣的幽默，很不容易了。

寒風似乎越括越猛。有時，陣陣飛雪像刀子、像尖針落在人們的頭上，他們擠成一團，發著殘酷而絕望的美國式毒誓（而非暗夜刺客的毒誓），這是千真萬確的事，儘管當中帶著一種神秘、不可言喻的奇妙氣氛。在這個刮風下雪的夜晚，彷彿這個悲慘的夜晚還有某種噱頭。

對街那家大布店窗子裡的一個景象，還一度讓人們暫時忘了現況。明亮的窗戶裡出現一個男人的身影，這個人身材肥胖，穿著很講究，還留著英國親王那種漂亮而時髦的鬢角。

He stood in an attitude of magnificent reflection. He slowly stroked his moustache with a certain grandeur of manner, and looked down at the snow-encrusted mob. From below, there was denoted a supreme complacence in him. It seemed that the sight operated inversely, and enabled him to more clearly regard his own environment, delightful relatively.

One of the mob chanced to turn his head and perceive the figure in the window. "Hello, look-it 'is whiskers," he said genially.

Many of the men turned then, and a shout went up. They called to him in all strange keys. They addressed him in every manner, from familiar and cordial greetings to carefully-worded advice concerning changes in his personal appearance. The man presently fled, and the mob chuckled ferociously like ogres[25] who had just devoured something.

They turned then to serious business. Often they addressed the stolid[26] front of the house.

"Oh, let us in fer Gawd's sake!"

"Let us in or we'll all drop dead!"

"Say, what's th' use o' keepin' all us poor Indians out in th' cold?"

And always some one was saying, "Keep off me feet."

The crushing of the crowd grew terrific toward the last. The men, in keen pain from the blasts, began almost to fight. With the pitiless whirl of snow upon them, the battle for shelter was going to the strong.

那個男人若有所思地站在那裡，優雅地捻著嘴上的小鬍子，低頭看著風雪中的遊民。從遊民悽慘的處境來看，他足以沾沾自喜，這相反的兩幕對照起來，更烘托出他幸福的生活。

　　人群中有一個人這時轉過頭來，瞄到了窗戶裡的這個男人。「嘿，你們看，是鬚角仔。」他開心地說。

　　許多人跟著轉過頭來，隨之一陣喊叫聲，用各式各樣的聲音和方式和他打招呼，有些人熱誠地跟他打招呼，有些人細心地勸他換換打扮，男人連忙逃開，遊民看得吃吃狂笑，他們笑的樣子就像剛吃下食物的巨人一樣。

　　之後，大家又把心思擺回正事上，不時對著毫無動靜的大門大喊。

　　「噢，看在老天爺的份上，讓我們進去！」

　　「讓我們進去，我們都快要凍死啦！」

　　「喂，把我們這群可憐、窮酸的人關在外面受凍有啥好處？」

　　而且總是會聽到有人說：「不要踩我的腳。」

　　人群的推擠邁向高潮。被陣陣刺骨寒風折騰的人群，都快打起來了。無情紛飛的大雪下，大家爭著避寒，愈爭愈兇。

25 ogre ['ougər] (n.)（童話故事中）會吃人的巨人
26 stolid ['stɑːlɪd] (a.) 無動於衷的

It became known that the basement door at the foot of a little steep flight of stairs was the one to be opened, and they jostled[27] and heaved in this direction like laboring fiends. One could hear them panting and groaning in their fierce exertion.

Usually some one in the front ranks was protesting to those in the rear: "O—o—ow! Oh, say, now, fellers, let up, will yeh? Do yeh wanta kill somebody?"

A policeman arrived and went into the midst of them, scolding and berating[28], occasionally threatening, but using no force but that of his hands and shoulders against these men who were only struggling to get in out of the storm. His decisive tones rang out sharply: "Stop that pushin' back there! Come, boys, don't push! Stop that! Here, you, quit yer shovin'! Cheese that!"

When the door below was opened, a thick stream of men forced a way down the stairs, which were of an extraordinary narrowness and seemed only wide enough for one at a time. Yet they somehow went down almost three abreast. It was a difficult and painful operation. The crowd was like a turbulent water forcing itself through one tiny outlet.

27 jostle ['dʒɑːsəl] (v.) 撞；推；擠
28 berate [bɪ'reɪt] (v.) 訓斥

　　一聽到收容所要打開的是小陡梯腳下地下室的門,人們便窮凶惡極地你推我擠地湧過來,你可以聽到他們費力的喘息和呻吟。

　　前面總會有人在向後面的人抗議說:「喔——喔——噢!喂,老兄們,別擠了,好不好?想擠死人啊?」

　　這時來了一名警察,他走到人群中間又訓又罵,偶爾也威脅一下,但沒有動用武力,頂多用雙手和肩膀推開那些掙扎著要進屋子裡避寒的人。他嚴厲地大聲命令道:「後面的,別擠了!男人,別擠了!別那樣!嘿,你,別推了!」

　　地下室的門打開後,一股人流擠下樓梯。樓梯很窄,只容得下一人通過,卻並肩擠了三個人。這是一個艱辛的過程,人群像一股洶湧的水流,奮力擠出一個小小的出口。

The men in the rear, excited by the success of the others, made frantic exertions, for it seemed that this large band would more than fill the quarters and that many would be left upon the pavements. It would be disastrous to be of the last, and accordingly men with the snow biting their faces, writhed[29] and twisted with their might.

One expected that from the tremendous pressure, the narrow passage to the basement door would be so choked and clogged with human limbs and bodies that movement would be impossible. Once indeed the crowd was forced to stop, and a cry went along that a man had been injured at the foot of the stairs.

But presently the slow movement began again, and the policeman fought at the top of the flight to ease the pressure on those who were going down.

A reddish light from a window fell upon the faces of the men when they, in turn, arrived at the last three steps and were about to enter. One could then note a change of expression that had come over their features. As they thus stood upon the threshold of their hopes, they looked suddenly content and complacent. The fire had passed from their eyes and the snarl had vanished from their lips. The very force of the crowd in the rear, which had previously vexed[30] them, was regarded from another point of view, for it now made it inevitable that they should go through the little doors into the place that was cheery and warm with light.

後面的人一看到前面的人進屋，便激動起來，開始瘋狂地推擠，深怕收容所要是容不下這多麼的人，許多人就得留在外面。要是在人群中吊車尾就太慘了，所以他們不顧紛飛的冰雪刺痛臉頰，使盡全力往前擠。

你可能會想，在這麼大的壓力下，狹窄的樓梯一定會被這些人的手腳身體塞住，最後誰也動不了。有一度，人群的確被逼得停下來了，有人大喊說，樓梯下有人受傷了。

但沒不久，緩慢的移動又開始了，警察也仕樓梯口奮戰，舒緩後面湧來的壓力。

這些人一一走到樓梯的最後三階，準備進屋時，窗戶裡的一盞紅燈映照在他們臉上。你可以看到他們臉上的表情變了。一旦站在這希望的門檻上了，人們會頓時感到心滿意足。他們眼中的怒火消失，嘴邊的怒吼也停歇了。後面的推擠剛剛還令人惱怒，現在卻具有不同意義，因為正是這股推擠的力量，確保他們一定會穿過那扇小門，走進這個舒適、溫暖、明亮的地方。

29 writhe [raɪð] (v.) 蠕動；扭動身體
30 vex [veks] (v.) 使惱怒

The tossing crowd on the sidewalk grew smaller and smaller. The snow beat with merciless persistence upon the bowed heads of those who waited. The wind drove it up from the pavements in frantic forms of winding white, and it seethed[31] in circles about the huddled forms, passing in, one by one, three by three, out of the storm.

人行道上扭動的人群越來越小了，大雪依舊無情地打在這些等待的人蜷縮的頭上。人行道上的飄雪不斷被狂風捲起，在這些挨在一起的身影邊翻騰盤旋，只見他們一個接一個，三三兩兩，鑽進屋裡，走出這場暴風雪。

---

31 seethe [siːð] (v.) 翻騰

Jack London (1876-1916)

熱愛生命

Love of Life

This out of all will remain—
They have lived and have tossed:
So much of the game will be gain,
Though the gold of the dice has been lost.

They limped[1] painfully down the bank, and once the foremost of the two men staggered[2] among the rough-strewn rocks. They were tired and weak, and their faces had the drawn expression of patience which comes of hardship long endured.

They were heavily burdened with blanket packs which were strapped to their shoulders. Head-straps, passing across the forehead, helped support these packs. Each man carried a rifle. They walked in a stooped posture, the shoulders well forward, the head still farther forward, the eyes bent upon the ground.

"I wish we had just about two of them cartridges that's layin' in that cache[3] of ourn," said the second man.

His voice was utterly and drearily expressionless. He spoke without enthusiasm; and the first man, limping into the milky stream that foamed over the rocks, vouchsafed[4] no reply.

The other man followed at his heels. They did not remove their foot-gear, though the water was icy cold—so cold that their ankles ached and their feet went numb. In places the water dashed against their knees, and both men staggered for footing.

在一切之中，這一點將繼續下去———
他們在生命中打滾，下著人生的賭注：
雖然已經弄丟了金骰子，
可以贏得的賭注何其多。

　　他們兩個人緩慢吃力地走下河岸，踏在碎石上時，走在前面男人差一點摔了跤。他們走了好長一段艱辛的路，已經筋疲力竭，臉上露出硬撐著的憔悴表情。

　　他們揹著沉重的毛毯行囊，用皮繩把它們綁在肩頭上，並把繩子套在頭上繞過額頭，分攤重量。他們各自持著一把來福槍，彎著腰、駝著背，肩膀往前傾，頭垂得更前面，眼睛直視著地上。

　　「我們藏在石頭下面的那些子彈，要是手邊能有幾發就好了。」走在後面的男人說。

　　他說話的語氣冷冰冰的，一點感情也沒有。走在前面男人，只顧緩緩地走進被石頭激得起泡沫的白色溪水中，一語不發。

　　後面的男人緊緊跟著。他們沒有脫下鞋，溪水很冰，凍得腳踝發疼，腳也都麻了。有幾處溪水對著膝蓋猛沖，沖得他們搖搖晃晃，努力保持平衡。

1　limp [lɪmp] (v.) 跛行
2　stagger [ˈstægər] (v.) 搖搖晃晃地走
3　cache [kæʃ] (n.) 隱藏處
4　vouchsafe [vaʊtʃˈseɪf] (v.) 賜予

The man who followed slipped on a smooth boulder, nearly fell, but recovered himself with a violent effort, at the same time uttering a sharp exclamation of pain. He seemed faint and dizzy and put out his free hand while he reeled[5], as though seeking support against the air. When he had steadied himself he stepped forward, but reeled again and nearly fell. Then he stood still and looked at the other man, who had never turned his head.

The man stood still for fully a minute, as though debating with himself. Then he called out: "I say, Bill, I've sprained my ankle." Bill staggered on through the milky water. He did not look around. The man watched him go, and though his face was expressionless as ever, his eyes were like the eyes of a wounded deer.

The other man limped up the farther bank and continued straight on without looking back. The man in the stream watched him. His lips trembled a little, so that the rough thatch[6] of brown hair which covered them was visibly agitated. His tongue even strayed out to moisten them.

"Bill!" he cried out. It was the pleading cry of a strong man in distress, but Bill's head did not turn. The man watched him go, limping grotesquely and lurching[7] forward with stammering gait up the slow slope toward the soft sky-line of the low-lying hill. He watched him go till he passed over the crest and disappeared. Then he turned his gaze and slowly took in the circle of the world that remained to him now that Bill was gone.

　　後面的男人在一塊光滑的圓石上滑了一下，差點摔倒。他猛力一掙，痛苦地大叫一聲，又站穩身子。他似乎有些頭昏眼花，在搖搖晃晃快摔倒的時候，伸出手在空氣中想抓住什麼支撐物。他站穩後，繼續前進，不料又晃了一下，差點沒摔倒。最後，他在原地站定，看著前面的男人，前面的男人連個頭都沒回。

　　他在那裡一動也不動地站了整整一分鐘，好像在天人交戰著。接著他喊道：「嘿，比爾，我的腳踝扭傷了。」比爾繼續在白色的溪水中蹣跚前進，沒有回頭。他看著前面的男人越走越遠，臉上雖然仍舊毫無表情，眼神卻像一隻受傷的鹿。

　　前面的男人慢慢地走上對面的河岸，頭也不回，繼續往前走。溪裡的人望著他的背影，嘴唇開始輕輕顫抖，散亂在嘴前的棕色鬍子跟著明顯地抖動起來。他甚至不知不覺地伸出舌頭，濡濕嘴唇。

　　「比爾！」他大聲喊道。這是硬漢在絕望當中懇求的哭喊聲，但是比爾沒有回頭。他看著比爾繼續往前行，踩著怪異的踉蹌步子，搖搖晃晃地爬上緩和的斜坡，走向矮山丘頂模糊的天際線。他看著他越走越遠，直到他跨過山丘頂端，消失不見。他把目光移開，慢慢環顧比爾走後所留下的這片天地。

5　reel [ri:l] (v.) 搖搖晃晃
6　thatch [θætʃ] (n.) 又髒又亂的毛髮
7　lurch [lɜ:rtʃ] (v.) 搖搖晃晃地移動

Near the horizon the sun was smoldering[8] dimly, almost obscured by formless mists and vapors, which gave an impression of mass and density without outline or tangibility.

The man pulled out his watch, the while resting his weight on one leg. It was four o'clock, and as the season was near the last of July or first of August,—he did not know the precise date within a week or two,—he knew that the sun roughly marked the northwest.

He looked to the south and knew that somewhere beyond those bleak hills lay the Great Bear Lake; also, he knew that in that direction the Arctic Circle cut its forbidding way across the Canadian Barrens. This stream in which he stood was a feeder to the Coppermine River, which in turn flowed north and emptied into Coronation Gulf and the Arctic Ocean. He had never been there, but he had seen it, once, on a Hudson Bay Company[9] chart.

Again his gaze completed the circle of the world about him. It was not a heartening spectacle. Everywhere was soft sky-line. The hills were all low-lying. There were no trees, no shrubs[10], no grasses—naught but a tremendous and terrible desolation that sent fear swiftly dawning into his eyes.

"Bill!" he whispered, once and twice; "Bill!"

He cowered[11] in the midst of the milky water, as though the vastness were pressing in upon him with overwhelming force, brutally crushing him with its complacent awfulness. He began to shake as with an ague[12]-fit, till the gun fell from his hand with a splash.

地平線上，太陽昏暗地燃燒著，幾乎被飄忽朦朧的霧氣遮住，看上去就像一團只有質量與密度、卻沒有輪廓或形體的東西。

溪裡的男人把身體的重量歇在一隻腳上，掏出手錶。四點了，現在這時節大概是七月底或八月初——他並不知道確切的日期，可能跟實際的日期差個一、兩個星期——他知道現在太陽大約在西北方的位置。

他向南方望去，知道在那群荒涼的山丘背後某處，就躺著大熊湖；他還知道，往那個方向，北極圈的禁區界線會劃過加拿大凍原。他站著的這條溪，會匯入科珀曼河，而科珀曼河會一路向北流，流入加冕灣和北極海。他沒去過那裡，但他曾經有一次在哈德遜灣公司的地圖上看過那個地方。

他又環顧四周的天地，眼前的景色並不怎麼鼓舞人心，到處都是模糊的天際線。低矮的山丘，沒有樹木，沒有灌木，也沒有草——什麼都沒有，只有一片空曠可怕的荒原，他的眼裡頓時充滿了恐懼。

「比爾！」他輕聲喊，然後又喊了一聲：「比爾！」

他在乳白色的溪水中縮起身子，彷彿巨大的空曠正重重地壓在他身上，用傲人的氣勢殘酷地壓垮他。他開始打寒戰，抖得手裡的槍啪啦一聲地掉進水裡。

8 smolder ['smoʊldər] (v.) 悶燒
9 Hudson Bay Company 哈德遜灣公司（加拿大歷史最悠久的百貨公司）
10 shrub [ʃrʌb] (n.) 灌木
11 cower ['kaʊər] (v.)（因恐懼而）退縮
12 ague ['eɪgjuː] (n.)（瘧疾的）發燒打寒戰

This served to rouse him. He fought with his fear and pulled himself together, groping in the water and recovering the weapon. He hitched[13] his pack farther over on his left shoulder, so as to take a portion of its weight from off the injured ankle. Then he proceeded, slowly and carefully, wincing[14] with pain, to the bank.

He did not stop. With a desperation that was madness, unmindful of the pain, he hurried up the slope to the crest of the hill over which his comrade had disappeared—more grotesque and comical by far than that limping, jerking comrade.

But at the crest he saw a shallow valley, empty of life. He fought with his fear again, overcame it, hitched the pack still farther over on his left shoulder, and lurched on down the slope.

The bottom of the valley was soggy[15] with water, which the thick moss held, spongelike, close to the surface. This water squirted[16] out from under his feet at every step, and each time he lifted a foot the action culminated in a sucking sound as the wet moss reluctantly released its grip. He picked his way from muskeg[17] to muskeg, and followed the other man's footsteps along and across the rocky ledges[18] which thrust like islets through the sea of moss.

Though alone, he was not lost. Farther on he knew he would come to where dead spruce and fir, very small and weazened[19], bordered the shore of a little lake, the titchin-nichilie, in the tongue of the country, the "land of little sticks." And into that lake flowed a small stream, the water of which was not milky.

這時他才回過神來。他壓住心中的恐懼，勉強地鎮定下來，在水裡摸索，找回了槍。他把肩上的行囊拉向左邊的肩膀，以減輕受傷的那隻腳踝的負擔。接著，他繼續前進，慢慢地、小心地走向河岸，臉上強忍著痛苦。

他一步也沒停下來，不顧疼痛、發瘋似地急忙爬上斜坡，爬到同伴消失不見的山丘頂——他跟蹌的步子，比搖搖晃晃、跌跌撞撞前進的同伴還要怪誕可笑。

到了山丘頂，他只看到一片淺淺的山谷，沒有人煙。他心裡又一陣驚慌，等鎮定下來之後，他把行囊再往左肩挪了些，然後蹣跚地走下山坡。

山谷的底端都是水，水下濃密的苔蘚像海綿一樣把水鎖在地面上。他每走一步，水就從腳底噴出，潮濕的苔蘚吸住了他的腳，他每一勉力抬腳，就聽到一個「叭塔」的聲音。他小心翼翼地走過一塊塊青苔沼澤地，沿著同伴所留下的腳印走過石塊。遍布的石塊，看起來就好像在這片苔蘚之海上聳起的一座座小島。

他一個人走著，並未迷路。他知道，再往前走，就會遇到一座小湖，湖邊是乾枯的雲杉和冷杉，一棵棵的又小又細，當地人管那個地方叫「提金齊力」，意思是「枯枝之地」。有一條小溪流入這座小湖，但是溪水不是乳白色的。

---

13 hitch [hɪtʃ] (v.) 拴住；鉤住
14 wince [wɪns] (v.) 因疼痛而扭曲臉孔
15 soggy [ˈsɑːɡi] (a.) 溼透的
16 squirt [skwɜːrt] (v.) 噴射
17 muskeg [ˈmʌskɛɡ] (n.) 青苔沼澤地
18 ledge [lɛdʒ] (n.) 石頭平滑的表面
19 weazened [ˈwiːzənd] (a.) 枯萎細瘦的（= wizened）

8
熱愛生命

There was rush-grass on that stream—this he remembered well—but no timber, and he would follow it till its first trickle ceased at a divide. He would cross this divide to the first trickle of another stream, flowing to the west, which he would follow until it emptied into the river Dease, and here he would find a cache under an upturned canoe and piled over with many rocks. And in this cache would be ammunition for his empty gun, fish-hooks and lines, a small net—all the utilities for the killing and snaring[20] of food. Also, he would find flour,—not much,—a piece of bacon, and some beans.

Bill would be waiting for him there, and they would paddle away south down the Dease to the Great Bear Lake. And south across the lake they would go, ever south, till they gained the Mackenzie. And south, still south, they would go, while the winter raced vainly after them, and the ice formed in the eddies, and the days grew chill and crisp, south to some warm Hudson Bay Company post, where timber grew tall and generous and there was grub[21] without end.

These were the thoughts of the man as he strove onward. But hard as he strove with his body, he strove equally hard with his mind, trying to think that Bill had not deserted him, that Bill would surely wait for him at the cache. He was compelled to think this thought, or else there would not be any use to strive, and he would have lain down and died.

　　在那條小溪上會飄著燈心草,而且不會飄著浮木,這一點他記得很清楚。他會溯溪而上,一直走到小溪源頭的分水嶺。他會翻過這道分水嶺,來到另外一條小溪的源頭,這條溪往西流,他會沿著水流一路走到小溪匯入迪斯河的地方。在那個地方,有一個倒翻過來的獨木舟,獨木舟下有一堆石頭,石頭下面就藏有他們的東西。裡頭有空槍用的子彈,還有魚鉤、釣線和一張小漁網,都是一些用來獵殺和誘捕食物的工具。此外,還藏有一些麵粉、一塊培根和一些豆子。

　　比爾會在那裡等他,然後他們會順著迪斯河,一路向南划到大熊湖。到了湖的南岸,他們會繼續往南走,一直走到麥肯錫河。之後再往南繼續走下去,冬天會在他們身後追趕,湍流會結冰,天氣會變得又乾又冷,然而冬天追不上他們,因為他們會往南走到哈德遜灣公司某個暖和的驛站,那裡的樹木高大茂盛,不愁沒有得吃。

　　他吃力地走著,心裡想的就是這些。他一方面努力地前進,一方面內心也在掙扎著,他跟自己說,比爾應該不會丟下他,他一定會在獨木舟那裡等他。他只能這麼想了,不然一切的工夫都會白費,他也就會撐不下去而倒下了。

20 snare [snɛr] (v.) 設陷阱捕捉
21 grub [grʌb] (n.) 食物

And as the dim ball of the sun sank slowly into the northwest he covered every inch—and many times—of his and Bill's flight south before the downcoming winter. And he conned[22] the grub of the cache and the grub of the Hudson Bay Company post over and over again. He had not eaten for two days; for a far longer time he had not had all he wanted to eat.

Often he stooped and picked pale muskeg berries, put them into his mouth, and chewed and swallowed them. A muskeg berry is a bit of seed enclosed in a bit of water. In the mouth the water melts away and the seed chews sharp and bitter. The man knew there was no nourishment in the berries, but he chewed them patiently with a hope greater than knowledge and defying experience.

At nine o'clock he stubbed[23] his toe on a rocky ledge, and from sheer weariness and weakness staggered and fell. He lay for some time, without movement, on his side. Then he slipped out of the pack-straps and clumsily dragged himself into a sitting posture. It was not yet dark, and in the lingering twilight he groped about among the rocks for shreds of dry moss. When he had gathered a heap he built a fire,—a smoldering, smudgy[24] fire,—and put a tin pot of water on to boil.

---

22 con [kɑːn] (v.) 仔細研究
23 stub [stʌb] (v.) 把（腳趾）碰在……上
24 smudgy [ˈsmʌdʒi] (a.) 模糊不清的

　　昏暗的太陽慢慢地往西北方落下，那個方向他踏遍了好幾次，他和比爾要趁著冬天降臨之前逃往南方。他滿腦子都是藏在石頭下的食物，還有哈德遜灣公司驛站裡的美食。他已經兩天沒吃東西了，而且好久未曾飽食一頓了。

　　他有時會彎下腰，撿起沼地上蒼白的莓果，把它們放到嘴裡嚼一嚼，然後吞下去。這種沼地的莓果只有一小粒種子，外面是一層漿水。一進到嘴裡，水就化掉了，種子咬起來又澀又苦。他知道這種莓果沒有營養，但他總得忍著咬下，雖然沒有營養又難吃，但總是一絲生機。

　　九點左右，他的腳趾頭踢到一塊石頭，因為他已經太虛弱，就摔了個跟斗。他側躺在那裡，有好一會兒一動也不動。之後，他撥下行囊的皮帶，笨重地掙扎著坐起來。天色還沒黑，在夕陽的餘暉中，他在石頭間摸索，尋找乾苔蘚。他收集了一堆乾苔蘚，生起一團朦朧的小火，然後把一個馬口鐵鍋擺在上面，開始煮水。

He unwrapped his pack and the first thing he did was to count his matches. There were sixty-seven. He counted them three times to make sure. He divided them into several portions, wrapping them in oil paper, disposing of one bunch in his empty tobacco pouch, of another bunch in the inside band of his battered hat, of a third bunch under his shirt on the chest. This accomplished, a panic came upon him, and he unwrapped them all and counted them again. There were still sixty-seven.

He dried his wet foot-gear by the fire. The moccasins[25] were in soggy shreds. The blanket socks were worn through in places, and his feet were raw and bleeding. His ankle was throbbing, and he gave it an examination. It had swollen to the size of his knee.

He tore a long strip from one of his two blankets and bound the ankle tightly. He tore other strips and bound them about his feet to serve for both moccasins and socks. Then he drank the pot of water, steaming hot, wound his watch, and crawled between his blankets.

He slept like a dead man. The brief darkness around midnight came and went. The sun arose in the northeast— at least the day dawned in that quarter, for the sun was hidden by gray clouds.

At six o'clock he awoke, quietly lying on his back. He gazed straight up into the gray sky and knew that he was hungry. As he rolled over on his elbow he was startled by a loud snort[26], and saw a bull caribou[27] regarding him with alert curiosity.

他打開行囊，先數數還有多少根火柴。總共還有六十七根。他一連數了三遍，確定數目之後，他把火柴分成幾堆，用油紙包起來，然後把一包放進空煙袋裡，一包放在一頂破帽子的帽圈裡，還有一包放在貼胸的上衣裡面。弄好之後，他突然一陣慌張，又取出那幾包油紙，把它們打開再數過一遍。還是六十七根。

他在火邊把濕掉的鞋襪烘乾。軟底鞋已經溼得裂成一片一片，氈襪子磨破了好幾個洞，兩隻腳凍得又紅又痛，還在流血。一隻腳踝脹得血管直跳，他檢了一下，腳踝已經腫到跟膝蓋一樣粗了。

他從他那兩條毯子當中撕下一個長條，把腳踝裹緊。然後又撕下幾條，裹在腳上，充當鞋子和襪子。最後他把那鍋滾燙的水喝了，然後上好手錶的發條，爬進兩條毯子的中間。

他睡得像死人一樣。午夜前後短暫的黑暗，來了又走。太陽從東北方升起，至少天空是從這個方位亮起來的，因為太陽被灰雲遮住了。

他在六點鐘的時候醒了過來，靜靜地躺在地上。他望著灰色的天空，知道自己肚子餓了。他撐著手肘轉過身來，突然被一個響亮的鼻息聲嚇了一跳，接著看到一隻公馴鹿正機警而好奇地看著他。

25 moccasin [ˈmɑːkəsɪn] (n.) 鹿皮製軟鞋（原為北美印地安人穿的鞋）
26 snort [snɔːrt] (n.) 從鼻孔噴氣的聲音
27 caribou [ˈkærɪbuː] (n.) 北美馴鹿

The animal was not more than fifty feet away, and instantly into the man's mind leaped the vision and the savor of a caribou steak sizzling and frying over a fire. Mechanically he reached for the empty gun, drew a bead[28], and pulled the trigger. The bull snorted and leaped away, his hoofs rattling and clattering as he fled across the ledges.

The man cursed and flung the empty gun from him. He groaned aloud as he started to drag himself to his feet. It was a slow and arduous task. His joints were like rusty hinges. They worked harshly in their sockets, with much friction, and each bending or unbending was accomplished only through a sheer exertion of will. When he finally gained his feet, another minute or so was consumed in straightening up, so that he could stand erect as a man should stand.

He crawled up a small knoll and surveyed the prospect. There were no trees, no bushes, nothing but a gray sea of moss scarcely diversified by gray rocks, gray lakelets, and gray streamlets.

The sky was gray. There was no sun nor hint of sun. He had no idea of north, and he had forgotten the way he had come to this spot the night before. But he was not lost. He knew that. Soon he would come to the land of the little sticks. He felt that it lay off to the left somewhere, not far—possibly just over the next low hill.

28 draw a bead (on . . .) 瞄準

　　這頭動物離他頂多十五公尺遠，他腦海裡立刻浮現鹿排在火堆上滋滋作響的畫面和香味。他本能地抓起空槍，瞄準，扣板機。馴鹿用鼻子呼哧一聲跳開，奔過岩石逃走，蹄下發出踢躂躂的聲音。

　　他大罵一聲，把空槍丟開。他一邊大聲咒罵，一邊掙扎著站起來。他吃力緩慢地爬起身子，關節就像生鏽的門軸，在骨臼裡嘎吱嘎吱地摩擦，每個彎曲和伸直的動作，都得費上很大的心力來完成。等到他不好容易站起來，還得花一會兒的工夫才能挺起腰，像個人類一樣挺直地站著。

　　他慢慢爬上一個小圓丘，觀察四周的地形。那裡看不到樹木或樹叢，什麼都沒有，只有一片一望無際的灰色苔蘚，偶爾點綴著幾塊灰色的岩石、幾片灰色的水潭，和幾條灰色的水流。

　　天空灰濛濛一片，看不到太陽，連太陽的影子也找不到。他看不出來哪一邊是北方，也忘了昨天晚上是怎麼走到這裡的。但是他沒有迷路，這一點他很明白，他很快就會走到那片枯枝之地。他覺得它就在左邊不遠的某個地方，說不定翻過下一座小山丘就到了。

He went back to put his pack into shape for traveling. He assured himself of the existence of his three separate parcels of matches, though he did not stop to count them. But he did linger, debating, over a squat[29] moose-hide[30] sack. It was not large. He could hide it under his two hands. He knew that it weighed fifteen pounds,—as much as all the rest of the pack,—and it worried him.

He finally set it to one side and proceeded to roll the pack. He paused to gaze at the squat moose-hide sack. He picked it up hastily with a defiant glance about him, as though the desolation were trying to rob him of it; and when he rose to his feet to stagger on into the day, it was included in the pack on his back.

He bore[31] away to the left, stopping now and again to eat muskeg berries. His ankle had stiffened, his limp was more pronounced, but the pain of it was as nothing compared with the pain of his stomach. The hunger pangs[32] were sharp. They gnawed and gnawed until he could not keep his mind steady on the course he must pursue to gain the land of little sticks. The muskeg berries did not allay this gnawing, while they made his tongue and the roof of his mouth sore with their irritating bite.

He came upon a valley where rock ptarmigan[33] rose on whirring[34] wings from the ledges and muskegs. Ker—ker— ker was the cry they made. He threw stones at them, but could not hit them. He placed his pack on the ground and stalked them as a cat stalks a sparrow.

他回到原地，整理行囊，準備出發。他確定一下三包分開放好的火柴還在，但是沒有停下來再數一遍。不過他還是為了一個寬寬短短的鹿皮袋子猶豫了一下，他想了又想，拿不定主意。那個袋子不大，兩隻手就可以抓住，大概有十五磅重，跟剩下的行囊一樣重，這讓他感到猶豫。

最後，他把袋子放到一旁，繼續打包。沒多久他又停下來，盯著袋子，然後連忙把它撿起來，用帶著敵意的眼神看看四周，好像那片荒原想把袋子搶走似的。接著，當他站起來跟跟蹌蹌、準備展開一天的路程時，袋子已經放在他背上的行囊裡了。

他朝著左方走，又不時地停下來撿沼地的莓果吃。他扭傷的腳踝已經僵硬，腳步變得更加一跛一跛。不過，痛歸痛，還比不上胃的難受。他餓得肚子發疼，一陣一陣絞得厲害，讓他難以冷靜地趕路前往枯枝之地。沼地的莓果安撫不了這種疼痛，而且莓果的苦澀還讓他的舌頭和口腔也痛了起來。

他來到一個山谷，山谷裡有松雞，牠們呼呼拍著翅膀，從石塊和沼地上飛起，發出咯咯咯的叫聲。他拿石頭扔向松雞，沒扔著。他把行囊放到地上，像貓捕麻雀那樣地偷偷靠近松雞。

29 squat [skwɑːt] (a.) 矮胖的
30 hide [haɪd] (n.) 獸皮
31 bear [ber] (v.) 朝……方向走
32 pang [pæŋ] (n.) 陣陣劇痛
33 ptarmigan ['tɑːrmɪɡən] (n.) 松雞類
34 whirr [wɜːr] (v.) 呼呼作響

❽
熱愛生命

The sharp rocks cut through his pants' legs till his knees left a trail of blood; but the hurt was lost in the hurt of his hunger. He squirmed[35] over the wet moss, saturating his clothes and chilling his body; but he was not aware of it, so great was his fever for food.

And always the ptarmigan rose, whirring, before him, till their ker—ker—ker became a mock to him, and he cursed them and cried aloud at them with their own cry.

Once he crawled upon one that must have been asleep. He did not see it till it shot up in his face from its rocky nook. He made a clutch as startled as was the rise of the ptarmigan, and there remained in his hand three tail-feathers. As he watched its flight he hated it, as though it had done him some terrible wrong. Then he returned and shouldered his pack.

As the day wore along he came into valleys or swales[36] where game was more plentiful. A band of caribou passed by, twenty and odd animals, tantalizingly[37] within rifle range. He felt a wild desire to run after them, a certitude that he could run them down. A black fox came toward him, carrying a ptarmigan in his mouth. The man shouted. It was a fearful cry, but the fox, leaping away in fright, did not drop the ptarmigan.

Late in the afternoon he followed a stream, milky with lime[38], which ran through sparse patches of rush-grass. Grasping these rushes firmly near the root, he pulled up what resembled a young onion-sprout no larger than a shingle-nail.

尖鋭的岩石劃破他的褲子，割破了膝蓋，在地上滴出一道血跡，不過他已經餓得不知道疼痛。他在潮濕的苔蘚上往前爬，衣服都濕透了，全身冰冷，但他已經餓得發狂，對這些事情毫無知覺。

不斷有松雞在他面前呼呼飛起，牠們咯咯的叫聲彷彿在嘲弄他。他咒罵牠們，對著牠們的叫聲大吼回去。

有一次，他沒發現自己爬到了一隻正在睡覺的松雞旁邊，等到松雞忽然從石頭角落朝他的臉飛過來時，他才看到松雞。松雞嚇得飛起來，他也嚇得伸手亂抓，結果抓到了三根尾巴上的羽毛。他看著松雞飛走，心裡恨得牙癢癢的，好像松雞跟他有仇似的。之後，他走回原地，背起行囊。

他沿途走過溪谷和沼澤，獵物也跟著變多。一群馴鹿緩緩走過，有二十多隻，而且都在他的射程內。他有一股強烈的欲望想追上去，覺得自己可以撞倒牠們。後來還有一隻黑狐狸朝他走過來，嘴裡叼著一隻松雞。他大吼一聲，嚇得狐狸趕緊開溜，只不過牠口中的松雞並未掉出來。

接近傍晚的時候，他沿著一條小溪走，溪水裡含有石灰，是乳白色的，流過稀稀疏疏的燈心草叢。他緊緊抓住燈心草的最底部，拉出跟瓦釘差不多大、長得有點像嫩洋蔥芽的東西。

---

35 squirm [skwɜːrm] (v.) 蠕動；扭動
36 swale [sweɪl] (n.) 潮濕的低地
37 tantalizingly [ˈtæntəlaɪzɪŋli] (adv.) 令人著急地
38 lime [laɪm] (n.) 石灰

It was tender, and his teeth sank into it with a crunch that promised deliciously of food. But its fibers were tough. It was composed of stringy filaments saturated with water, like the berries, and devoid of nourishment. He threw off his pack and went into the rush-grass on hands and knees, crunching and munching[39], like some bovine[40] creature.

He was very weary and often wished to rest—to lie down and sleep; but he was continually driven on—not so much by his desire to gain the land of little sticks as by his hunger. He searched little ponds for frogs and dug up the earth with his nails for worms, though he knew in spite that neither frogs nor worms existed so far north. He looked into every pool of water vainly, until, as the long twilight came on, he discovered a solitary fish, the size of a minnow[41], in such a pool.

He plunged his arm in up to the shoulder, but it eluded him. He reached for it with both hands and stirred up the milky mud at the bottom. In his excitement he fell in, wetting himself to the waist. Then the water was too muddy to admit of his seeing the fish, and he was compelled to wait until the sediment had settled.

The pursuit was renewed, till the water was again muddied. But he could not wait. He unstrapped the tin bucket and began to bale[42] the pool.

　　那個東西很嫩，他一口咬下去，發出嘎吱嘎吱的聲響，好像很美味的樣子，只不過它的纖維很硬，而且跟莓果一樣，只有飽含水分的纖維質，缺乏營養。他扔下行囊，趴到燈心草叢裡，像隻牛一樣嘎吱嘎吱地使勁嚼起來。

　　他累得時而想停下來休息，躺下來睡一覺，但也一直有什麼驅使著他繼續前進，倒不是因為他想去枯枝之地，而是飢餓感在驅策著他。他在小池塘找青蛙，用指甲挖泥土找蟲子，即使他也知道在這種北國之地根本不會有青蛙或蟲子。他每個水坑都找，都沒找著。不過，當漫長的暮色降臨後，他在水坑裡找到了一條小鯉魚般大小的魚。

　　他把整隻手臂伸進水裡，水都淹到了肩膀，結果魚還是溜掉了。他用兩隻手去抓，把池底的白色泥漿都攪了起來。最後他因為一個激動，跌進了池子裡，腰際以下都弄濕了。這下子池水混濁得根本看不到魚在哪裡，他只好先等著，等泥漿沉澱下來。

　　之後他再度開始抓魚，結果又把池水弄得一片混濁。但他等不及了，便從行囊上取下馬口鐵罐，把池水舀出來。

39　munch [mʌntʃ] (v.) 大聲咀嚼；使勁咀嚼
40　bovine ['boʊvaɪn] (a.) 牛一般的
41　minnow ['mɪnoʊ] (n.) 鯉科小魚
42　bale [beɪl] (v.) 把……裡面的水舀出來

He baled wildly at first, splashing himself and flinging the water so short a distance that it ran back into the pool. He worked more carefully, striving to be cool, though his heart was pounding against his chest and his hands were trembling.

At the end of half an hour the pool was nearly dry. Not a cupful of water remained. And there was no fish. He found a hidden crevice among the stones through which it had escaped to the adjoining and larger pool—a pool which he could not empty in a night and a day. Had he known of the crevice, he could have closed it with a rock at the beginning and the fish would have been his.

Thus he thought, and crumpled up[43] and sank down upon the wet earth. At first he cried softly to himself, then he cried loudly to the pitiless desolation that ringed him around; and for a long time after he was shaken by great dry sobs.

He built a fire and warmed himself by drinking quarts[44] of hot water, and made camp on a rocky ledge in the same fashion he had the night before. The last thing he did was to see that his matches were dry and to wind his watch.

The blankets were wet and clammy[45]. His ankle pulsed with pain. But he knew only that he was hungry, and through his restless sleep he dreamed of feasts and banquets and of food served and spread in all imaginable ways.

He awoke chilled and sick. There was no sun. The gray of earth and sky had become deeper, more profound. A raw wind was blowing, and the first flurries[46] of snow were whitening the hilltops.

他一開始就猛舀水，把自己都潑濕了，舀出來的水卻潑得不夠遠，流回了池子裡。於是他放慢動作，努力讓自己冷靜下來，儘管他的心臟砰砰地撞著胸口，兩隻手一直在發抖。

　　過了半小時之後，池子裡水被舀得只剩下不到一杯的水，可是卻什麼魚影都沒有。他這才發現，石頭間有個暗縫，魚就從那裡溜進旁邊的大水潭裡了——那個水潭很大，舀一天一夜也舀不完。如果他早一點看到這條隙縫，那他一開始只要用石頭把隙縫堵住，那麼那條魚現在就是他的了。

　　他一邊這麼想著，不料身子一坍，就陷進了潮濕的泥土裡。起初，他只是小聲地唉叫了一下，接著就對著周圍那片孤寂的荒原號啕大哭起來，抖著身子抽噎了好一陣子。

　　他升起一團火，喝了幾鍋熱水來暖和身子，然後跟昨晚一樣露宿在一塊平坦的岩石上。他睡前又檢查了一下火柴是不是乾的，然後上好手錶的發條。

　　兩條毯子又冷又濕又黏，他的腳踝隨著脈搏，一陣一陣地抽痛，不過他現在只有飢餓感。他整夜都沒睡好，還夢到了大餐，一道道的美食以各種方式端到他面前，擺滿整桌。

　　他醒來的時候，又冷又難受。天上看不到太陽，大地和天空的灰色變得更深、更濃了。一陣刺骨的寒風襲來，第一批大雪下得山頂都覆蓋上一層白雪。

43　crumple up 垮掉；崩潰
44　quart [kwɔːrt] (n.) 夸脫（容量單位，約相當於一公升）
45　clammy [ˈklæmi] (a.) 冷而濕黏的
46　flurry [ˈflɜːri] (n.) 小陣雪

The air about him thickened and grew white while he made a fire and boiled more water. It was wet snow, half rain, and the flakes were large and soggy. At first they melted as soon as they came in contact with the earth, but ever more fell, covering the ground, putting out the fire, spoiling his supply of moss-fuel.

This was a signal for him to strap on his pack and stumble onward, he knew not where. He was not concerned with the land of little sticks, nor with Bill and the cache under the upturned canoe by the river Dease. He was mastered by the verb "to eat." He was hunger-mad.

He took no heed of the course he pursued, so long as that course led him through the swale bottoms. He felt his way through the wet snow to the watery muskeg berries, and went by feel as he pulled up the rush-grass by the roots. But it was tasteless stuff and did not satisfy.

He found a weed that tasted sour and he ate all he could find of it, which was not much, for it was a creeping growth, easily hidden under the several inches of snow.

He had no fire that night, nor hot water, and crawled under his blanket to sleep the broken hunger-sleep. The snow turned into a cold rain. He awakened many times to feel it falling on his upturned face.

　　他在升火煮水時，周圍的空氣變得白濛濛的。天空下起了挾帶著雨水的濕雪，雪花又濕又大。雪花一落到地上就化了成水，接著越下越多，最後地面上覆蓋了一層雪花，澆熄了火，也弄濕了他要用來做燃料的乾苔蘚。

　　這表示他應該把行囊綁上，繼續蹣跚前進，只是他不知道要往哪裡走去。他不管什麼枯枝之地了，還有什麼比爾、什麼迪斯河邊獨木舟下藏的東西。他現在一心只想吃東西，他餓瘋了。

　　他不管該怎麼走了，只要走在沼澤谷底就行了。他在潮濕的雪地中摸索前進，尋找稀軟的沼地莓果，或是拉出燈心草根，只不過燈心草根沒有味道，也吃不飽。

　　後來他找到一種野草，吃起來酸酸的，他只要一看到就會把它吃掉，只是這種野草並不多。這種草貼著地面長，幾公分的雪一下子就把它蓋住了。

　　這天晚上，他沒有火，也沒有熱水。他鑽進毯子裡睡覺，不時地被餓醒。雪變成了冰冷的雨。他好幾次醒過來，感覺到雨水落在他仰著的臉上。

Day came—a gray day and no sun. It had ceased raining. The keenness of his hunger had departed. Sensibility, as far as concerned the yearning for food, had been exhausted. There was a dull, heavy ache in his stomach, but it did not bother him so much. He was more rational, and once more he was chiefly interested in the land of little sticks and the cache by the river Dease.

He ripped the remnant of one of his blankets into strips and bound his bleeding feet. Also, he recinched[47] the injured ankle and prepared himself for a day of travel. When he came to his pack, he paused long over the squat moose-hide sack, but in the end it went with him.

The snow had melted under the rain, and only the hilltops showed white. The sun came out, and he succeeded in locating the points of the compass, though he knew now that he was lost. Perhaps, in his previous days' wanderings, he had edged away too far to the left. He now bore off to the right to counteract the possible deviation from his true course.

Though the hunger pangs were no longer so exquisite[48], he realized that he was weak. He was compelled to pause for frequent rests, when he attacked the muskeg berries and rush-grass patches. His tongue felt dry and large, as though covered with a fine hairy growth, and it tasted bitter in his mouth.

---

47 recinch [rɪ'sɪntʃ] (v.) 重新綁緊
48 exquisite ['ekskwɪzɪt] (a.) （疼痛）嚴重的；極度的

　天亮了，又是灰濛濛的一天，看不到太陽。雨已經停了。他強烈的飢餓感消失了，最起碼，他渴望食物的知覺已經疲乏了。他只覺得胃隱隱作痛，但沒那麼難受了。他比較清醒了，又開始關心起枯枝之地和迪斯河邊藏的東西了。

　他把撕剩的毯子撕成長條，包裹流著血的雙腳，並且把受傷的腳踝也重新包紮過，準備好好走上一天的路。整理行囊時，他對著那個寬短的鹿皮小袋猶豫許久，最後還是一起帶上了路。

　下過雨後，積雪都融化了，只有山丘頂上還有白雪。太陽露出了，他終於能夠定出羅盤的方位了，儘管他知道自己迷路了。也許在前兩天的遊蕩中，他往左邊走太多了，他開始朝右邊走，想走回原來的路線。

　雖然飢餓所帶來的疼痛不再那麼強烈，但他發覺自己還是很虛弱。在撿沼地莓果或拔燈心草吃的時候，不時得停下來休息一下。他的舌頭又乾又腫，彷彿覆上了一層茸毛，吃的東西都變苦了。

His heart gave him a great deal of trouble. When he had traveled a few minutes it would begin a remorseless thump[49], thump, thump, and then leap up and away in a painful flutter[50] of beats that choked him and made him go faint and dizzy.

In the middle of the day he found two minnows in a large pool. It was impossible to bale it, but he was calmer now and managed to catch them in his tin bucket. They were no longer than his little finger, but he was not particularly hungry. The dull ache in his stomach had been growing duller and fainter. It seemed almost that his stomach was dozing.

He ate the fish raw, masticating[51] with painstaking care, for the eating was an act of pure reason. While he had no desire to eat, he knew that he must eat to live.

In the evening he caught three more minnows, eating two and saving the third for breakfast.

The sun had dried stray shreds of moss, and he was able to warm himself with hot water. He had not covered more than ten miles that day; and the next day, traveling whenever his heart permitted him, he covered no more than five miles. But his stomach did not give him the slightest uneasiness. It had gone to sleep.

He was in a strange country, too, and the caribou were growing more plentiful, also the wolves. Often their yelps drifted across the desolation, and once he saw three of them slinking[52] away before his path.

他的心臟也帶給他不少負擔。他只要走上幾分鐘，心臟就一陣無情的重捶[49]，砰砰砰地，然後猛地往上一頂，開始快速亂跳[50]，痛得他喘不過氣來，頭暈目眩的。

中午的時候，他在一個大水潭裡看到兩條小鯉魚。水潭的水是不可能舀光的，但現在他比較冷靜了，兩條魚都被他抓進了馬口鐵罐裡。這兩條魚跟他的小指頭差不多長，不過他倒沒那麼餓了。隱隱的胃痛已經越來越模糊，彷彿胃已經睡著了一樣。

他把魚生吃下去，仔細地咀嚼[51]，對他來說，吃東西現在純然是一種理性的行為。他並沒有胃口，但是他知道，為了活下去，他一定要吃東西。

傍晚的時候，他又抓到了三條小鯉魚。他吃了兩條，留下一條當作第二天的早餐。

太陽已經把地上零星散漫的苔蘚曬乾了，他可以喝點熱水暖暖身子了。這一天，他走了不到十六公里的路。隔天，只要心臟還撐得住，他就繼續走，但只走了不到八公里的路。他的胃再也沒有難受的感覺了，它已經睡著了。

他現在走到了一個陌生的地帶，馴鹿越來越多，野狼也越來越多。荒原上經常迴蕩著牠們的嗥聲，有一回，他還看到三隻野狼從他面前鬼鬼祟祟地走過[52]。

---

49 thump [θʌmp] (n.) 重擊；猛捶
50 flutter [ˈflʌtər] (n.) 快速不規則的跳動
51 masticate [ˈmæstɪkeɪt] (v.) 咀嚼
52 slink [slɪŋk] (v.) 鬼鬼祟祟地走

Another night; and in the morning, being more rational, he untied the leather string that fastened the squat moose-hide sack. From its open mouth poured a yellow stream of coarse gold-dust and nuggets[53]. He roughly divided the gold in halves, caching one half on a prominent ledge, wrapped in a piece of blanket, and returning the other half to the sack.

He also began to use strips of the one remaining blanket for his feet. He still clung to his gun, for there were cartridges in that cache by the river Dease. This was a day of fog, and this day hunger awoke in him again. He was very weak and was afflicted with a giddiness[54] which at times blinded him.

It was no uncommon thing now for him to stumble and fall; and stumbling once, he fell squarely into a ptarmigan nest. There were four newly hatched chicks, a day old— little specks[55] of pulsating life no more than a mouthful; and he ate them ravenously, thrusting them alive into his mouth and crunching them like egg-shells between his teeth.

The mother ptarmigan beat about him with great outcry. He used his gun as a club with which to knock her over, but she dodged out of reach. He threw stones at her and with one chance shot broke a wing. Then she fluttered away, running, trailing the broken wing, with him in pursuit.

又過了一晚。第二天早上，他比較清醒了，便把那個寬短的鹿皮袋子的皮繩解開，從裡面倒出黃色的粗砂金和塊金。他把黃金分成兩半，其中一半用毯子包起來，藏在一塊顯眼的大石頭上，另外一半則裝回袋子裡。

他還從剩下的毯子撕下幾段長條，包裹雙腳。他還是捨不得他的槍，因為迪斯河邊的石頭下面有子彈。這天起了霧，而他的飢餓感又醒來了。他很虛弱，而且頭很暈，常常暈得眼花撩亂。

現在對他來說，絆倒摔跤不是什麼稀奇的事。有一次，他絆倒，直接摔進一個松雞巢裡。巢裡有四隻剛孵出來的小松雞，才一天大——這個在搏動中的生命，那麼小，還不夠吃一口。他狼吞虎嚥起來，把牠們活生生地塞進嘴裡，嘎吱嘎吱地咬，像咬蛋殼一樣地在齒間把牠們咬碎。

母松雞拍著翅膀在他身邊尖聲大叫，他拿起槍，像拿棍子一樣地打下去，但是母松雞躲開了。他拿石頭丟牠，投中了一次，把牠的翅膀給打傷了。母松雞拍著翅膀跑走，受傷的翅膀拖在地面上，他在後面追著跑。

53 nugget ['nʌgɪt] (n.) 天然塊金
54 giddiness ['gɪdɪnɪs] (n.) 眩暈
55 speck [spɛk] (n.) 微小物

The little chicks had no more than whetted his appetite[56]. He hopped and bobbed[57] clumsily along on his injured ankle, throwing stones and screaming hoarsely at times; at other times hopping and bobbing silently along, picking himself up grimly and patiently when he fell, or rubbing his eyes with his hand when the giddiness threatened to overpower him.

The chase led him across swampy ground in the bottom of the valley, and he came upon footprints in the soggy moss. They were not his own—he could see that. They must be Bill's. But he could not stop, for the mother ptarmigan was running on. He would catch her first, then he would return and investigate.

He exhausted the mother ptarmigan; but he exhausted himself. She lay panting on her side. He lay panting on his side, a dozen feet away, unable to crawl to her. And as he recovered she recovered, fluttering out of reach as his hungry hand went out to her. The chase was resumed.

Night settled down and she escaped. He stumbled from weakness and pitched head foremost on his face, cutting his cheek, his pack upon his back. He did not move for a long while; then he rolled over on his side, wound his watch, and lay there until morning.

Another day of fog. Half of his last blanket had gone into foot-wrappings. He failed to pick up Bill's trail. It did not matter. His hunger was driving him too compellingly—only—only he wondered if Bill, too, were lost.

那幾隻小松雞讓他開了胃。他拖著受傷的腳踝，一瘸一拐單腳跳著追上去，一邊對母松雞丟石頭，一邊粗聲吆喝。有時候，他就只是不出一聲地一路往前跳，摔倒了就咬著牙、耐心地爬起來，或是在快暈過去的時候，用手揉揉眼睛。

　　這場追逐領著他穿過谷底的沼地。在潮濕的苔蘚地上，他看到人的腳印。那不是他的腳印——他看得出來。那一定是比爾的腳印，但是他不能停下來，因為母松雞還在跑。他要先抓到牠，然後再回來研究腳印。

　　母松雞被他追得筋疲力竭，而他自己也追得累壞了。母松雞側躺在地上喘個不停，他也是。他離母松雞只有三、四公尺遠，卻沒有力氣爬過去。等到他恢復力氣了，母松雞也恢復力氣，當他飢餓的雙手伸過去，母松雞便拍著翅膀跑開。一場追逐遂又重新開始。

　　到了天黑時，母松雞逃過一劫。他因為渾身無力，絆了一跤，跌了個狗吃屎，割破了臉頰，讓行囊壓在背上。他靜靜躺在那裡好一陣子，之後才翻過身，側躺在地上，上好手錶的發條，然後就地躺到了早晨。

　　這一天又起霧了。他剩下的那條毯子，有一半都拿去包腳了。他沒有找到比爾的腳印，但這不打緊。他餓得受不了了——只是——只是他又在想，會不會比爾也迷路了。

56 whet somebody's appetite 激起食欲
57 bob [bɑ:b] (v.) 上下跳動

By midday the irk[58] of his pack became too oppressive. Again he divided the gold, this time merely spilling half of it on the ground. In the afternoon he threw the rest of it away, there remaining to him only the half-blanket, the tin bucket, and the rifle.

A hallucination began to trouble him. He felt confident that one cartridge remained to him. It was in the chamber[59] of the rifle and he had overlooked it. On the other hand, he knew all the time that the chamber was empty. But the hallucination persisted. He fought it off for hours, then threw his rifle open and was confronted with emptiness. The disappointment was as bitter as though he had really expected to find the cartridge.

He plodded[60] on for half an hour, when the hallucination arose again. Again he fought it, and still it persisted, till for very relief he opened his rifle to unconvince himself.

At times his mind wandered farther afield, and he plodded on, a mere automaton, strange conceits and whimsicalities[61] gnawing at his brain like worms. But these excursions out of the real were of brief duration, for ever the pangs of the hunger-bite called him back.

He was jerked back abruptly once from such an excursion by a sight that caused him nearly to faint. He reeled and swayed, doddering[62] like a drunken man to keep from falling. Before him stood a horse. A horse! He could not believe his eyes. A thick mist was in them, intershot with sparkling points of light.

走到了中午時，他覺得行囊太重，又把黃金分成兩半。這一次，他直接把一半的黃金灑在地上。到了下午時，他把剩下的那一點黃金也扔掉，身上只剩下半條毯子、一個馬口鐵罐和一枝槍。

一種幻覺開始折磨他。他覺得自己身上一定還有一發子彈，就裝在槍膛裡，只是他沒看到。但另一方面，他又始終都知道槍膛裡是空的。這種幻覺縈繞不去，他掙扎了好幾個小時，想擺脫幻覺，最後，他把槍膛甩開，看到裡面什麼都沒有。他內心的失望難以言喻，彷彿他真的認為會在裡面發現子彈。

他拖著沉重的步伐繼續往前走，走了半小時，幻覺又出現了。他奮力想擺脫，但是幻覺揮之不去，直到他又把槍膛打開，用事實說服自己。

有時候，他的心思一路飄遊到遠方，一方面繼續拖著沉重的腳步，無魂地往前走，各種奇異的想像如蟲子一般啃咬著他的腦袋。這些脫離現實的幻想都很短暫，因為陣陣的胃痛總會把他喚回來。

有一次，一個差點令他昏厥的幻覺，把他猛然拉回現實。當時他跟跟蹌蹌、搖搖擺擺，像個醉漢要倒不倒地蹣跚前進。這時，他看到眼前站著一匹馬。一匹馬！他不敢相信自己的眼睛。他的眼睛一片矇矓，有時還會看到光點。

58　irk [ɜːrk] (n.) 負擔
59　chamber [ˈtʃeɪmbər] (n.) 槍膛
60　plod [plɑːd] (v.) 步履艱難地走
61　whimsicality [ˌwɪmzɪˈkælɪti] (n.) 奇想
62　dodder [ˈdɔːdər] (v.) 搖搖晃晃地走

He rubbed his eyes savagely to clear his vision, and beheld, not a horse, but a great brown bear. The animal was studying him with bellicose[63] curiosity.

The man had brought his gun halfway to his shoulder before he realized. He lowered it and drew his hunting-knife from its beaded sheath at his hip.

Before him was meat and life. He ran his thumb along the edge of his knife. It was sharp. The point was sharp. He would fling himself upon the bear and kill it. But his heart began its warning thump, thump, thump. Then followed the wild upward leap and tattoo[64] of flutters, the pressing as of an iron band about his forehead, the creeping of the dizziness into his brain.

His desperate courage was evicted[65] by a great surge of fear. In his weakness, what if the animal attacked him? He drew himself up to his most imposing[66] stature, gripping the knife and staring hard at the bear.

The bear advanced clumsily a couple of steps, reared up, and gave vent to a tentative growl. If the man ran, he would run after him; but the man did not run. He was animated now with the courage of fear. He, too, growled, savagely, terribly, voicing the fear that is to life germane[67] and that lies twisted about life's deepest roots.

The bear edged[68] away to one side, growling menacingly, himself appalled by this mysterious creature that appeared upright and unafraid. But the man did not move. He stood like a statue till the danger was past, when he yielded to a fit of trembling and sank down into the wet moss.

他用力揉揉眼睛，看清楚了面前站的不是一匹馬，而是一隻大棕熊。那頭動物正用著一副好奇而挑釁的眼神在打量他。

他抓起槍，但槍還沒舉到肩上他就想起來了裡頭沒有子彈。他把槍放下，從臀後的鑲珠刀鞘裡拔出獵刀。

站在他面前的，是一個血肉之軀。他用大拇指滑過刀刃，刀刃很利，刀鋒也很利。他會一把撲上去，把熊刺死。然而，他的心臟開始響起警告的砰砰聲，接著猛地往上一頂，開始快速亂跳，他的頭像是被鐵箍緊緊箍住，一陣暈眩襲來。

他孤注一擲的勇氣，被一陣極度的恐懼驅散。他這麼虛弱，如果那頭熊攻擊他，怎麼辦？他使出全身力氣，盡可能擺出最具威嚴的姿態，手裡握著獵刀，狠狠地瞪著那頭熊。

那頭熊笨拙地往前走了幾步，然後站直身子，試探性地大吼一聲。如果前面的這個人類跑了，牠就會追上去，但人類並沒有跑開。此時恐懼反而激起了他的勇氣，他也大吼了一聲，又兇又狠，在這個生死關頭，把生命最深層的恐懼都吼了出來。

大棕熊轉身慢慢往旁邊移動，一邊發出威脅的低吼，這個直立而毫無恐懼的神秘動物震住了牠。這個人類紋風不動，像個雕像一樣地站著。最後等到危險解除了，他才一陣哆嗦，在潮濕的苔蘚地上跪了下來。

63 bellicose [ˈbelɪkoʊs] (a.) 好鬥的
64 tattoo [təˈtuː] (n.) 連續而快速的鼓聲
65 evict [ɪˈvɪkt] (v.) 驅逐
66 imposing [ɪmˈpoʊzɪŋ] (a.) 威嚴的；氣勢雄偉的
67 germane [dʒɜːrˈmeɪn] (a.) 貼切的；恰當的
68 edge [edʒ] (v.) 慢慢往某個方向移動

8

熱愛生命

He pulled himself together and went on, afraid now in a new way. It was not the fear that he should die passively from lack of food, but that he should be destroyed violently before starvation had exhausted the last particle of the endeavor in him that made toward surviving.

There were the wolves. Back and forth across the desolation drifted their howls, weaving the very air into a fabric of menace that was so tangible that he found himself, arms in the air, pressing it back from him as it might be the walls of a wind-blown tent.

Now and again the wolves, in packs of two and three, crossed his path. But they sheered[69] clear of him. They were not in sufficient numbers, and besides they were hunting the caribou, which did not battle, while this strange creature that walked erect might scratch and bite.

In the late afternoon he came upon scattered bones where the wolves had made a kill. The debris had been a caribou calf an hour before, squawking[70] and running and very much alive. He contemplated the bones, clean-picked and polished, pink with the cell-life in them which had not yet died.

Could it possibly be that he might be that ere the day was done! Such was life, eh? A vain and fleeting thing. It was only life that pained. There was no hurt in death. To die was to sleep. It meant cessation, rest. Then why was he not content to die?

　　他振作起來，繼續往前走，心裡又有了新的恐懼。他不怕自己會因為沒得吃而慢慢餓死，但他擔心自己在還沒餓到喪盡求生的力氣之前，就會被大塊朵頤。

　　荒原上有野狼，牠們的嗥叫聲四處迴盪，瀰漫著險惡的氣息，隨時逼近過來，就像風將帷幕徐徐吹過來一樣，他意識到自己舉起了雙臂，想把帷幕擋開。

　　偶而可以看到三三兩兩的野狼，從他面前走過，不過狼隻們都繞過他。牠們的數量還不夠多，況且牠們的目標是馴鹿。馴鹿不會反抗，而這個直立的奇怪動物可能會抓、會咬。

　　接近傍晚時，他在路上看到野狼獵食後所留下的一堆骨頭。在一個小時之前，這堆殘骸還是一隻小馴鹿，又叫又跑，活蹦亂跳的。他端詳著這堆骨頭，骨頭被啃得乾淨光亮，骨頭裡是粉紅色的，那裡還有一些尚未死掉的細胞。

　　他自己會不會在天黑之前也成為一堆骨頭？生命就是如此嗎？虛無又短暫？有生命，才會令人痛苦，死了，就毫無知覺。死去，就是睡去，就是停下來，就是休息。既然如此，他有什麼不甘心的？

69 sheer [ʃɪr] (v.) 避開
70 squawk [skwɑːk] (v.) 發出又尖又響的叫聲

❽
熱愛生命

But he did not moralize[71] long. He was squatting in the moss, a bone in his mouth, sucking at the shreds of life that still dyed it faintly pink. The sweet meaty taste, thin and elusive almost as a memory, maddened him. He closed his jaws on the bones and crunched. Sometimes it was the bone that broke, sometimes his teeth.

Then he crushed the bones between rocks, pounded them to a pulp, and swallowed them. He pounded his fingers, too, in his haste, and yet found a moment in which to feel surprise at the fact that his fingers did not hurt much when caught under the descending rock.

Came frightful days of snow and rain. He did not know when he made camp, when he broke camp. He traveled in the night as much as in the day. He rested wherever he fell, crawled on whenever the dying life in him flickered up and burned less dimly.

He, as a man, no longer strove. It was the life in him, unwilling to die, that drove him on. He did not suffer. His nerves had become blunted, numb, while his mind was filled with weird visions and delicious dreams. But ever he sucked and chewed on the crushed bones of the caribou calf, the least remnants of which he had gathered up and carried with him.

He crossed no more hills or divides, but automatically followed a large stream which flowed through a wide and shallow valley. He did not see this stream nor this valley. He saw nothing save visions. Soul and body walked or crawled side by side, yet apart, so slender was the thread that bound them.

他才思索了一下子，就在苔蘚上蹲下來，嘴裡放著一根骨頭，吸吮著骨頭裡還帶有血色的骨髓。這種肉的鮮味，像矇矇矓矓的記憶，令他發狂。他往骨頭一口咬下，嘎吱嘎吱啃了起來，嘴裡咬碎的有時候是骨頭，有時候是他自己的牙齒。

他拿起石頭對著骨頭砸下去，然後把骨頭輾碎，吞下肚子裡。他急急忙忙的，石頭砸到了自己的手指頭，不過他嚇了一跳，因為手指頭好像不太會痛。

接下來的幾天，下起了大雪和大雨。他也搞不清楚自己紮營拔營的時間到底是什麼時候，他在夜晚和白天的活動時間差不多長。他只要摔了跤，便就地休息；等到他奄奄一息的性命又有了一點點氣力，他就繼續緩慢地前進。

身為人，他其實已經不再掙扎了。不甘心死去的，是他體內的生命本能，驅策著他繼續前進。他並不痛苦，他的神經已經遲鈍、麻木，他腦海裡只有奇幻的畫面，還有大塊朵頤的白日夢。他就這樣一路啃吮著小馴鹿的碎骨頭，他把那些殘屑骨骸收集起來，帶在身上。

他不再翻越小山丘或分水嶺，只是無意識地沿著一條大河走。大河流過一片寬闊平淺的山谷，但他看不到大河，也看不到山谷，他只看得到幻象。他的靈魂和身體已經分離，各自肩並肩地走著或爬行著，兩者之間的連繫非常微弱。

71 moralize [ˈmɔːrəlaɪz] (v.) 說教

He awoke in his right mind[72], lying on his back on a
rocky ledge. The sun was shining bright and warm. Afar off
he heard the squawking of caribou calves. He was aware of
vague memories of rain and wind and snow, but whether
he had been beaten by the storm for two days or two
weeks he did not know.

For some time he lay without movement, the genial
sunshine pouring upon him and saturating his miserable
body with its warmth. A fine day, he thought. Perhaps he
could manage to locate himself.

By a painful effort he rolled over on his side. Below him
flowed a wide and sluggish river. Its unfamiliarity puzzled
him. Slowly he followed it with his eyes, winding in wide
sweeps[73] among the bleak, bare hills, bleaker and barer
and lower-lying than any hills he had yet encountered.

Slowly, deliberately, without excitement or more than
the most casual interest, he followed the course of the
strange stream toward the sky-line and saw it emptying
into a bright and shining sea. He was still unexcited. Most
unusual, he thought, a vision or a mirage[74]—more likely a
vision, a trick of his disordered mind.

He was confirmed in this by sight of a ship lying at
anchor in the midst of the shining sea. He closed his eyes
for a while, then opened them. Strange how the vision
persisted! Yet not strange. He knew there were no seas
or ships in the heart of the barren lands, just as he had
known there was no cartridge in the empty rifle.

他躺在一塊岩石上醒來時，意識正常。這時陽光明亮而溫暖，他聽到遠處傳來一群小馴鹿又尖又響的叫聲。他還隱約記得有下過雨，有刮過風，也有下過雪，但他不記得已經被風雨吹打了兩天，還是兩個星期。

他靜靜地躺了半晌，和煦的陽光灑在身上，溫暖他可憐的身軀。他想，今天天氣真好，搞不好可以找出方位。

他咬著牙吃力地翻過身，側躺在岩石上。岩石下緩緩流過一條寬闊的河流，這條河看起來很陌生，令他困惑了起來。他慢慢地沿著河流望去，只見河流蜿蜒穿過一座座荒涼光禿的山丘，這是他見過最荒涼、最光禿禿、最低的山丘了。

他心情並不激動，也不特別好奇，只是從容緩慢地沿著陌生的河流一路望向天際，看見它流入一片明亮閃耀的大海。他內心還是很平靜，他想，這麼不尋常，這是幻象還是海市蜃樓——應該是幻象吧，他心智不正常時才會看到的。

看到那片閃耀的大海上停著一艘大船時，他就更加確信是幻象。他把眼睛閉上一會兒後再張開，怪了，幻象還在！但這也不是什麼怪事啦，他心裡明白，在這片荒涼的凍原上，沒有大海，也沒有大船，就跟他知道那把空槍裡沒有子彈一樣。

72 in one's right mind 精神正常
73 sweep [swi:p] (n.) 連綿彎曲的河流
74 mirage [mɪˈrɑːʒ] (n.) 海市蜃樓

He heard a snuffle[75] behind him—a half-choking gasp or cough. Very slowly, because of his exceeding weakness and stiffness, he rolled over on his other side. He could see nothing near at hand, but he waited patiently.

Again came the snuffle and cough, and outlined between two jagged[76] rocks not a score of feet away he made out[77] the gray head of a wolf. The sharp ears were not pricked so sharply as he had seen them on other wolves; the eyes were bleared[78] and bloodshot, the head seemed to droop limply and forlornly. The animal blinked continually in the sunshine. It seemed sick. As he looked it snuffled and coughed again.

This, at least, was real, he thought, and turned on the other side so that he might see the reality of the world which had been veiled from him before by the vision. But the sea still shone in the distance and the ship was plainly discernible. Was it reality, after all?

He closed his eyes for a long while and thought, and then it came to him. He had been making north by east, away from the Dease Divide and into the Coppermine Valley. This wide and sluggish river was the Coppermine. That shining sea was the Arctic Ocean. That ship was a whaler, strayed east, far east, from the mouth of the Mackenzie, and it was lying at anchor in Coronation Gulf.

He remembered the Hudson Bay Company chart he had seen long ago, and it was all clear and reasonable to him.

他聽到身後有吸鼻子的聲音，像是有點哽住的喘氣聲或是咳嗽聲之類的。他因為身體很虛弱僵硬，很慢很慢地才翻過身來，轉到另一側。他沒看到附近有什麼東西，但是他耐心地等待著。

他又聽了到吸鼻子和咳嗽的聲音，他在六公尺外兩塊尖突的大石頭之間，隱約看到一個灰色的野狼頭。那隻野狼的一雙尖耳朵不像其他野狼那樣地垂直豎起，牠的兩隻眼睛昏暗無光，充滿血絲，有氣無力地垂著頭，可憐兮兮的。這頭動物在陽光下不停地眨著眼睛，看起來是生病了。他盯著牠看時，牠又開始吸鼻子和咳嗽。

這次可不是幻象了吧，他一邊想著，一邊翻身回去。這下不會再看到剛剛的幻象，而是可以看到真實的世界了吧。然而，遠處依然有一片大海在閃耀著，那艘大船依舊清晰可辨。莫非，這是真的？

他閉上眼睛，想了好一會兒，然後他想通了：他一直朝著東北方走，離迪斯分水嶺越來越遠，最後走到科珀曼河谷了。這條寬闊緩慢的河流，正是科珀曼河。那片閃耀的大海，就是北極海。那艘大船，是一艘捕鯨船，從麥肯錫河口一路向東駛過來，現在停泊在加冕灣。

他想起很久以前看過的那張哈德遜灣公司的地圖，現在，一切都變得清楚合理了。

---

75 snuffle [ˈsnʌfəl] (n.) 吸鼻子的聲音
76 jagged [ˈdʒæɡɪd] (a.) 尖突的；邊緣不整齊的
77 make out 勉強看出
78 bleared [blɪrd] (a.)（因疲勞）眼睛發紅而視力模糊

❽ 熱愛生命

He sat up and turned his attention to immediate affairs. He had worn through the blanket-wrappings, and his feet were shapeless lumps of raw meat. His last blanket was gone. Rifle and knife were both missing. He had lost his hat somewhere, with the bunch of matches in the band, but the matches against his chest were safe and dry inside the tobacco pouch and oil paper. He looked at his watch. It marked eleven o'clock and was still running. Evidently he had kept it wound.

He was calm and collected. Though extremely weak, he had no sensation of pain. He was not hungry. The thought of food was not even pleasant to him, and whatever he did was done by his reason alone.

He ripped off his pants' legs to the knees and bound them about his feet. Somehow he had succeeded in retaining the tin bucket. He would have some hot water before he began what he foresaw was to be a terrible journey to the ship.

His movements were slow. He shook as with a palsy[79]. When he started to collect dry moss, he found he could not rise to his feet. He tried again and again, then contented himself with crawling about on hands and knees.

Once he crawled near to the sick wolf. The animal dragged itself reluctantly out of his way, licking its chops[80] with a tongue which seemed hardly to have the strength to curl. The man noticed that the tongue was not the customary healthy red. It was a yellowish brown and seemed coated with a rough and half-dry mucus.

他坐起來，轉而注意到切身的問題：裹在腳上的毯子已經被他磨破了，他光著兩隻腳，腳變得奇形怪狀的；他僅存的一條毯子已經用完了；槍和刀，都不見了；帽子也不知掉在哪裡了，帽圈裡那包火柴也跟著不見了，不過放在胸口的火柴還在，它還用油紙包著裝在小煙袋裡，很安全，而且還是乾燥的。他看看手錶，時針指著十一點鐘，還在走，顯然他一直都有記得要上發條。

　　他現在很冷靜、很沉著。雖然身體很虛弱，但不會痛。他也不餓，甚至光是想到食物就會不舒服。他現在做的任何事，純粹都是基於理性。

　　他把膝蓋以下的褲腳撕下來，拿來裹腳。沒想到，那個馬口鐵罐子竟然還安在。出發之前，他要先喝點熱水，他知道要走到船那裡，會費上好一番工夫。

　　他的動作很慢，還會像中風病人一樣地發著抖。他想採集乾苔蘚，卻發現腳抬不起來。他試了幾次，最後只得四肢著地用爬的。

　　有一次，他爬到了那隻病狼的附近，那頭動物拖著身子不情願地讓開了，然後伸出像是連捲舌都沒力氣的舌頭，舔拭著嘴巴四周。他注意到狼的舌頭沒有健康的血色，而是黃黃暗暗的，而且覆蓋著一層粗粗乾乾的黏液。

---

79 palsy [ˈpɔːlzi] (n.) 麻痺；癱瘓
80 chops [tʃɔːps] (n.) 嘴巴四周

After he had drunk a quart of hot water the man found he was able to stand, and even to walk as well as a dying man might be supposed to walk. Every minute or so he was compelled to rest. His steps were feeble and uncertain, just as the wolf's that trailed him were feeble and uncertain; and that night, when the shining sea was blotted out[81] by blackness, he knew he was nearer to it by no more than four miles.

Throughout the night he heard the cough of the sick wolf, and now and then the squawking of the caribou calves. There was life all around him, but it was strong life, very much alive and well, and he knew the sick wolf clung to the sick man's trail in the hope that the man would die first.

In the morning, on opening his eyes, he beheld it regarding him with a wistful[82] and hungry stare. It stood crouched[83], with tail between its legs, like a miserable and woe-begone dog. It shivered in the chill morning wind, and grinned dispiritedly when the man spoke to it in a voice that achieved no more than a hoarse whisper.

The sun rose brightly, and all morning the man tottered and fell toward the ship on the shining sea. The weather was perfect. It was the brief Indian Summer[84] of the high latitudes. It might last a week. Tomorrow or next day it might be gone.

　　喝下一夸脱的熱水後，他發現自己可以站起來了，甚至還可以用垂死者的走路樣子來走路。他每走一、兩分鐘，就得停下來休息一下。他的腳步很虛弱，走不穩，跟在他後頭的那隻狼，也跟他一樣。當天晚上，當黑夜籠罩住那片閃耀的大海時，他知道自己離船更近了，儘管今天還走不到六公里半。

　　這一夜，他不時聽到那隻病狼的咳嗽聲，偶爾還有小馴鹿的尖叫聲。他的四周充滿了生命，而且都是強壯的生命，健康而活躍；他知道，那隻病狼就跟在他這個病人的後面，寄望著他會先死去。

　　早晨，他睜開眼睛，看到那隻狼正用著飢渴的眼神覬覦著他。牠趴在地上，尾巴夾在兩腿之間，像一條可憐而悲哀的狗。牠在早晨的寒風中直發抖，他對牠說話，聲音很微弱，像沙沙的耳語，牠無精打采地對他咧了咧嘴。

　　旭日東升，照亮了大地。整個上午，他跟跟蹌蹌、走走跌跌，朝著閃爍海面上的那艘船前進。天氣很好，這是高緯度地區短暫的秋老虎時節，會持續個一星期左右，而明天或後天大概就會結束。

81　blot something out 遮住；掩蓋
82　wistful ['wɪstfəl] (a.) 渴望的；苦思妄想的
83　crouch [kraʊtʃ] (v.) 蹲伏
84　Indian Summer 秋老虎（小陽春，深秋時節突然特別暖活的天氣）

In the afternoon the man came upon a trail. It was of another man, who did not walk, but who dragged himself on all fours. The man thought it might be Bill, but he thought in a dull, uninterested way. He had no curiosity. In fact, sensation and emotion had left him. He was no longer susceptible[85] to pain. Stomach and nerves had gone to sleep.

Yet the life that was in him drove him on. He was very weary, but it refused to die. It was because it refused to die that he still ate muskeg berries and minnows, drank his hot water, and kept a wary eye on the sick wolf.

He followed the trail of the other man who dragged himself along, and soon came to the end of it—a few fresh-picked bones where the soggy moss was marked by the foot-pads of many wolves.

He saw a squat moose-hide sack, mate to his own, which had been torn by sharp teeth. He picked it up, though its weight was almost too much for his feeble fingers. Bill had carried it to the last. Ha! ha! He would have the laugh on Bill.

He would survive and carry it to the ship in the shining sea. His mirth[86] was hoarse and ghastly, like a raven's croak, and the sick wolf joined him, howling lugubriously[87]. The man ceased suddenly. How could he have the laugh on Bill if that were Bill; if those bones, so pinky-white and clean, were Bill?

下午的時候，他在路上看到一道蹤跡，那是別人留下的，而且那個人不是用走的，而是趴在地上用爬的。他想這個人可能是比爾，但是他只是冷冷地閃過這個念頭罷了。他沒有什麼好奇心了，事實上，感覺和情感早已經離開他了。他已經不會感覺到疼痛，胃和神經都睡著了。

　　是他體內的生命本能，驅策他繼續前進的。他很累，但生命的本能不肯就這樣死去。正因為不肯死去，他才繼續吃沼地的莓果和小鯉魚，繼續喝他的熱水，小心提防那隻病狼。

　　他一路跟著那個趴在地上往前爬的人的痕跡，不久就走到了痕跡的盡頭——潮濕的苔蘚上，攤著幾根才剛被啃光的骨頭，旁邊是一群野狼的腳印。

　　他看到一個寬短的鹿皮袋子，就跟他自己的一樣，袋子已經被尖利的牙齒撕裂。他把袋子撿起來，他虛弱的手指還差一點拿不動。比爾到最後一刻，都還帶著袋子。哈！哈！現在反倒是他嘲笑起比爾了。

　　而他會活下去的，會把袋子帶到閃閃海面上的那艘船上。他的笑聲沙啞而可怕，就像烏鴉的叫聲，而那隻病狼也加入他，悲嗥起來。但他突然又停了下來，如果，那個人真的是比爾，如果這堆被啃個精光、帶著血色的白骨是比爾的，他怎麼笑得出來？

---

85 susceptible [səˈseptəbəl] (a.) 易受影響的；敏感的

86 mirth [mɜːrθ] (n.) 歡笑

87 lugubriously [luˈgjuːbrɪəsli] (adv.) 憂傷地；悲哀地

He turned away. Well, Bill had deserted him; but he would not take the gold, nor would he suck Bill's bones. Bill would have, though, had it been the other way around, he mused as he staggered on.

He came to a pool of water. Stooping over in quest of minnows, he jerked his head back as though he had been stung. He had caught sight of his reflected face. So horrible was it that sensibility awoke long enough to be shocked.

There were three minnows in the pool, which was too large to drain; and after several ineffectual attempts to catch them in the tin bucket he forbore[88]. He was afraid, because of his great weakness, that he might fall in and drown. It was for this reason that he did not trust himself to the river astride one of the many drift-logs which lined its sand-spits[89].

That day he decreased the distance between him and the ship by three miles; the next day by two—for he was crawling now as Bill had crawled; and the end of the fifth day found the ship still seven miles away and him unable to make even a mile a day.

Still the Indian Summer held on, and he continued to crawl and faint, turn and turn about; and ever the sick wolf coughed and wheezed[90] at his heels. His knees had become raw meat like his feet, and though he padded them with the shirt from his back it was a red track he left behind him on the moss and stones.

他轉身走開了。沒錯，比爾是丟下了他，但他不會把那袋黃金帶走，也不會啃比爾的骨頭。就算情況如果反過來，比爾會帶走他的黃金、啃他的骨頭，他一邊搖搖晃晃地往前走，一邊這麼想著。

他來到一個水坑前。他彎下腰，想看看裡面有沒有小鯉魚，卻又突然把頭縮回來，像是被什麼叮到了一樣。他看到了自己映在水面上的臉！那張臉那麼可怕，他的知覺被嚇得都醒了過來。

水坑裡有三隻小鯉魚。水坑很大，不可能把水舀光。他想用馬口鐵罐把魚撈起來，但撈了好幾次都撈不起來，就放棄了。他擔心自己這麼虛弱，不小心摔下去就會溺死，也因為這樣，他沒有坐上河流岸邊的浮木順流而下。

這一天，他離那艘船的距離縮短了五公里；第二天，縮短了三公里多——因為他現在就跟比爾一樣，是趴在地上用爬的；到了第五天晚上，他發現自己離船還有十一公里左右，而他現在一天連一公里半也爬不了了。

秋老虎還持續著，他繼續爬行，繼續昏厥，繼續翻滾掙扎。那隻病狼也一直跟在他後面，不停地咳嗽和喘息。他的膝蓋已經和雙腳一樣，成了一個肉團，他雖然撕下背上的上衣來墊膝蓋，但是苔蘚和石頭上還是留下了一條紅色的血跡。

88 forbear [fɔːrˈber] (v.) 克制
89 spit [spɪt] (n.)（伸入水域的）岬
90 wheeze [wiːz] (v.) 喘息

❽
熱愛生命

Once, glancing back, he saw the wolf licking hungrily his bleeding trail, and he saw sharply what his own end might be—unless—unless he could get the wolf. Then began as grim a tragedy of existence as was ever played—a sick man that crawled, a sick wolf that limped, two creatures dragging their dying carcasses[91] across the desolation and hunting each other's lives.

Had it been a well wolf, it would not have mattered so much to the man; but the thought of going to feed the maw[92] of that loathsome and all but dead thing was repugnant[93] to him. He was finicky[94]. His mind had begun to wander again, and to be perplexed by hallucinations, while his lucid intervals grew rarer and shorter.

He was awakened once from a faint by a wheeze close in his ear. The wolf leaped lamely back, losing its footing and falling in its weakness. It was ludicrous[95], but he was not amused. Nor was he even afraid. He was too far gone for that.

But his mind was for the moment clear, and he lay and considered. The ship was no more than four miles away. He could see it quite distinctly when he rubbed the mists out of his eyes, and he could see the white sail of a small boat cutting the water of the shining sea.

91 carcass ['kɑːrkəs] (n.) 軀體
92 maw [mɑː] (n.) 動物的咽喉或胃
93 repugnant [rɪ'pʌgnənt] (a.) 令人反感的
94 finicky ['fɪnɪki] (a.) 挑剔的
95 ludicrous ['luːdɪkrəs] (a.) 滑稽可笑的

有一次，他回頭一瞥，看到那隻病狼正貪婪地舔著他的血跡，他立刻清楚地看到自己可能的下場——除非——除非他先下手為強。一齣殘酷的生存悲劇於是上演——一個爬行的病人，一隻跛行的病狼，兩頭生物在荒原上各自拖著垂死的身軀，想要獵取彼此的性命。

　　如果那是一頭健康的狼，他也不會那麼在乎了。但是一想到要給一頭垂死的噁心動物當食物吃，他就反感。他就是這麼挑剔。他又開始神遊了，他被幻覺弄得迷迷糊糊的，而且清醒的時間越來越少、越來越短。

　　有一次，他昏倒後被耳邊一陣喘息聲驚醒。那頭狼一跛一跛地跳回去，又因為太虛弱，一個沒站穩跌在地上。那畫面很滑稽，但是他不覺得好笑，甚至也沒被嚇到，他早就不怕這種事了。

　　在這一刻，他的頭腦很清醒，他躺在那裡，開始思考。他離船已經不到六公里半了。他把眼裡的髒東西揉掉後，清楚地看到了那艘大船，還看到了一艘小船的白帆劃過那片閃耀大海的海面。

But he could never crawl those four miles. He knew that, and was very calm in the knowledge. He knew that he could not crawl half a mile. And yet he wanted to live. It was unreasonable that he should die after all he had undergone. Fate asked too much of him. And, dying, he declined to die. It was stark madness, perhaps, but in the very grip of Death he defied Death and refused to die.

He closed his eyes and composed himself with infinite precaution. He steeled himself to keep above the suffocating languor[96] that lapped[97] like a rising tide through all the wells of his being. It was very like a sea, this deadly languor, that rose and rose and drowned his consciousness bit by bit. Sometimes he was all but submerged, swimming through oblivion with a faltering stroke; and again, by some strange alchemy of soul, he would find another shred of will and strike out more strongly.

Without movement he lay on his back, and he could hear, slowly drawing near and nearer, the wheezing intake and output of the sick wolf's breath. It drew closer, ever closer, through an infinitude of time, and he did not move.

It was at his ear. The harsh dry tongue grated like sandpaper against his cheek. His hands shot out—or at least he willed them to shoot out. The fingers were curved like talons[98], but they closed on empty air. Swiftness and certitude require strength, and the man had not this strength.

但是他永遠也爬不了那六公里半的路了。他知道這一點，內心也很平靜。他知道自己連一公里都爬不了，但是，他想活下去。都經歷過了這一切了，如果還死去，就顯得荒謬了。命運對他太苛刻了，他命已垂危，但他不肯死。一切顯得瘋狂，死神緊緊抓住他，但他反抗死神，不肯死去。

他閉上眼睛，慎戒地讓自己保持冷靜。會讓人失去呼吸的疲憊感，像上漲的潮水一樣，從身體各處湧上來，他要打起精神，不能沉下去。這種會讓人死去的疲憊感，就像海水一樣，不斷地拍打上來，一點一點地淹沒他的意識。有時候，他整個被淹沒，他兩手無力地游著，游過茫茫的一片，然而生命奇異的力量，會讓他又找到一絲求生的意志，然後奮力游出去。

他靜靜地躺著，可以聽到那隻病狼一呼一吸的喘息聲，正慢慢地靠近他。聲音越靠越近、越靠越近，時間變得好長好長，但他還是沒有移動。

牠就來到他的耳邊了。牠粗糙乾燥的舌頭，像砂紙一樣刮著他的臉頰。他猛地伸出手——起碼他心裡是想這樣的。他的手指彎曲得像鷹爪一般，但是撲了空。敏捷準確的動作是需要氣力的，但是他沒有那個力氣。

96　languor [ˈlæŋgər] (n.)（身體或心理的）倦怠
97　lap [læp] (v.)（波浪）沖刷；輕輕拍打
98　talon [ˈtælən] (n.) 猛禽的利爪

The patience of the wolf was terrible. The man's patience was no less terrible. For half a day he lay motionless, fighting off unconsciousness and waiting for the thing that was to feed upon him and upon which he wished to feed. Sometimes the languid[99] sea rose over him and he dreamed long dreams; but ever through it all, waking and dreaming, he waited for the wheezing breath and the harsh caress of the tongue.

He did not hear the breath, and he slipped slowly from some dream to the feel of the tongue along his hand. He waited. The fangs[100] pressed softly; the pressure increased; the wolf was exerting its last strength in an effort to sink teeth in the food for which it had waited so long. But the man had waited long, and the lacerated[101] hand closed on the jaw. Slowly, while the wolf struggled feebly and the hand clutched feebly, the other hand crept across to a grip.

Five minutes later the whole weight of the man's body was on top of the wolf. The hands had not sufficient strength to choke the wolf, but the face of the man was pressed close to the throat of the wolf and the mouth of the man was full of hair. At the end of half an hour the man was aware of a warm trickle in his throat. It was not pleasant. It was like molten lead being forced into his stomach, and it was forced by his will alone. Later the man rolled over on his back and slept.

99 languid ['læŋgwɪd] (a.) 懶洋洋的
100 fang [fæŋ] (n.) 尖牙
101 lacerated ['læsəreɪt] (a.) 撕裂的；割破的

那頭狼的耐心真是可怕，但是這個人的耐心也一樣可怕。有半天的時間，他一動也不動地躺著，掙扎著不陷入昏迷，等著那頭動物。他們彼此互懷鬼胎，想吃掉對方。 有時候，那片疲憊的大海淹沒了他，他陷入長長的夢境，但是醒醒睡睡的，始終等著那個喘息聲和那舌頭刺人的舔舐。

他並沒有聽到那個呼吸聲，他慢慢從夢裡醒過來，感覺到舌頭在舔他的手。他靜待著。那頭狼的尖牙輕輕地往下壓，接著用更大的力氣往下壓，使盡全身最後一絲的力氣，把牙齒插入等了這麼久的獵物裡。而這個人也等了很久了，他用被咬裂的手，抓住狼的下巴。慢慢地，就在狼無力地掙扎著、那隻手無力地抓著牠時，另外一隻手悄悄地伸過來，揪住了狼。

五分鐘後，這個人把全身的重量壓在了狼的身上。這個人的雙手沒有力氣掐死狼，但他的臉已經緊緊壓在狼的脖子上，而且滿嘴都是毛。半個小時後，他感覺到一股溫血緩緩地流進他的喉嚨裡，味道不是很好，有點像是把鉛液灌進胃裡頭一樣，他只能靠意志力硬把它灌進去。隨後，他翻過身、仰躺在地上，入睡了。

There were some members of a scientific expedition on the whale-ship Bedford. From the deck they remarked a strange object on the shore. It was moving down the beach toward the water. They were unable to classify it, and, being scientific men, they climbed into the whale-boat alongside and went ashore to see.

And they saw something that was alive but which could hardly be called a man. It was blind, unconscious. It squirmed along the ground like some monstrous worm. Most of its efforts were ineffectual, but it was persistent, and it writhed and twisted and went ahead perhaps a score of feet an hour.

Three weeks afterward the man lay in a bunk[102] on the whale-ship Bedford, and with tears streaming down his wasted cheeks told who he was and what he had undergone. He also babbled incoherently of his mother, of sunny Southern California, and a home among the orange groves and flowers.

The days were not many after that when he sat at table with the scientific men and ship's officers. He gloated over[103] the spectacle of so much food, watching it anxiously as it went into the mouths of others. With the disappearance of each mouthful an expression of deep regret came into his eyes. He was quite sane, yet he hated those men at meal-time.

---

102 bunk [bʌŋk] (n.)（船上）靠牆的床鋪
103 gloat over . . . 貪婪地看著……

　　培福號捕鯨船上有幾個科學遠征隊的人員，他們從甲板上望見岸上有個奇怪的東西，那個東西正在沙灘上往大海移動，他們無法辨識出那是什麼。身為科學家，他們登上大船旁邊的小捕鯨船，駛向岸邊，想一探究竟。

　　他們看到一個活物，但他長得根本不像人。他的眼睛都瞎了，而且沒有什麼意識，像條巨蟲一樣在地上蠕動，白費著很多力氣，卻仍堅持不懈，又扭又爬，一小時大概可以爬個六公尺遠。

　　三個星期後，這個人躺在培福號捕鯨船的床舖上，一邊任眼淚順著他削瘦的臉頰往下淌，一邊訴說著自己的身世，以及所經歷的一切。他還語無倫次地提起他的母親，說起陽光燦爛的南加州，還有那個坐落在柑橘園和花叢間的家園。

　　沒過幾天，他就跟科學人員和船員同桌吃飯了。他貪婪地看著滿桌的食物，焦急地盯著食物被送進別人的嘴裡。每消失一口食物，他的眼裡就流露出萬分的惋惜。他的神智很清楚，但在吃飯時，他痛恨那些人。

He was haunted by a fear that the food would not last. He inquired of the cook, the cabin-boy, the captain, concerning the food stores. They reassured him countless times; but he could not believe them, and pried cunningly about the lazarette[104] to see with his own eyes.

It was noticed that the man was getting fat. He grew stouter with each day. The scientific men shook their heads and theorized. They limited the man at his meals, but still his girth increased and he swelled prodigiously[105] under his shirt.

The sailors grinned. They knew. And when the scientific men set a watch on the man, they knew too. They saw him slouch for'ard after breakfast, and, like a mendicant, with outstretched palm, accost[106] a sailor.

The sailor grinned and passed him a fragment of sea biscuit[107]. He clutched it avariciously, looked at it as a miser looks at gold, and thrust it into his shirt bosom. Similar were the donations from other grinning sailors.

The scientific men were discreet. They let him alone. But they privily examined his bunk. It was lined with hardtack[108]; the mattress was stuffed with hardtack; every nook and cranny[109] was filled with hardtack. Yet he was sane. He was taking precautions against another possible famine—that was all.

He would recover from it, the scientific men said; and he did, ere the Bedford's anchor rumbled down in San Francisco Bay.

他擔心食物會不夠吃，這樣的恐懼在他心裡揮之不去。他跟廚師、服務生、船長都問過船上有多少食物，大家已經無數次地跟他擔保食物不缺，但是他還是不相信，一定要偷溜到儲藏室親眼見了才放心。

大家注意到這個人胖了起來，一天比一天胖。科學人員搖搖頭，提出各自的說法。他們限制他的飯量，但是他的腰圍還是越來越粗，衣服下的身體胖得驚人。

水手們咧著嘴笑，他們知道他為什麼會胖，而且也知道科學人員何時在觀察他。吃完早餐後，他們看到他懶洋洋地走著，然後對著一個水手，像乞丐那樣地伸出手。

那位水手咧嘴笑笑，給他一小片硬餅乾。他貪婪地抓過餅乾，像守財奴盯著黃金一樣看地盯著餅乾，然後把餅乾塞進胸口處的上衣裡。其他咧著嘴笑的水手，也給了他餅乾。

科學人員很謹慎，他們隨他去，但是也暗中檢查他的床舖。他的床舖上面擺著一排硬餅乾，床墊裡也塞滿了餅乾；每個角落，每個隙縫，都是餅乾。但是他的神智很清楚。他只是防患未然，怕又會鬧饑荒——如此罷了。

他會恢復正常的，科學人員如是說道。而他也的確恢復了，培福號的鐵錨在舊金山灣裡隆隆一聲拋下去時，他就已經恢復了。

---

104 lazarette [ˌlæzəˈret] (n.) 船上的儲藏間（= lazaret = lazaretto）
105 prodigiously [prouˈdɪdʒəsli] (adv.) 巨大地；驚人地
106 accost [əˈkɑːst] (v.) 上前攀談
107 sea biscuit （昔日船員出海時吃的）硬餅乾
108 hardtack [ˈhɑːrdtæk] (n.) （船員出海時吃的）硬餅乾
109 cranny [ˈkræni] (n.) （牆上的）裂縫；縫隙

8
熱愛生命

國家圖書館出版品預行編目資料

走進李伯大夢：美國短篇小說精選（英漢對照）/ Washington Irving 等著
；羅慕謙 譯 . 一初版 . 一 [臺北市]：寂天文化，2011.12　面；公分 .

ISBN 978-986-184-951-5 (25K 平裝)

874.57　　　　　　　　　　　　　　　　　　　　　100024901

■作者 _ Washington Irving 等著　■譯者 _ 羅慕謙　■主編 _ 黃鈺云　■製程管理 _ 黃敏昭
■出版者 _ 寂天文化事業股份有限公司　■電話 _ 02-2365-9739　■傳真 _ 02-2365-9835
■網址 _ www.icosmos.com.tw　■讀者服務 _ onlineservice@icosmos.com.tw　■出版日期 _ 2011 年 12 月 初版一刷（250101）
■郵撥帳號 _ 1998620-0 寂天文化事業股份有限公司
■訂購金額 600（含）元以上郵資免費　■訂購金額 600 元以下者，請外加郵資 60 元